GRANITE AND BONES

A PYKE ISLAND MYSTERY IN DOWNEAST MAINE

MOE CLAIRE

Inquiries should be addressed to:
moeclairemystery@gmail.com
www.moeclairemystery.com

Map by Dan Kirchoff | www.dankirchoff.com
Interior Formatting: Mariella Travis | www.alleiram.com
Large Print and eBook Conversion: Sam Sheng | linkedin.com/in/samsheng

ISBN
978-1-961905-50-4 (Paperback)
978-1-961905-52-8 (Large Print Edition)
978-1-961905-51-1 (eBook)

12 Willows Press
Winterport, Maine
www.12willowspress.com

BOOKS BY MOE CLAIRE

In the "Pyke Island Mystery in Downeast Maine" Series:

A Fickle Tide
Granite and Bones
Black Veil, White Rose
A Blind Spider (forthcoming)

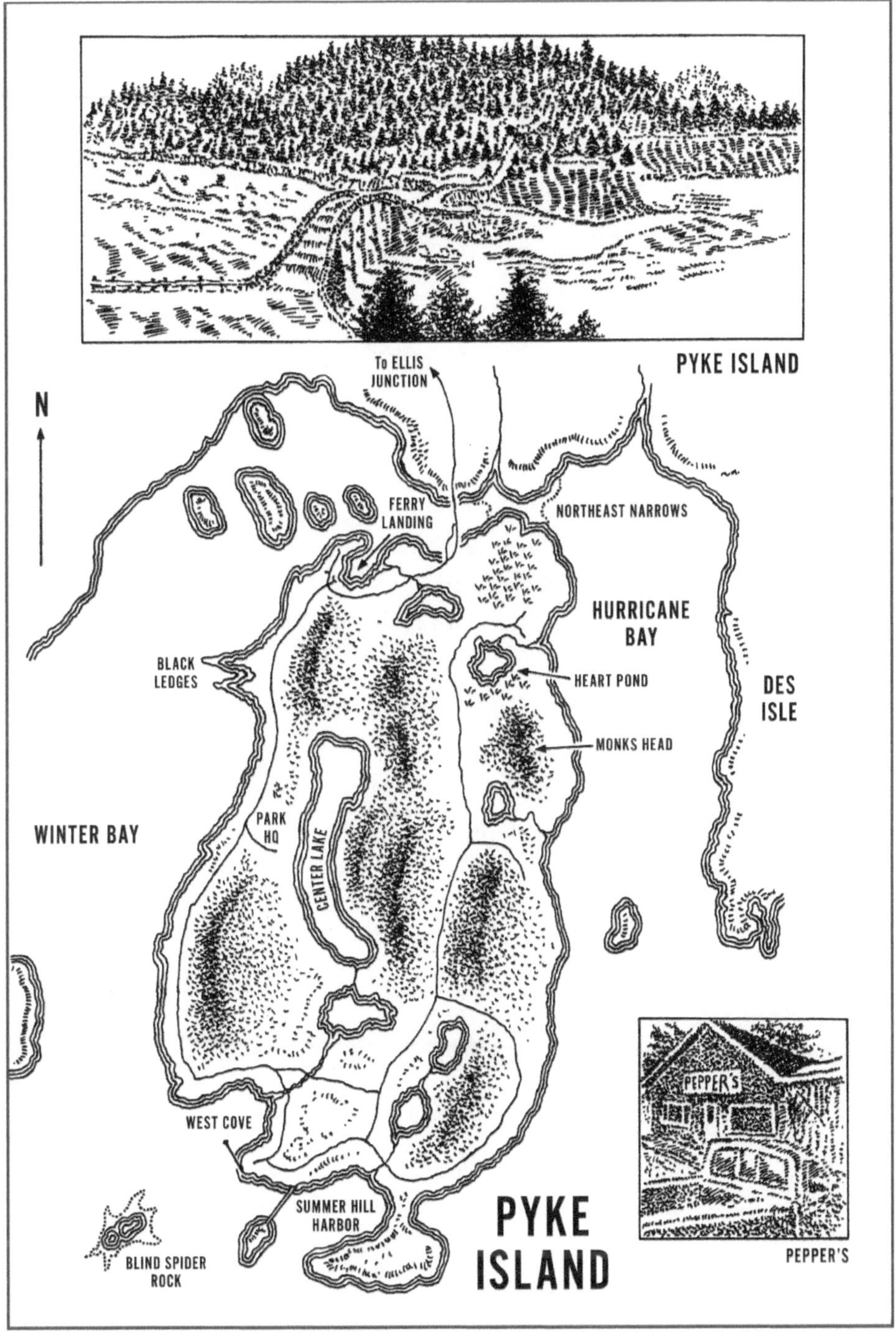

PYKE ISLAND
To ELLIS JUNCTION
N
FERRY LANDING
NORTHEAST NARROWS
HURRICANE BAY
BLACK LEDGES
HEART POND
DES ISLE
MONKS HEAD
WINTER BAY
PARK HQ
CENTER LAKE
WEST COVE
SUMMER HILL HARBOR
PYKE ISLAND
BLIND SPIDER ROCK
PEPPER'S
PEPPER'S

Love

Love is a wild wonder
And stars that sing,
Rocks that burst asunder
And mountains that take wing.

John Henry with his hammer
Makes a little spark.
That little spark is love
Dying in the dark.

—Langston Hughes

Prelude

What he heard next was a cry—long, shrill, heartrending. It surged from his throat and took with it the strength from his lungs. Minutes went by as the cry dissolved into a hiss, like air leaking from a pipe. Then he became aware of the drumming, deep and hollow, as if the drums were in the belly of the mountain. The beating was steady, not rushed but insistent. He felt it in his temples and on his chest, pressed to the earthen floor.

A voice spoke. He could barely hear it above the drumming.

"I have lived here since words began," it whispered. "Long ago, I conquered the ice creatures by melting their hearts." The voice rose to a song that kept time with the drumming. "I sing for Mother Beaver, for Grandmother Woodchuck, for Turtle and his brothers. I sing for the spirits of caribou and elk. They are ghosts, shadows in their own land."

The song made him soften his face and slowly open his eyes. Yes. Yes. There in a shaft of light he saw them, back from the dead, the caribou and elk, giant beavers and bears, all moving across the surface in waves of color. Some of the animals paused to gaze down at him. Others moved away to dark corners.

With every ounce of willpower he had left, he raised one finger. The pace of the drumming was becoming slower, and slower still as he struggled to make his mouth form the words, "Help me."

The drumming stopped.

The last sound he heard was someone weeping.

ONE

He was late but she didn't mind waiting, because every sense in her body was indulging in the beauty of this fine Maine day in late June. Relishing the noontime sun, Del was stretched out on a large granite boulder. It was that time of the year when, by bathing the island in more than sixteen hours of glorious solar energy, the sun finally won the tug-of-war against the frigid waters encircling Pyke Island. Every living thing was celebrating—along roadsides, lupine sprang into bloom, pines released waves of yellow pollen, birds gulped down seeds and insects for their young, sleek does browsed on belly-high grass, followed by their spotted fawns.

Del pulled her baseball cap over her face and closed her eyes, listening to the creek behind her bubble and splash over rocks. She inhaled the sweet scent of the wild roses that edged the gravel parking area. A cool, gentle breeze ruffled her shorts and T-shirt. It carried a trace of salt air mixed with a funk of old suntan lotion from the sweatband of her cap. Her tongue poked at her teeth for the sticky remains of a granola bar lunch. She smoothed the hair near her neck, this winter's pixie growing out shaggy and unruly with a tendency to stick out at various angles. She yawned.

If he doesn't show up soon, I could fall asleep here.

She heard the crunch of tires on gravel. Lazily turning her head and opening one eye, Del saw Tyler Holden's Lexus SUV pull off the main road into the parking area by the creek. He was coming from the wrong direction.

She closed her eyes again. She heard the car door slam and footsteps on the gravel, then his voice. "Hey, Adele Corriveau, my favorite geology expert. Is this where the tour starts?"

"The tour was supposed to start an hour ago," said Del, from under her cap. "It's okay because I'd rather be sunning myself than finishing my bachelor's degree. But now that you're here …"

She sat up and slid down the rock. Del gave him a full, two-arm hug and a kiss on each cheek, which was almost exactly how they had said goodbye except *that* time she went light on the hug because his ribs were still broken. Ty's arms held her closely and perhaps a little longer than most friends who greet each other after three months. She stepped back and looked him over. It was what she remembered: stylishly slender, taller than her by a few inches, fair, closely cropped reddish-blond hair, light-blue eyes, a precisely edged darker red beard outlining a square jaw, a slightly lopsided smile, the mysterious thin scar in front of his left ear. And not even bruised or bandaged like the last time she'd seen him. *But what's with the outfit?*

"Ty, we're going on an afternoon hike, not a safari in Africa," she teased. "Are those new boots? And that pack looks heavy. What're you bringing?"

He glanced down at his mid-calf hunting boots and the trail pants tucked into them. "Pretty new," he said, smiling. "I don't get a lot of use for this gear in Portland. It's why I need to visit you and your rocky island." He opened his pack to show her a sweatshirt, windbreaker, coil of rope, flashlight, whistle, utility knife, and first aid kit, in addition to a quart of water. "Just normal safety equipment for any hike. What're *you* bringing?"

Del pointed to her small daypack. "Water, another granola bar, plastic baggies for samples, a tape measure, my hand lens, and my rock hammer. My phone"—she patted her cargo shorts pocket—"is for emergencies."

"Half the time I don't get any bars on this side of Pyke Island. How can you depend on that in an emergency?"

Del swung on her daypack and turned toward the creek. "Today let's not have any emergencies," she said over her shoulder.

He slipped into his backpack and secured the straps while Del leapt across the creek using a ragged line of rocks. She waited while he jogged to catch up with her in the woods.

They were quickly enclosed in the bright green of tall cedar trees, their steps swallowed by the spongy forest floor, lush with moss-covered roots and stones. There was no marked trail through these woods, but Del could make out the depression of a footpath. She knew to keep the marshy area to her right while following glimpses of the peak in front of her.

Slowly, the ground began to rise and change from spongy green to a golden-brown layer of dried pine needles, last fall's crop shed by the magnificent white pines in this part of the forest. Del stopped at the edge of a small pond. She snapped a picture with her phone of a rock dome framed by the opening in the trees. The top was rounded and bare, arched like a skull. A ring of thin trees partway down the peak encircled it like fuzz around a bald pate.

"There's my independent research project," she said. "It's called Monks Head. Early French explorers called it 'Le Moine Chauve,' meaning 'the bald monk.'"

"I can see why," Ty said. "Am I imagining this or is it sort of pink?"

"Exactly. A granite dome just under seven hundred feet showing lots of potassium feldspar, or K-spar, not like the gray granite on most of Pyke Island."

"Sure, it looks different, but is it?"

"Yup. We think it formed separately from the Whaleback Mountains on the other side of the valley. But why is Monks Head alone here? Why is the composition different?"

Ty slipped his water bottle out of his pack. "How will you figure that out?" he asked between sips.

"First, I need to document the 'whats,' like the specific minerals, relative hardness. I'll map major physical features, cliffs, crevasses, and boundaries where the two granites come together, if I can find them. Hopefully, I get a grant to pay for radiometric dating of my rock samples to find the age of the granite."

"You can take rocks from the park?"

"With permission from the director of Granite Coast Park herself." Del patted her back pocket. "Once I assemble the data, I'll work with my faculty advisor to develop an explanation of how it formed and why it's alone on this side of the valley."

Farther along the trail, boulders were scattered everywhere, some the size of panel trucks, broken from the peak by the most recent glaciation ten thousand years ago. Now the boulders were just part of the forest, platforms for ferns and lichens and anchors for the trees that grew close around them. The land rose in a series of steps until Del and Ty came to the base of an almost vertical cliff. On one side of the cliff was a long tumble of rocks in many sizes and shapes leaning up against the precipice.

"This is a talus slope, the accumulation of many rockfalls," Del said, stopping to take a picture and record the GPS coordinates. "And the easiest way up, like giant stairs."

Del and Ty climbed the edge of the talus, pulling themselves up with their hands as much as pushing with their legs. The tumble of rocks tapered as they climbed, and it ended at a narrow shelf fringed with low-growing, twisted jack pines. They had already hiked for over an hour and were still only partway up Monks Head.

Breathing hard from the climb, Del sat down at the edge of the shelf. "Time for a water break. I've only been here a few times before.

The sea to the east. Forest and lakes at our feet. It's one of the best views in Granite Coast Park for a short hike."

"Short but straight up." Ty took off his pack and made himself comfortable on a broken log wedged against a clump of spindly huckleberry. "I can see why there're no official trails here. The park wants visitors to come back year after year, not kill themselves."

He pivoted to open his pack. The log under him suddenly shifted and part of it dropped out of sight. "What the—" A loud crack covered up his expletive. Ty reached out to steady himself, but his arm disappeared almost to his shoulder. His feet kicked out for balance. By then Del was at his side and hauled him up by the other arm. The log slipped completely into a hole, and they heard it thumping down the inside, the thumps getting progressively deeper.

"Hey, I thought we were avoiding emergencies today," she teased.

"A fucking deep hole," he grumbled. "I guess you get to document that."

They cleared dry branches and debris around the hole to reveal a crescent-shaped opening, just wide enough for someone to fall through. Del took a snapshot and noted the GPS coordinates.

"Nice work," she said, stepping away to take a photo of the rock above them. "You found the top edge of an exfoliated slab that broke off from there"—she pointed to a long, jagged gouge—"and slipped down at least twenty feet. Like a layer pulled off an onion. Made a cave, I bet. Technically, it's called a rock shelter. The talus we climbed must cover part of it."

Ty was shining his flashlight into the hole. "Freaking deep. I can't see the bottom."

"Let's check this out." Feet first, Del started a controlled skid on her backside, tracking the slab where it leaned against the main rock face. The stone flared out as they descended. In many places, ferns, low-growing shrubs, and jack pine had taken hold in the thin layer of organic material caught in the edge. After twenty-five feet they came to another talus slope, granite blocks completely obscuring the slab's edge, except for one dark cavity—a triangular hole like a dormer window looking out at the night sky, a void where there should have been rock.

Del scrambled down to the opening. It was about three feet high and just wide enough for one person to slip through sideways. A big guy with a beer belly might not fit through at all. She sat balancing near the edge of a block that formed the lower lip of the opening.

"Maybe you could point your flashlight in and check it out first," she said. "See if we can get in, if it has a floor."

"Maybe I should check for wildlife first. You know, lions, tigers, and bears?"

She laughed. "Oh my! We haven't seen any lions or tigers here since the Pleistocene. I'm sure there are black bears, but I've never actually seen one on the island. This is too steep even for a coyote den."

With a wave of his hand, Ty dismissed the spider's web across the opening. Then, after slipping his pack off one shoulder, feetfirst he gradually let himself slide in. His pack made a scraping sound. Everything but the top of his head disappeared into the darkness. Then that disappeared too.

"There's a floor, big rocks, and gravel," he called back.

"No wildlife?" Del asked as she lowered herself into the hole.

"Not anymore." His voice seemed far away.

The first thing Del noticed about the interior of the cave was the profound tomb-like silence. She couldn't hear the wind rustling in the trees, birds chirruping, or the hum of a distant engine—all normal background sounds when hiking in the park. Using the flashlight setting on her phone, Del looked around at the sheer walls on both sides. She stepped carefully, feeling for her footing on the uneven floor. Deeper in the shelter she saw Ty's silhouette in the bright circle made by his flashlight. With her next step, she banged her shin against something and fell on one knee.

"Ow!"

Ty swung the beam toward her. Sections of the shattered log, the one that had fallen from above, were scattered around a cluster of chair-sized jagged rocks. Looking up, Del saw a crescent of daylight thirty feet directly above. Now the opening that had almost swallowed Ty seemed incredibly small, but it would make a fine chimney hole if someone wanted to build a fire.

She stood, wiping grit from her shin. "What do you mean 'not anymore'? Something used to live here?"

"Nope. Died here. Come see."

Ty led her with the beam of light so Del could avoid other rocks and catch up to where he was standing. Toward the closed end of the shelter, the floor smoothed out into a bed of dirt and gravel.

"You found animal bones?"

He turned with the flashlight toward the black interior and danced the light back and forth until it revealed a dirty white skull, turned sideways, jawbone wide open, long yellow teeth leering at them. He ran the shaft of light along a complete human skeleton—backbone, ribs, arms, and legs—the collapsed bones organized in the pose of a person who was on his stomach with one arm reaching forward and one knee raised to the side.

He said, "Definitely human."

Although streaked and soiled, the bones were perfectly organized so that Del could imagine the human being who took his or her last breath there. What she didn't want to think about was how every speck of flesh had been erased.

TWO

"I should've brought a bigger flashlight," Ty said as he moved the beam along the skeleton in front of them.

"How long does it take for the bones to get like that?" Del looked up again at the hole which was now far behind them. Her eyes were beginning to get used to the dark.

"Years, but I'm not sure how many. Depends on the humidity."

Ty slipped off his pack and pulled out his phone. "No service here. Hold this flashlight while I take pictures. Back of the skull is broken. I see scraps of fabric under some of the long bones, a chain with a pendant around the neck, chunks of what might be leather around the feet."

"I'm sure we can get a signal if we climb back up." She scanned the walls of the rock shelter. It was formed like a lean-to, the outside wall slightly curved and tapered, exactly as one would expect if a layer slipped off an onion. The inside wall was mostly vertical, fissured and rough at the base, but at waist height it was smoother, and the small amount of light from the chimney hole above reflected on the surface.

"Hey!" Ty called to her. "Where'd you go with the light? I can't take pictures."

"You need to see this."

She moved the beam of light over to what looked like a group of caribou racing upward across the stone. The animals with huge heads and amazing antlers were scratched and chipped into the stone, in places smudged with black. Beyond the caribou were several large beavers, slightly below them the hulking shapes of two bears, then a group of what she guessed might be elk as their antlers were thin and swept back. By holding the flashlight at an angle below the carvings, she clearly saw the animals' features made by a combination of grooves, gouges, and pecks.

Ty stood and they both crept closer to the cave art. He took several pictures, following the animal shapes from left to right, where they disappeared in a hanging garden of twisted roots.

"Petroglyphs. Awesome," Del said after a few minutes. She studied an area by holding the flashlight at different angles and examining the gouges though her hand lens. "I'm sure this is old, really old. There's stuff filling in the depressions, charcoal maybe, dust and dirt, some fungus."

"Time to call in the cops."

"I'd like to get measurements and stone samples from the cave before we leave. No one's going to let us in here again."

Ty was shaking his head. "I don't know how the hell they're going to keep this place secure once word gets out."

"Oh, yeah. Speaking of word getting out, did I tell you Marco's coming for dinner?"

"That being Marco, the grad student in history, or Marco, the more-often-broke freelance journalist?"

"You know those are two sides of the same Marco, although he hasn't done much reporting since winter. He's been really busy, working on his dissertation and prepping to teach a class next semester. But he said he'd come down and hang out with us for a couple of days."

"Knowing Marco, he'll smell a story here and hang around for weeks."

Del sensed that Ty made his last comment with a cutting edge, not what anyone would call enthusiasm.

THREE

Over the next few hours, they used everything Ty had brought on the hike, and Del had to admit he was better prepared for the unexpected than she was.

They had climbed out of the rock shelter and back to the shelf near the chimney hole before either of them noticed that Del's shin was bleeding. Ty used his first aid kit to patch her up, applying antiseptic and three bandages where Del thought one might be fine. Then they had to climb even higher on Monks Head before they got a signal. After Ty exchanged a phone call with the county sheriff, Mike Hodgkins, he sent the pictures, and they climbed back down most of the talus slope until they found sections of tree branches, which they carried back up. Ty used his rope and utility knife to work the branches together like a teepee. They placed the assembly over the chimney hole, making, according to Ty, "damn sure only an idiot would fall in."

Then Ty and Del climbed back up to where they got the signal, a place they dubbed "Monks Forehead." It was now late afternoon.

Del called her Grandpa Gabe to explain they would be late for dinner, without telling him what they'd found. Grandpa told her it was no problem because the plan was to steam lobster, which would only take a few minutes. He said Marco had texted from Ellis Junction to say he was about thirty-five minutes from the bridge to Pyke Island, and Evie just finished making coleslaw. Grandpa, a widower for about three years, had met Evie at a garden club meeting in April. He called her his "gardening consultant," but Del knew they were actually dating in the style of seventy-somethings, by being friends first.

Kind of like Marco and me, friends with occasional benefits. Actually, I can't imagine Grandpa and Evie having those *kinds of benefits.*

Ty's phone buzzed with messages. The sheriff's office was sending officers, accompanied by park rangers, to secure the area. The sheriff asked them to stay until the first officers arrived.

Finally, there was nothing to do but wait. Del and Ty sat side by side, quietly looking across the waters of Hurricane Bay to the next peninsula east of Pyke Island. The wind had freshened, and whitecaps appeared on the waves. Even though it was a few days after the start of astronomical summer, the Gulf of Maine held on to its winter chill well into July. Ty put on the windbreaker and gave Del the sweatshirt.

"Well, buddy," he said, "here we are with another mystery."

She sighed. "I've got a project to finish. Even though it might be fun, I'm going to let you and Marco handle this one."

Another mystery on Pyke Island had brought the three of them—Del, Ty, and Marco—together in January, just six months earlier: Del as a victim of assaults and threats, Ty as the private investigator hired to protect her, and Marco as the journalist eager for the story. As it turned out, they all had knowledge and connections that helped the police solve the case. There were discoveries, secret interviews, undercover work, and a rescue. In the end, the police had their arrests, Marco got his story, and Ty got a little beat up but with a hero's reward. At least, that's what he called an all-expenses-paid hospital stay and recuperation vacation. And Del got on with the next phase of her life, exchanging a career as a carpenter for a return to college.

"Right. Tell me you're not curious to find out who died in the cave."

Hugging herself, Del smiled slowly. "Okay." Even in Ty's sweatshirt she felt chilly in the wind. "But what I'm really curious about is how he or she died."

He changed his focus toward the wind-whipped bay, watching a lobster boat chug its way south. "This view is amazing. Tell me again how you know we're sitting on an old volcano."

"Not on. *In.* We're sitting deep inside the magma chamber. This granite, like all granite, formed as magma cooled far below the earth's surface. Geologists estimate that the top of the volcano was two miles above us."

Squinting, he craned his neck upward. "Where'd that all go?"

She swept a hand in an arc. "Downhill. Three hundred million years or so of erosion transported the overlying layers into valleys and canyons offshore."

"Two miles is a lot of material."

"Three hundred million years is a lot of time."

Ty gave her his smug smile. "I get it. Never underestimate the slow but steady force of erosion."

"Ah, geology neophyte, it's time you moved up to the next level. Erosion is a geological process, not a force. *Gravity* is behind the curtain, and you should always pay attention to it."

"Good advice when you're sitting on top of a cliff. Then the reason these mountains are still here—"

"Is because they're hard, relatively speaking."

"I don't need a lesson to understand that. My butt is getting sore." Ty shifted his weight, leaning back on his hands. "Is Marco planning on staying through the Fourth of July?"

"I'm not sure what his schedule is."

"Your parents coming up?"

"No, I talked with my mom last week. My brother Ben is getting engaged. She's in full planning mode for a big party in Boston in September. We haven't seen them for months."

"I was hoping to spend some time with you," he said, turning his attention back to her. "We haven't had much chance to talk, just the two of us."

"Really? You want to talk?" Del felt the prick of suspicion. "About yourself?" The Ty Holden she knew never talked about his personal life and was adamant about his privacy.

"Sure." He hesitated as if he wasn't sure. "I've got some time."

"Yeah, I'd like that. You want to talk on a boat ride or a hike?"

"I was hoping you'd show me the park for a few days. I brought my gear for a reason."

"There's a couple hundred miles of trails." Facing the granite peaks across the valley, Del stretched her arms wide. "We need more than a few days."

"Maybe I need to stay longer." His cheeks colored a little, and he looked away again.

How curious he was. Ty, who could be arrogant and smug, now seemed somewhat shy and nervous. The man sitting next to her was a different Ty Holden in more ways than one. A gust of wind plastered the windbreaker against his chest and arms, distinctly outlining lean but defined muscles. Del stole a good look while his attention was elsewhere.

A little extra bodybuilding during recuperation, or maybe I wasn't paying attention last winter?

"Hey, um, I think I should work my way back down to where I can see the opening, in case they come up that way," Del said. "The GPS coordinates you gave them might be off by several yards, enough that they might not see one dark entrance in the jumble of rocks."

"I don't know," he said. "I won't be able to see you and we can't talk by phone."

She held out her hand. "You brought that whistle for a reason. One long tweet means the police have come and you can climb down. Lots of tweets means I'm being hauled off by a lion or tiger or bear and you're on your own."

Back down the rockslide by the cave opening, Del felt she got the better deal because it was out of the wind. Because there was no comfortable place to sit, she used the wait time to take more photos and measurements.

After the first police and rangers arrived, one long whistle brought Ty down from Monks Forehead, and the officers politely but firmly shooed them off.

FOUR

While Del, Ty, and Marco cleaned up from their summer feast, Grandpa Gabe drove Evie home. It was a forty-minute round trip from the Corriveau homestead in the village of Ferry Landing to where Evie lived just off the main road near Summer Hill Harbor, the only other real village on the island. Grandpa described her house as a cute English-style cottage surrounded by gardens.

His summer project building a garden in the open yard area between his cottage and the old Corriveau family house was still a work in progress. It was completely fenced off from deer, but most of the beds weren't framed yet. Weeds were sprouting from a waiting pile of topsoil. It was unusual, but Del's fit and energetic grandpa was taking his time with building that garden. After Grandma Marjorie passed away, Del and Grandpa worked on multiple remodeling projects together, including turning the loft over the garage into Del's apartment, updating his cottage, and remodeling the old Corriveau family house to be a rental. Evie was helping him with design details on the garden project. Del assumed she was a welcome distraction.

After the dishes were washed, the lobster pot scrubbed, and the outdoor cooker stowed away in Grandpa's shed, they dragged lawn chairs closer to the lip of the rocky ledge that separated the Corriveau property from Winter Bay on the island's western side. Marco handed out beers. They were quiet, enjoying the view of the water and the islands marking the inner bay. Lazy waves lapped at the pebbly shore just below them. It was after eight with the sun still well above the horizon.

"Nice how calm and warm it is here compared to sitting on top of Monks Head," Ty said casually. He was checking his phone frequently and thumbing through messages.

"The wind changed to the southeast today," said Del. "By morning, it'll be foggy over on the eastern side."

Marco slapped his hands on his thighs. "Sweet Jesus, are you two going to tell me what happened today? When you got here, we asked about the hike and you said 'nice hike.' We asked about what you found and you said 'nice views.' Could you be more evasive? Del *never* misses an opportunity to talk about rocks."

Del slouched in her chair and smiled at him. She turned to Ty. "Do we tell him before Grandpa gets back? You know how his imagination can overheat, and that might damage his self-control."

Ty shook his head. "Let's wait or else we'll have to do it twice." He got up and walked to the cottage. He was paying serious attention to something on his phone.

Del was happily enjoying the trio's reunion. When Ty said he was coming to visit for a couple of weeks, she had coordinated with Marco so that he would take time from his work at the university. Grandpa gladly offered Ty and Marco beds in the bunk room of his cottage. Her apartment above the garage was too small, and having both guys sleep in her living room was definitely too complicated. In addition to having hiking buddies, Del planned on taking them out on the *Margie B*, her grandpa's lobster boat, and visiting some of the special areas on Pyke Island. She hoped the skeletal remains in the rock shelter wouldn't upset the fun too much.

"What's wrong with him?" Marco asked.

"Don't know," she said. "If I wanted to connect the dots, I'd say he's hiding something." She closed her eyes, enjoying the sensation of the low sun on her face.

"Isn't that a major personality trait with Ty?"

Del felt a soft kiss on her lips and the tickle of Marco's unruly boyish locks on her cheeks. Inhaling his scent of coffee and salt air, which was Marco's scent even when he was miles inland, she opened her eyes and scowled. "Hey, we had an agreement. None of this stuff while we're all here."

Bending over the back of her chair, Marco gently pushed a strand of hair away from her eyes. The caramel-colored complexion he wore over the winter had become a deeper reddish brown making his toothy, dimple-cheeked grin even more attractive. "So, we're alone right now. You don't want me to damage my self-control, do you?"

She was tempted to say maybe later, but she knew that would be a mistake with Ty and Grandpa around. They did have an agreement.

Del tried to duck but he managed to place another wet kiss on her forehead. "Hey, you need to practice that self-control," she said, reaching up to swat him while Marco danced away.

He laughed, drained his beer, and tipped the empty bottle to the west. "Going to be another fabulous sunset. Where's my tripod and camera?"

FIVE

"I don't know how the hell we're going to keep the place secure once word gets out." Sheriff Mike Hodgkins was on the phone the following morning with a senior detective from the Maine State Police. "I can get the park to close a fire road on the south side. Settlement Creek Farm agreed to close the parking area and woodland trails on the north and east. The other abutter is the Wilson family, owners of Heart Pond, on the west. I'll alert them, but they already chase people off their property. Problem is, Monks Head is surrounded by a couple hundred acres, all unposted. It'll be crawling with the curious and reporters in no time. We have to keep at least two officers exposed on a rockslide day and night watching the area for how long? You got to find us some help."

Mike had arrived early at his satellite office on Pyke Island to organize assignments and shuffle personnel for the next few days. Officers from the state police's Evidence Response Team and a medical examiner were still at Monks Head, and it might be another day or two before the skeletal remains could be removed. Even then, the police must keep the cave secure until investigators complete their work.

What's more, the prehistoric petroglyphs certainly were an important archeological find and seemed to be near the boundary separating Granite Coast Park and the Settlement Creek property. Mike had yet to tell anyone in those organizations about them. Because he wasn't sure who owned the cave, he planned to tell them both in a face-to-face meeting scheduled for later that afternoon.

As for the skeleton, Mike had his own hunch—a case that went cold over five years ago. He shared his thoughts with the state cop at the scene yesterday.

As requested, Del and Ty came into the sheriff's Pyke Island office at ten. He led them to the interview room and, with the video equipment turned on, asked them to describe how they found the cave and what they saw. Because Ty had already sent in most of the details with pictures, the interview was quick.

Ty told the sheriff about the cut on Del's shin and that they might find her blood and DNA on the log and rocks in the cave. Del had provided elimination samples to the police in January, and Mike was pretty sure they were still in the state database.

"Depending on what the techs find for human DNA besides the skeleton, we might need samples from you, Ty," Mike explained. "You want to do that now or wait? You planning on being around for a while?"

"I'll be around," Ty said. "I usually refuse to provide a DNA sample, but in this case I will if you agree not to retain it beyond the investigation."

Mike nodded, turned off the recording equipment, and yawned. "Long morning already. Let's grab some coffee and move to my office. Is Marco here?"

"We left him in the parking lot chatting with Jessica Ouellette," Del said. "I think she's flirting with him."

"Ahem." Mike cleared his throat with intentional exaggeration. "Deputy Sheriff Ouellette is a respected county police officer, and she is on duty." He wiped his mug with a napkin and filled it with coffee from the office machine. "Go get him so I only have to go through this once."

Mike sipped his coffee while Del, Ty, and Marco found and arranged seats in front of his desk. He leaned back in his chair with an ear-to-ear grin. "Can't believe I'm sitting across from you three again."

"Come on, Sheriff Mike," Del said brightly. "You know things were getting a little boring around here."

"With the Fourth of July coming up?" Mike rolled his eyes. "Every year I pray it's cold and rainy so everyone stays home." He leaned forward, placed his cup on his desk, rested his elbows, and pointed an index finger at them. "I need a solemn promise from each of you that you'll stay away from the cave, that you don't write about it, don't publish those photos, don't discuss it with anyone." He glared at Marco. "With anyone *else* until we give you permission. Can I trust you?"

Marco shifted in his seat. "Sheriff, any idea when the medical examiner might be done at the cave?"

Mike slammed his palm on the desk, causing a small coffee geyser. "You'll know when everyone else knows." A little overacted, he thought, but it had the effect of shutting Marco up. Del stopped smiling, and Ty sat immobile with his arms crossed. He was a hard nut to crack. "This is not a game. I need those promises."

"At some point the news will get out," Ty said, turning to Del and Marco. "But it won't be from us." They both nodded.

"Even after the ME is done, we need to keep the archeological site secure as long as possible until ownership is clear." Mike stood. "With this island crawling with tourists every summer for the last hundred and thirty years, it's hard to believe that no one found it before."

Del raised her hand like a sheepish student.

"What?" Mike said curtly. He really wanted them to leave. He had a pile of paperwork to get through.

"Look at this picture I took yesterday. There's a lighter pinkish streak down the northeast side of Monks Head. That's the color of the granite when it's not covered with biofilm—you know, lichens and stuff that grows on surfaces exposed to the air and sun. Recent rockslides have that color—'recent' meaning in years, not centuries. When I was waiting for you guys yesterday, I noticed many of the blocks around the opening were that color. Grandpa said there was a magnitude four or so earthquake here about six years ago that rattled homes and damaged chimneys."

"I remember it," Mike said. "It was before dawn, sometime in November. By the flood of calls we got, I know it woke up hundreds of folks. The park closed some trails until they were able to reroute them. Did you send us this picture?"

"Just did." She nodded and put her phone away. "While the quake might explain why it remained hidden for a long time, it doesn't tell us how many people have known about it since."

Del stood to leave, reaching for the office door with Ty and Marco just behind her, when a loud, excited voice came from the outer office.

"Hey, Sheriff, hey, I got a message. Your hunch was right." One of his new recruits, a young, fresh-faced uniformed officer, leaned into the opening of Mike's office, never missing a syllable. "Medical examiner thinks it's Chief George. He wants—ohhhhh—" The last sound he made when he saw Del, Ty, and Marco was as much an exhale as a word.

Practicing his controlled breathing, Mike pointed toward the waiting area and the trio left quickly. He signaled to the young officer to come inside and close the door.

SIX

Del and Marco had laptops open next to each other on Grandpa Gabe's dining table. Grandpa stood behind Marco, peering over his shoulder, holding his glasses away from his face to read what was on their screens. Ty was leaning against the doorway to the kitchen, mostly focused on finishing a beer.

"Five and a half years ago. I've found four weeks of news articles on Chief George's disappearance," Marco said, clicking through the list a little too fast for Grandpa, who was adjusting his glasses up and down and craning his neck looking, Del thought, a bit like a near-sighted vulture. "They say the same thing. Reported missing by neighbors in Settlement Creek in mid-December. Didn't seem to take any personal effects with him, left his car. There were several searches of the property and woods, including the park. Divers searched Heart Pond. But nothing, no trace. And then winter set in. By the way, his full name was George Tozur. The articles called him the island's most vocal Native American, although some people claimed he was full of blather. There were reports of a feud between George and a neighbor. Those reports were never confirmed or denied by the police."

Grandpa cleared his throat and nodded. "That's pretty much what I remember. That side of the island was crawling with searchers for a few weeks, at least until the snow fell. The neighbor the article is referring to is Wilson, who took a strong disliking to George."

"What do you remember about him—Chief George, I mean?" Del asked.

"I never met him, but once in a while our weekly would print a letter to the editor from him describing how we stole everything from his native people. I saw him and Wilson get into a shouting match at one town meeting." Grandpa grinned. "Old Man Wilson actually took a swing at George's head until some good citizens pulled them apart before he hurt himself. Wilson was none too steady on his feet even then, arthritis and a bad hip."

"Old Man Wilson?" Marco asked.

"A mean SOB Wilson was, if you ask me. Always quick to find fault in others," Grandpa said. "He died two years ago of a stroke, I think. That would be three years after George disappeared. Some folks speculated that Wilson killed George."

Del nodded. "I remember you saying, Grandpa, that the island was better off without that feud."

Grandpa pushed his glasses up his nose and crossed his arms. "Well, the remaining Wilsons aren't troublemakers, anyway."

"There are more Wilsons?" Marco asked.

"His daughter Charlotte still lives in the family house on Heart Pond. She's always been very private, a recluse. I'm not sure I've ever seen her about, but I know she's in a wheelchair. One of the Fairlie daughters has been her private nurse for a few years. I've known Pete Fairlie since we moved back here and I had my tax business. He was one of my clients. Thinking about retiring, he stopped by the boatyard this spring. He's looking to buy a cruiser and wanted some advice." Grandpa pushed up his glasses and jabbed a finger at Marco's shoulder. "Here's a tip for you. You want gossip? Skip the woman's club. The old farts hanging out at the harbor know all the chitchat. They're saying Charlotte's son is living with her now."

Marco started slapping his pockets, which he always did when he was looking for his little notebook. "I'll have to find out more about Wilson."

Del squinted at her screen. "I don't see much about the tremor on the Weston Observatory website except a map showing the epicenter, which was east of the island out in the Gulf. I can't make anything out of the satellite images. Sheriff Mike said the park closed some trails. I wonder if they have any records describing the damage. I know the administrator at park headquarters. She'll be able to find out."

"Gabe, what do you know about Settlement Creek?" Marco asked, pulling his notebook from a cargo pocket. "From what I can tell, it's some kind of planned community run by an executive council who call themselves 'elders.' People who want to live there need to apply and show some—what it says here—'Indigenous American roots,' whatever that is. But they're not listed as a tribe."

"All I can tell you is that people were talking about it when Del's grandma, Marjorie, and I moved back here in the nineties. Some of my neighbors were worried that the American Indian thing was a cover for a bunch of hippies who wanted to grow pot, but there was never any trouble like that. They keep to themselves. They're not part of the fishing community. They're the best organic farmers around."

"Gotcha. Their website makes them look like a farm commune." Marco read from another web page. "Currently eighteen families. Organic gardens, egg production, fishing elvers and smelts in the creek. We can find them at the Ellis Junction farmer's market on Saturdays. Here's a list of local markets they sell to."

"They had some of the early licenses to harvest baby eels. I bet that paid off," Grandpa said. "Last winter elvers were going for two thousand dollars a pound." He cleared his throat. "Do the math on a thirty- to fifty-pound harvest and you get some real money for a few weeks of work."

Del clicked through several web pages. "Huh, says they run their own school. Here's a few success stories, a list of colleges and what they're studying. Hey, I recognize him, the dark-eyed, dark-haired, tanned hunk with a ponytail. Listen to this: Ryan has a PhD in archeology, currently doing postgraduate work at the University of Wisconsin. I remember him hanging out at the bars last summer for a few weeks. Who wouldn't?"

Del turned her laptop to show Marco, who glanced and curled his lip. She took that to mean he wasn't as impressed as she was.

Marco was jotting notes. "Let's see. Del needs a report from the park. We'll visit Settlement Creek and see if we can talk to an officer. We should find out more about other Wilsons. Does this town keep tax maps online?"

"Town of Pyke Island," Grandpa said, directing Marco to the town website.

There was a rather loud "Who said *we* were starting an investigation?" from the doorway leading to the kitchen. Ty, with ears edged in pink making his thin scar look very white, was wagging his beer bottle at them. "As I recall, *we* promised the sheriff we wouldn't."

Marco rubbed his chin. "I recall promising not to publish or print or televise. I didn't agree to not snoop, did you, Del?"

"Not me," she said.

"You think you're going to start asking questions about Chief George and no one's going to wonder why?"

"We'll have a cover story," Marco answered. "We'll say we're interested in organic farming."

"Sure, that'll look innocent enough." Ty turned to an invisible companion. "Hi. How are the gardens? Can you tell me who killed Chief George?"

"I already sent an email to Lucy Irwin, admin at the park, about any records on the earthquake," Del said. "I still have a research project to finish."

Ty scowled at her. "I guess that won't set off alarms."

"Ty, what are you hiding?" Del slapped her laptop closed. "When you pulled into the parking area yesterday, you were coming from the wrong direction. That road is a dead end. You also said something about not getting 'any bars on this side of Pyke Island,' which is strange because *you and I* never went near that side of the island when you were here last winter."

"And you've been real grumpy since I got here," added Marco.

"And you left the house this morning before four and came back before six," added Grandpa. "You were pretty quiet about it, but I heard you over Marco's snoring."

"Huh?" Del looked over her shoulder at her grandpa.

"Hey, *I* don't snore," insisted Marco. Both Del and Grandpa slapped his shoulders lightly for that.

Ty was working his face to keep it serious but his eyes were smiling. "Busted." He turned into the kitchen and called over his shoulder, "Anyone up for another beer?"

"You bet," came from Marco.

Del's jaw almost dropped on the table. "Ty Holden is having a second beer? In one day? Just 'cause you're on vacation, don't go crazy now."

He brought out two beers and took a seat at the table. "Well, I'm not on vacation, exactly. I'm working."

"Working for?" Del swooped her hand in the air like a conductor trying to bring in the violins.

"The Settlement Creek Elder Council."

Marco gagged on a swallow of beer and coughed some into his hand. "Sweet Jesus, how long were you planning on keeping *that* secret?" He started licking the beer from his cupped hand until Grandpa threw a paper towel at him.

Ty sat back in his chair. "I wasn't going to tell you at all because it should be a simple surveillance job. Finding the skeleton changed everything."

Gabe peered at him over his glasses. "You going to tell us what happened this morning?"

"I had to check on a security camera that stopped sending updates."

"What're you watching?" Marco asked.

"I'll tell you this much because it's all in a police report even though the sheriff has been keeping it quiet. Since April, Settlement Creek has been experiencing off-and-on nighttime vandalism. They lost a large part of their elver harvest because their nets were ripped open. The chicken coop was broken into and several birds were killed. Two newborn goats just disappeared. Sheriff's officers set up watches and their own people volunteered for watches. But whenever an area was being guarded, nothing happened. As soon as they took a few nights off, the vandalism started again. Mike recommended security cameras and gave them my name."

"They're not using electric fencing?" Grandpa asked.

"The hot wires were broken multiple times, and their deer fencing was sliced clean through," Ty explained.

"A bear can tear up fencing pretty badly."

Ty shook his head. "No, investigators said that some of the damage might have been a bear, but not the fencing, cut cleanly, something only a sharp blade can do. Mike said he thought the vandal was trying to make it look like a bear."

"Sounds mean enough," Grandpa agreed with raised eyebrows and a nod.

"And so far?" Del asked.

"Nothing. But then I just finished installing everything the day before yesterday." Ty's phone buzzed with a text message, which he thumbed to immediately. "Lucky for the investigation you're *not* doing, Mike already informed the current president of Settlement Creek about the skeletal remains, and she's willing to talk to you tomorrow night."

Del thought Marco was going to jump up and do a happy dance.

"To us *three*, you mean, right, Ty?" she said. "You think I might meet Ryan?" She elbowed Marco, who responded with a snort.

"I'll be there, but on this case—I'm working for her, not you. By the way, her name is Pale Moon Smith."

"Seriously?" Del chuckled. "Or is that her pick-my-own-name-that-sounds-kinda-Indian name?"

"It's the name on the law degree hanging in her office. And don't forget, we say nothing about what we found. We're there because Marco's interested in an article on Chief George."

"And maybe some advice on organic farming." She elbowed Marco again.

SEVEN

At the Granite Coast Park Visitor Center, Del met Lucy Irwin near the information counter. A handful of volunteers in dark-green uniforms were politely instructing clumps of tourists sporting backpacks and hiking boots on how to read maps and pamphlets, which contained all the information they needed, if they would just take the time to read them. It was definitely the start of high season in the park.

Lucy signaled to Del, punched a code that opened the Staff Only door, and ushered her into the office area. "Phew! Thanks for getting me out of there for a few minutes," she said in a booming voice. "Every year it's the same thing. We train the volunteers before the crowds show up, but under pressure some forget everything. Follow me. They created a detailed report on the damage from that earthquake. I've got a copy on my desk."

Del almost had to break into a trot to keep up with Lucy's quick-step through a short hall lined with offices. For someone working on her second career, Lucy had more than enough energy. She was a pint-sized dynamo in orthopedic shoes, her head topped by bright orange hair gelled into spikes. If it weren't for the spiked hair, you wouldn't be able to find her in a crowd. Lucy stopped abruptly in a large room with one neatly organized desk in front of a small nest of cubicles. She slapped her palm loudly on the desk's only empty corner. The top half of a head popped up over a nearby cubicle wall and then ducked.

"Dammit, this morning I put it right here with a sticky with your name on it," she boomed, then ratcheted up the volume even more. "Hey! Anyone take a report off my desk?"

A much softer woman's voice came from the cubicle with the disappearing head. "Not me."

"The other rangers are all out already. I won't see them until tomorrow." Lucy unlocked her desk and pulled out a spiral-bound document. "I'll chew out whoever took it later. Here, you can have the copy I was going to read over dinner. I never knew about an earthquake. It happened before I started."

"If this is your only copy, I'll scan it and bring it back," Del said.

"Don't bother, there's a couple others in the file cabinet."

"Thanks a lot, Lucy. I really appreciate it." Del paged quickly through the report. "This is really detailed—maps, photos, diagrams."

"The director at the time, Hiram Lemuel, was looking for extra funding, so they wanted to highlight the damage and repairs we needed." Lucy tapped Del lightly on the forearm. "You haven't volunteered here in a while. You free on Sunday morning? It's the start of the week of the Fourth and we need all the help we can get."

"With no orientation training?"

"You already know how to read a map and I heard you spent weeks here every summer with your grandparents. You hardly helped out last year, but I forgive you because you were working at the pub in Ferry Landing." She pointed to a large scheduling calendar. "Where can I write you in?"

From the public area a man's voice called down the hall. "Lucy? Lucy, we got a problem here. Can you come?"

"Don't move. I'll be right back." Lucy marched away shouting, "This better be a real problem!" and slammed the door to the public area, leaving the office amazingly quiet.

The cubicle with the jack-in-the-box occupant spoke up in a normal tone. "She's really loud but we love her. This place was a disorganized mess before Lucy took over."

Del walked back through the cubicles to find the voice's owner, who turned out to be Kay Levant, a middle-aged park ranger with reddish-gold tanned arms and face, cropped honey-colored hair, and deep creases around her eyes, the kind people call laugh lines but were mostly due to a career spent in the great outdoors. Kay Levant was a well-known naturalist. In May, Del had attended a presentation she gave on invasive insects and the potential damage to Maine's forests, but she didn't know Kay personally and introduced herself.

Ranger Levant shook Del's hand with a strong grip. "Nice to meet you. Call me Kay. I saw you at Monks Head yesterday, briefly. Sheriff Hodgkins got rid of you and your friend pretty quickly."

"Yeah, that's his job."

The ranger turned back to her keyboard and monitor. "You know, Lucy will have you roped into volunteering before you think to say no."

Del grinned. "I know she's very, um, forceful."

"That's one way of putting it."

On the wall behind Kay was a three-by-two-foot section of rough barn board mounted with a collection of a dozen or more antique hand tools—various hammers, chisels, and points. "Can I look at the tools?" Del asked. "One looks like my rock hammer, except heavier and much older. Are these yours?"

"Uh, no. I share this desk with Garth. They were his grandfather's, a stonecutter who worked in the quarries around here. If you come by when he's here, he might tell you more. He's really proud of them, but then he's Garth."

"I don't understand." Del snapped a picture of the tool display.

"Well, Garth is not much for talking. The only reason he tolerates sharing this space with me is that we're in the office writing reports on different days."

"Does he know about old, abandoned quarries on Pyke Island?"

"No doubt. He's been a ranger here forever. I think Granite Coast Park is his first and only love."

"I'd like to talk to him."

A door banged and Lucy's voice was heard booming from the hall. "Is it fall yet? Someone, tell me it's fall!"

Kay lowered her voice. "Check Lucy's calendar to see Garth's schedule, but you might have to put in some volunteer time."

EIGHT

On historical maps, Settlement Creek is the name of the stream that empties a basin of ponds and marshes nestled in the belly of the island's longest glacier-carved valley. As it approaches the sea, the creek seems to forget where it's going, and the last five miles meander around grassy flats and scrubby islands. Early settlers dug ditches and swales to drain the muddy soils, making lush meadows for agriculture. It was the only land on Pyke Island worth farming.

Because Granite Coast Park occupies much of the island's center and eastern part, the public road to the Settlement Creek community is circuitous, hugging the coast, the park, and the creek. Del realized that, although she'd lived on the island full-time for over three years, she'd never been to the very end of this road, only as far as the falls at Heart Pond. The land beyond that was all private.

It was after nine, close to sunset, and the coast was heavy with fog when Del and Marco arrived at a tall metal gate marking the private entrance. On either side of the gate, a six-foot chain-link fence lined with dark trees formed a wall that merged into the black woods. From outside, they couldn't see anything beyond the fencing.

Ty met them at the gate, which swung open when he inserted a card into a reader. The community at Settlement Creek called itself a village even though it was just twenty or so buildings evenly spaced around a circular drive. In the fading light, Del saw a series of one-story houses, vinyl-sided double-wide mobile homes set on cement slabs with neat yards and small covered porches leading to the front doors. Toward the middle of the loop sat a much larger steel-frame building with a softly lit sign out front that read: COMMUNITY CENTER. As they approached, two boys left the building laughing and ran playfully across the drive toward the houses.

Marco, Del, and Ty entered a foyer with a public restroom on one side and an office on the other. Coming from double doors at the end, Del heard the echo of a basketball being dribbled then hitting a backboard, and the squeak of sneakers on a wood floor.

On a bulletin board outside the office was a large poster with the headline:

VISITORS MUST RESPECT OUR COMMUNITY RULES:

NO ALCOHOLIC BEVERAGES

NO SMOKING OR VAPING

NO FIREWORKS

NO ILLEGAL DRUGS

NO HUNTING

NO FIREARMS OF ANY KIND

NO VIDEO GAMES

NO UNAUTHORIZED PETS OR ANIMALS

Underneath, it read: TVs AND VIDEOS ARE NOT ALLOWED IN RESIDENCES; INTERNET ACCESS IS LIMITED TO PUBLIC COMPUTERS IN THE SCHOOLHOUSE. Below that, a bulletin: WEEKLY MOVIES AT THE COMMUNITY CENTER with a list of dates and titles. Above the door to the office, another poster decorated with handprints in a range of sizes and colors proclaimed: TOLERANCE STARTS WITH ME.

As Ty made the introductions, Pale Moon Smith rose from her chair behind a modest desk. With her father a lawyer and her brothers in law school, Del had grown up around people who studied law, and she found them generally to be a conservative crowd. She had never met one like Pale Moon. Her wispy gray hair with whiter streaks was long, almost to her waist, twisted into dreadlocks entwined with a scattering of turquoise-dyed feathers and beads. She was delicate, and actually quite tan, not pale at all, with washed-out blue eyes. She wore a billowing plain blue cotton dress that made her neck and arms seem like she was built out of chicken bones. Del towered over her and was very careful shaking Pale Moon's fragile hand. She thought, *I can see why islanders were worried about hippies.*

"Thank you for seeing us," Marco started. He placed his phone on the desk between them. "I'd like to record this interview, if you don't mind."

"Turn it off," Pale Moon said. "This is a conversation, not an interview. I know you're a reporter. None of what I say is to be quoted."

Marco slipped his phone into his pocket. "We're very sorry about Chief George. How is the community taking the news?"

Pale Moon folded her hands on the desk. "Sad but relieved. Not knowing for over five years was very trying. We're grateful to the sheriff for telling our council in private before the police make it public." She sighed. "When I think about how he died, falling into that hole, falling, I think they said thirty feet, into a dark cave and crawling on the floor until …" Another sigh. "I don't know what we're going to tell the children. Maybe it would have been better to never know."

Del leaned forward to ask a question, but Ty shot her a look that said *Don't.*

"At least there is closure," Marco said.

"The elders are very relieved because this past winter we started the process of having him declared legally dead. Now we save those legal fees."

Marco started a question "About a will—" but Pale Moon cut him off by raising her palm. "I can't and won't talk about any will until we file for probate."

Del started to see Pale Moon in a different light. *She may be delicate, but she's not wimpy.*

"You knew him well?" Marco asked. "How long have you been a member of Settlement Creek?"

Pale Moon's face lit up. "Yes, I was one of the first members. This farm saved my life. I was working a temporary job without benefits, studying law in the evenings, and got pregnant. The father was a complete jerk, no help financially. He disappeared the day he heard I was pregnant. I had no family to fall back on. I managed to finish my degree, but I knew I couldn't support a baby without going on welfare. Back then, no law firm would hire an unmarried pregnant woman, and they got away with it. Today we would sue their pants off. George's community welcomed me and I had my beautiful boy here. Speaking of my beautiful boy ..."

During Pale Moon's story, the ponytailed Ryan had stepped into the office. The website's picture didn't quite do him justice. He was tall with a frame and muscular build that said "college basketball," very dark eyes outlined by thick lashes the same color as his dark brown hair. He must have been playing in the gym. The shorts, sneakers, and towel he was using to dry his face were a dead giveaway. Pale Moon introduced him to Del and Marco, but he barely acknowledged anyone. Ryan asked his mother about setting up for something and she nodded. He left as abruptly as he'd arrived.

Marco seemed eager to ask more questions. "Can you tell me about the community's requirement to show Indigenous American heritage? How's that work? How do people who have no tribal affiliation prove that?"

"There's no requirement to be a Native American, although it helps," Pale Moon said. "George taught us his cultural values. Our vision is a community that follows the tribal organization of native people, such as common land, a respect for community, shared income and duties, wise elders who mediate disputes." She pointed a finger at Marco. "That you *can* quote me on. But there's not enough time tonight. I've got a meeting in ten minutes."

"When can we do a more in-depth interview?" Marco laid his business card on her desk. "I'd like to do an article on how Settlement Creek Farm evolved from George's vision."

"There's so much to tell you about the joys of living here. Come back on Sunday morning. We're going to have a memorial service for George in the gym. There will be wall-to-wall displays of photographs and memories, and everyone will want to talk about him."

She reached under her desk and brought out a poster-sized sheet of cardboard partially covered with photos, likely her own work-in-progress, and propped it up on her desk. There were two eight-by-ten head shots of Chief George, one as a young man with slicked-back dark hair, and one much older with a head of flowing silver and a bushy dark mustache. In another picture, he and a group of young men were standing in front of a playground holding tools. In each photo Chief George was wearing a western-style shirt, not typical Maine duds, and he wasn't grinning like the others. The look on his face could be described as lonely.

Del leaned in to study the photos. George was attractive in the weather-beaten cowboy style. When he looked directly at a camera, he was incredibly sexy. There was an expression coming from those smiling dark eyes and pursed lips that said "How about I make you happy tonight?" Del found herself smiling as she thought about how she might answer.

Pale Moon clapped her hands over her head and giggled. "There it is," she said. "Del sees it. I can show these photos to a hundred men and all they see is a handsome face and head of hair. But us women know that special look, that je ne sais quoi, when we see it." She was clapping and rocking in her chair when Ryan came back into the office. "Del, you see it? Admit it."

Del nodded, blushed, and laughed softly with her. Marco looked confused. Ty was deadpan.

Ryan caught most of the merriment, responding with a deep frown.

"It's really not funny. I've heard that the 'special look' comes with extra baggage, the kind that might be jealous enough to create a scene."

In an instant, Pale Moon's face changed from merriment to a mask. "Ryan, that's enough. We don't gossip and pass on rumors." She tucked the poster away.

Ryan flicked the towel he was holding over his shoulder. "Yeah, I know, don't insult the dead."

"We're done here. Ty will show you out." Pale Moon stood and handed them each a pale-yellow printed card. "The service is invitation-only. You'll need these to be let in at the gate." As she held up a card for Marco, she eyed him directly. "This is an invitation to attend. There will be no photography without my permission, and I need to review anything you write." She raised her eyebrows.

As he took the card from her fingers, Marco acknowledged agreement with a smile and a nod.

Pale Moon shot Ryan an evil look. "Come on Sunday and talk to people who loved him." In a billow of blue cotton, she breezed out the door as Ryan held it open. Behind her back he met Del's gaze for a brief moment. His frown changed into a wry smirk, seemingly for her benefit.

Once they were in the parking area out of hearing range, Del turned to Ty and said in a loud whisper. "What was that about Chief George falling into the chimney hole? That doesn't make any sense. You saw the jagged rocks where the log smashed into splinters. Even if he survived the fall, would he have crawled around those rocks toward the interior, or would he have crawled toward the light?"

"You were pretty sure that the back of his skull was broken," Marco said. "Couldn't that happen in a thirty-foot fall? So he survived, but barely, was so disoriented he didn't know where he was going?"

"No, you should have seen the rocks sticking up everywhere." Del shook her head. "No, a fall like that would have broken more than just his skull. Chief George was struck on the back of the head while looking at the cave art. He landed face-first, maybe tried to crawl away, and died."

Ty nodded. "I agree with Del. I suspect the cops told the council that it was an accident as a preliminary assessment or because they want the murderer to believe they're done."

"Don't forget, someone carried a log up to that lip of rock specifically to hide the hole you almost fell into," Del said. "We should have realized it was out of place before you sat on it. No tree that size ever grew anywhere near there. Chief George certainly didn't put it there after he *fell* in. To find the murderer, you need to find everyone who knew about the cave."

Ty nodded again.

Marco was jotting in his notebook. "I've been researching the Wilson family. Remember, their property abuts Settlement Creek on one side, and Gabe said there was a feud between them."

"But all that ended when George died," Del said.

"Maybe not. There's a history of trouble between Wilson and Settlement Creek for the whole time George was president, including lawsuits on illegal fishing. I found a few court decisions online."

"What's the status now? Are there still pending lawsuits?" Ty asked.

"As far as I can tell, his daughter Charlotte withdrew the last one. I'd kill to see what state detectives found when Chief George disappeared. I'm sure they saw Wilson as a suspect."

"Those records are confidential," Ty said. "Pale Moon told me she tried to get a copy, but the cops won't release any of it. Someone's privacy must be at risk."

Grinning broadly, Marco ran his fingers through his curly hair, pushing it away from his face. "So I have to do my own legwork."

"What does Pale Moon know about how the remains were found?" Del asked. "Does she know about the cave art?"

"Pale Moon and the elders were told that a ranger found the cave and the petroglyphs. There's some controversy about whether it's on park land or their land. I heard them discuss having a surveyor verify the boundary. In the meantime, the state cops are having both entrances to the cave closed over."

Ty's phone buzzed and he was quick to check it.

"How's the surveillance going?" Del asked.

"That's one of the alarms. Looks like I'm staying awhile tonight. This vandal is patient and elusive, uncanny. Seems he knows exactly what we're doing."

NINE

Watch and wait. The following day, Ty Holden mulled over how those words might become his new mantra. Gabe and Marco were clanking dishes in Gabe's kitchen, making lobster rolls for lunch. He smelled melted butter and toasted bread. Ty was the only one not busily getting ready for an afternoon of hauling lobster traps. Gabe wanted to leave by one to catch the slack tide. Yesterday's fog was finally burning off, and apparently slack tide was a good time to pick up pot buoys.

Marco had filled them in on the police announcement released that morning from the county office in Ellis Junction. The state police spokesperson had confirmed that the remains found on Pyke Island were identified as George Tozur, who disappeared five years and seven months earlier. He died of a depressed skull fracture, most likely from a fall. The initial assessment was that his death was accidental, but the investigation was ongoing. The remains were being moved to the medical examiner's office in Augusta for further analysis. It was a short announcement. Nothing about the remains being found in a cave near Monks Head. Marco said it was a waste of gas to drive all that way to Ellis Junction for a ten-minute announcement with no follow-up questions.

Ty watched as Del pulled the spiral binding out of the earthquake report and scanned the fifteen pages using Gabe's printer. She wanted a digital copy and almost tossed the paper copy into the recycling basket.

"By the way," she announced, "the report lists two new rockslides on Monks Head, the biggest one along the side of the slab cave, so it supports the theory that the quake in November created the opening before George disappeared."

"I'll give the sheriff that paper copy, if you don't need it," Ty said. "He might want to pass it to the state cops." Del stapled the sheets back together. He folded the document in half and tucked it into his back pocket.

While the others were going out to haul Gabe's traps, Ty had an appointment with the sheriff to fill him in on the surveillance at Settlement Creek. Overnight, someone had torn down one of the wildlife cameras. The strap holding it to the tree was shredded, and Ty found the crushed case in the creek. The memory card was useless, no video recording. Ty was waiting on a delivery so he could set up cameras to watch other cameras. *Watch and wait, but make the trap better each time.* Mentally, he was planning how to get the best coverage and outfox this vandal. The curious evidence was a pattern of scratches on the tree trunk, which one elder thought was cut by a knife, while others said they might be bear scratches. It seemed obvious that the vandal was trying to disguise their work to make it look like an animal's.

Of course, now that the vandal knew there were cameras, they might never come back. Ty discussed that situation with Pale Moon, and they agreed to keep watching for two more weeks. That worked out perfectly with his own plans.

Marco and Gabe came out of the kitchen with plates of lobster rolls and salad. Ty had to smile at Marco's new enthusiasm for cooking and cleaning. Ty wasn't sure whether he was trying to impress Gabe or Del.

"I wanted to head back to the university before the weekend," Marco said, "but now I'm going to stay through Sunday so I can attend George's memorial service. There's a story there, even if it's a lovefest."

"Sorry, I gotta pass," said Del. "I volunteered to work the next two Sundays at the information desk at the Visitor Center. But I have an ulterior motive, because Garth will be in the office."

"Rubin Garth?" Gabe asked.

"They told me everyone calls him just Garth."

"I've met him." Gabe nodded. "He's a character, probably the last ranger to have trained in the woods as a Maine Guide and not in college. You don't meet a real backwoods tracker anymore.

"He knows about abandoned quarries on the island. Finding any quarry near the edge of the Monks Head formation would be a big plus, like getting a free look deeper into the bedrock.

"The park is lucky to have him." Gabe cleared his throat twice. This was going to be a long speech for him. "Year before last, when that fellow's remains started showing up—you know, the one who disappeared in the snowstorm, only searchers couldn't find a trace until spring. Then someone found a human bone and they called for volunteers. Some of us from the firehouse pitched in. I tell you, the tracking dogs were going every which way. It was Garth that followed the coyote trail to find the rest of the body."

Del started searching on her phone. "I remember that."

"Then you're planning on hiking Monks Head again?" Ty asked.

"Soon as I can get permission. I really have to finish my project."

"Hmm, we watch and wait," mused Ty. He was scheming, figuring how to spend more time alone with Del. There was so much to tell her. For the last few months, he had been playacting conversations he wanted to have with her.

"Not me. Yum," Marco said, sucking butter off his fingers. "I'm going to do some digging on the backstories around George Tozur and the Wilson family. You want to come, Del?"

"Sorry, I scheduled time at the mineralogy lab on campus. If I don't finish before Saturday, I'll have to wait because the lab is closing for two weeks after the Fourth. I'd love to play detective, but I have a deadline."

Good girl, Ty thought. *Stay away from the mess at Settlement Creek. There's some ugly business going on—suspicions and half-truths about the security work they hired me for. I know Marco's getting himself involved, and I'll probably have to save his ass at some point, but then, I owe him one.*

TEN

A gloriously warm and dry Sunday—the last day of June—started the Fourth of July week. The weather forecast looked spectacular, highs in the low eighties and nights in the sixties. Del, in her newly pressed dark-green shirt, was hanging around Lucy's desk, ostensibly to chat with Lucy, but really hoping to catch Garth when he came in to write his weekly report. Lucy was always first in the office, by seven, no later. Most volunteers trickled in after eight. The ranger on duty at the information center would not unlock the doors to the public until nine, even though there were already a handful of tourists outside.

Garth stepped in from a back entrance and moved quietly to his cubicle. Del knew what he looked like because of a photo on the park website. But she didn't expect him to be a giant. He was broad-chested, fifty-plus-years old, with thick, curly strawberry-blond hair touched with gray, and a full beard. Del could picture him wearing a kilt and carrying a broadsword. She was surprised she had never met this ranger before, not in previous volunteer stints at the information counter, and never while hiking in the park. She certainly would have remembered meeting him.

She put her hand up to say hello. He glanced her way and quickly disappeared, more or less, into his cubicle. Less, because even seated, the crown of his head was visible.

She strolled down to where he was sitting. "Hi. I'm Del Corriveau. Lucy said I might find you here today."

"I'm here." He didn't look up, but continued writing with a pencil. His hands made the pencil look not much larger than a toothpick.

"I'm mapping the bedrock around Monks Head, and I heard that you might know about abandoned quarries in that area."

"Who told you that?"

"Kay Levant. I was here a couple of days ago picking up a report, and I was admiring your tool collection. They're pretty old, right?"

He put down his pencil and spun the chair so that he faced the tools on the wall plaque. "Hand-forged by quarry blacksmiths for my grandfather and his father."

"When was that?"

"Great-grandfather came to work in the quarries from Scotland in 1870. At fourteen, Grandfather was a tool boy, and later a stone cutter. Worked granite up and down the coast. Even worked slate near Borestone until that ran out."

"The one with the curved, chiseled end looks different from the others."

"Paving hammer."

"A what?"

"Called a paving hammer because it was used to lay granite paving blocks." He pivoted to her with an annoyed look. "What do you want—a lesson on stone working tools or to find old quarries?"

Del handed him a copy of the park's official topographic map showing the mountains, streams, ponds, and trails. "Do you know about the quarries around the base of Monks Head?"

He unfolded it and marked a circle on the southwest side between the base of the peak and a wetland. "Here, a small quarry, probably used for one project. Got the pink granite and some other stone." He marked two more circles far from the base on the southern side. "These might not help you. They're mostly filled in and I think the stone is all gray."

"Thanks, that'll really help my project. I'll start with the pink."

"No foot trails there."

"I know. I'm used to finding my way."

"Old dirt road cuts in from the Wilson property. It's private." He pointed to a dashed line.

"Okay, thanks."

Garth picked up his pencil and started writing.

Guess the conversation is over. A buzzer sounded. *Opening time.*

Del tucked the map into her shirt pocket. She heard Lucy's booming voice asking the volunteers to listen up for a few announcements.

By ten, there were no more campsites available, so the volunteers at the park information desk were handing visitors a list of camping areas along the lakes north of Ellis Junction. There was no reservation system for the park, just first come, first served, and that always led to many disappointed campers. Del spent most of the morning helping people deal with disappointment by suggesting they try a scenic hike and lunch at a lobster pound.

ELEVEN

Ty Holden observed the Sunday memorial service from the fringes, staying near the back of the gym, away from the door. He wasn't all that interested in how much these people loved Chief George. He was more interested in people who hated him, and it didn't seem likely that those people would get invitations to what Marco was calling a "lovefest." He estimated that there were about a hundred chairs in the gym, and most were filled, the majority taken by Settlement Creek families who brought many fidgety, whispering children. The women in the audience were dressed in colorful summer dresses, the men in summer shirts with jeans or shorts. After the service, everyone was invited to a community lunch.

There were a couple rows of special guests, including Sheriff Mike Hodgkins, Deputy Jessica Ouellette, two state police cops Ty recognized from the sheriff's Pyke Island office, and a handful of local business leaders. Marco Avila, who had been buzzing around the room before the service started, sat behind the sheriff and seemed a little fidgety himself—particularly when the sheriff stood up and left during the speeches.

The memorial service was mostly short talks with some poetry readings mixed in. Several older Settlement Creek members told nostalgic stories of the early years, when everyone had to work in the fields and keep part-time jobs outside the community, called the "dollar-driven world," in order to make ends meet. The audience laughed and clapped for each story. They lauded Chief George's vision and leadership and described how they'd elected him chief as a special honor. The next speaker pulled with a flourish, pulled the draping from a large poster set on a tripod in front of the stage. It showed a drawing of a plaque honoring Chief George's life. The speaker described the memorial in some detail for the audience. Besides George's name and profile, it listed the values he preached: honesty and integrity, respect for the land and its history, and respect for elders and community. The plaque was to be cast in bronze, mounted on a polished granite monument, and placed near the Community Center. The audience applauded, and some stood up and called out "Great job!" and "Beautiful!"

The final speaker was a soft-spoken man with a broad, tanned face framed by two long braids of black hair. Pale Moon introduced him as "Uncle," and Ty knew that was how everyone addressed him. He also thought some of the elders harbored resentment against Uncle, a resentment Ty was sure he saw behind their polite but cool deference.

Uncle's short speech never mentioned Chief George. Instead, he called upon the healing power of Mother Earth to help those who mourn. He told members to let the wind take away their grief, to watch it blow across the sea like the morning fog. Uncle's voice was deep and soothing. Some in the audience were wiping tears from their cheeks.

After Uncle, a group of schoolchildren took the stage to sing a song accompanied by a large drum and a flute played by energetic teenagers. Pale Moon, looking almost presidential in black pants, high-heeled boots, and a dark, purple tunic belted in silver, was the conductor. The song, introduced as her creation, was sung mostly in English but included bird calls and whistles.

When the song was done, the audience clapped vigorously, many rising to stand for an ovation. Pale Moon asked the children to bow, and she bowed herself. Clearly enjoying the applause, she extended her arms to the audience. Then something she saw changed her radiant expression to anger. With her hands clenched, Pale Moon stepped rapidly down the stairs in front of the stage and marched through the center aisle to the back of the gym. Everyone turned to watch her. Ryan stood up as she passed his seat. Her boot heels tapping a machine-gun rhythm on the floor, Pale Moon was moving like a well-aimed bullet speeding at a target.

Ty saw where the impact was about to happen. A woman in a wheelchair pushed by a tall, muscular man had come into the gym at some point during the singing. Ty assumed it was Charlotte Wilson. She sat hunched, knobby knees showing through a long, black skirt. She wore a black wig and a dark purple shawl over her bony shoulders. She was probably in her sixties, maybe a little older than Pale Moon. The man pushing her chair was buzz-cut and sunburnt, likely her son, Josh.

As in Josh, the possible vandal.

In their first meeting, Pale Moon had made it abundantly clear to Ty that she believed Josh Wilson was behind the vandalism. She said the problems had started just after he moved back to Pyke Island after several tours with the US Army. She thought the history of bad blood with the Wilsons was motivation enough.

For an instant, Ty thought he should step between them. He decided instead that it would be fun, and maybe useful, to let the confrontation play out.

"Get out!" Pale Moon screamed, even before she reached the wheelchair. "You have no right to be here! Turn her around and get her out!" Ryan was two steps behind her.

Charlotte Wilson watched Pale Moon approach without flinching. "We have every right." Her voice was soft but firm.

It was Josh who spoke next. He was loud, clear, and emphatic. "If we aren't welcome, why did we get an invitation?"

"That's a lie!" Pale Moon stopped just short of bumping into them. "I authorized no one to invite you."

Ryan caught up to her side. Ty saw Deputy Ouellette and the state cops rising to their feet.

"You'd better go," Ryan said, moving closer to Josh. "Ah, perhaps there's been a mistake."

"We go when my mother is ready." Josh was eyeball-to-eyeball with Ryan, showing no sign of backing down. Even though they were the same height, Josh carried at least twenty more pounds of muscle and an attitude that Ty had seen in career soldiers, a sign of the intense training and the confidence to do what was needed. If he wanted to, Josh could kill pretty boy Ryan before the police sprinted the twenty feet to stop him.

Army Ranger or one of the dark ops special forces?

"Get out!" Pale Moon stomped her foot and raised her hand as if to strike the wheelchair. Josh swiftly grabbed her wrist. She tried to pull away but didn't have the strength to do much more than vibrate in anger. Ryan put a hand on Josh's chest as if he wanted to push him away, but he hesitated, wisely. For a few heartbeats, everyone was immobile, all eyes on the quartet frozen in their various positions. The only sound in the gym was a soft sobbing coming from Charlotte Wilson. The once-fidgety children were as fascinated as their parents.

Before anyone made the next move, Deputy Ouellette stepped in the middle. Even though she was a foot shorter than both of them, she spoke quietly, firmly, disengaging Ryan from Josh. She ushered Pale Moon back to the stage. The state cops escorted the Wilsons to the door.

As the wheelchair moved past, Josh's left hand showed a slight tremor, so slight that most people might not notice. The well-trained machine was out of balance. Ty noticed because he had seen the tremor before, a result of too many "capture/kill" operations that were just "kill." It got worse when the final body count included women and children.

Might be useful to get his military history and discharge papers, if Mike can get them.

The audience began to murmur. Someone from the stage announced another poem and song.

Fun's over. Ty reflected on the confrontation. *Really, did Pale Moon almost lose it, or was that an act to call attention to the Wilsons? I wonder what Marco thought of the scene. Marco?*

Ty scanned the room. Marco's seat was empty. No sign of him. Ty walked out to the front steps where he could see the parking area and found his friend trying to talk to Charlotte, prancing around her wheelchair while Josh seemed to be running interference. At one point, Charlotte put her hands on Marco's arm, and he crouched down to hear her. In response, Josh shoved the wheelchair past him, knocking Marco off balance. Josh helped his mother stand and maneuvered her into the passenger seat of a large black SUV with darkened windows. Ty couldn't hear what was being said, but their pantomime was obvious. Just before getting into the driver's seat, Josh pointed forcefully at Marco and snapped something that made Marco take several steps back.

Marco, you fucking snoop. I can guess how the Wilsons got an invitation. You gave them the one that Del wasn't going to use. Isn't there some kind of journalism rule against manipulating a story?

TWELVE

On Monday, Marco was back at the university, and Ty said he would be busy all day testing his new security cameras. Evie talked Grandpa and Del into going to the local food festival in Summer Hill Harbor at the southern end of Pyke Island even though they knew the festival was another excuse to sell more stuff to tourists and keep them in town for a few hours. Del was going to pass until she saw that the vendor list included Settlement Creek Farm.

The festival was a series of tents, tables, and exhibits on the tree-shaded town common. Vendors were selling handcrafts and local foods, that is, if local is anywhere in Maine, not necessarily Pyke Island. The Settlement Creek booth was tended by young women in colorful tunics and beads. As it was too early in the growing season for most vegetables, they only had a few boxes of greens, onions, and sugar snap peas. Evie and Grandpa pinched, sniffed, sampled, and bought some of this and that. They were so cute together. Del wandered away and strolled around the sun-dappled common hoping to see Ryan.

It was Ryan who saw her first. "Hey, ah, Del, right?"

For the second time, she noticed how fine and buff he looked in a T-shirt and shorts.

She stopped strolling and pushed up her sunglasses. "Hi, Ryan. Are you selling vegetables today?"

"Not a chance," Ryan said, laughed. "They don't even encourage me to help in the gardens."

"And yet archeologists specialize in digging."

"Ha, good one. I volunteered for a month at a dig site in South Dakota once. It was wicked hot and dusty, not what I want to do again."

"What do archeologists do if not dig?"

"Study artifacts someone else excavated. The vault at the university is filled with them. My specialty is the chemistry of figurines, carvings, and art. You know, to identify the materials used and the process for making them. A nice, air-conditioned lab is where I like to work."

"Perfect." Del grinned with the thought of how fitting his expertise was with incredible cave art in his backyard. "Your mother must be ecstatic."

A noisy scrum of children delighted with some treat on a stick appeared out of nowhere. It was clear to Ryan and Del, standing in the middle of the green, that they were an obstacle, so they strolled to a side street off the common.

"God, no, she never liked my career choice," he said. "She wanted me to be a lawyer."

"Sure, but she must be pleased *now*. I bet you can't wait to see it?"

Ryan made a face, not exactly a scowl but close. "See what?"

"Oh, shit." She lowered her sunglasses over her eyes.

"Tell me," Ryan said. "Is this something everyone knows but me?"

Del led him to a quiet corner next to the church, where they found a stone bench that couldn't be seen from the tents on the common.

"I guess I screwed up," Del started, keeping her voice low. "I know that the elders of Settlement Creek know, and I assumed you did."

"Know what?" He leaned in and whispered, but in a harsh voice. He seemed to be moving beyond just being annoyed.

"Chief George's remains were found in a cave of sorts." Del paused trying to figure out how much to say.

"I heard a rocky place."

"A rock shelter, a cave made by slabs of rock broken from the dome." Del watched Ryan carefully. His expression changed from angry to curious. "His remains were found in front of a wall of very old cave art."

"Like what kind of art?"

"Petroglyphs—caribou, elk, bear."

Ryan jumped to his feet. "Pale Moon didn't tell me? She didn't *want* to tell me. She asked me yesterday when I was going back to Wisconsin. She wants me to leave. How could she keep that from me?" He wasn't whispering any longer.

"I'm sorry. I should go."

He made a tight circle of stiff-legged steps. "She is always in control, managing every move, everyone. It was that way even when Chief George was alive." He stopped with a jerk and swung to face her. "Want to hear a joke? *Chief* George was president, but the power belonged to Pale Moon. My mother was always on the council, for years as treasurer, then vice president. She knew his weaknesses and used them."

Del started backing away. "I really need to go."

Ryan waved his arms as if he could take flight. "Want to hear another joke? The whole Native American bullshit?"

"No, no. I don't want to hear another joke. But I need a promise from you."

His arms collapsed to his side. He stared at the ground.

"Don't tell anyone you found out from me. I'll be in deep shit. Tell them you overheard a park ranger talking." She turned onto the sidewalk heading toward the festival.

Three steps and Ryan was right behind her. He put his hand on Del's shoulder, firmly enough to make her stop. "You haven't told me how *you* found out."

Del shook her head and pulled away.

"Give me your number and I promise I won't tell." There was that sly smile again.

"That feels like extortion." She gave him her number.

"Wasn't the way I planned it, but I was hoping to meet you today. A couple of friends are planning my birthday drunk in a few weeks. It's the big three-oh this summer, in August. The guys from the university are driving out late July. We'll be doing the watering holes here in Summer Hill Harbor."

"Most drunks involve alcoholic beverages. Isn't that against the rules?"

Ryan snorted. "Off the farm I make my own rules. I'd like you to come, even if you bring your friends."

He didn't seem angry any longer, quite a personality shift from someone who just moments ago was throwing the adult version of a tantrum.

"Sure, send the invite. I can't promise."

Again, Del started slowly toward the town common and festival tents. Walking behind her, Ryan said, "I googled you."

"I haven't checked in a while," she said casually as they continued to stroll. "Learn anything interesting?"

"You were a soccer star on the Boston College roster a few years ago, and before that on the team that won the Massachusetts State Girls Championship. How come you don't play now?"

"I was never that good. An injury ended it all." *Not really an injury— a badly timed pregnancy, engagement, miscarriage, breakup, and months of … Shit, that chapter's closed.*

Ryan nodded his head vigorously. "Oh, yeah! Same with my basketball." He circled one shoulder slowly. "Rotator cuff."

Del pivoted to face him. "Is your mother's name really Pale Moon?"

He nodded and snickered. "Her parents were some of the original West Coast hippies."

"Was she in love with Chief George?"

Ryan looked surprised. "No, they fought all the time. Or more like she yelled at him a lot."

"What about?"

He was dismissive. "I never listened."

"He didn't, like, live with you?" Del asked.

"Well, kind of. When I was little, we all lived together in the old farmhouse. Pretty cozy, if you can imagine me and Pale Moon, three other families with a total of six kids, George, and Miss Ella, all in eight rooms. We shared bedrooms."

"Who's Miss Ella?"

"Ella Wilson. It was her farmhouse."

"Did George sleep with Miss Ella?"

"No way. If she slept, it was downstairs in the pantry off the kitchen. They put a bed in there for her."

"What do you mean, 'if she slept'?"

"God, she used to scare me, always walking like she was in a hurry but in circles. We all had to take care she didn't hurt herself or get lost. Sometimes she'd go into a room and not find her way out and start crying. I guess now you'd call it dementia."

"Did you always live in her farmhouse?"

Ryan thought for a moment, then shook his head. "Some time after Miss Ella died, they started putting up houses for the families. Every year there was some construction because they were accepting new members. I don't remember it all, but I was a kid."

"Was Chief George a good farmer?"

"Nah. I guess he put in his share of work, but I know he would just as soon play with Miss Ella's horses. He was really upset when, after she died, all the horses and carriages were sold to raise money."

"How did you and George get along?"

"He ignored me. I was fine with it." Ryan stuffed his hands into his pockets and hunched his shoulders. "Honestly, once I went away to high school, I stopped caring about what was happening at Settlement Creek as long as someone kept paying the bills."

Del saw Grandpa and Evie walking in her direction with as many bags as each could carry. "Here comes my grandfather. Really, I need to go." She smiled extra warmly at Ryan, hoping he wouldn't detect the overacting. "I'd like to talk more. Send me a text next time you're planning on being in town."

Like a happy stud, Ryan flicked his ponytail. "You bet."

THIRTEEN

The following afternoon, Ty eagerly agreed to help Del locate the quarry that Garth had marked on the park map. They started at the falls by Settlement Creek where they'd met eight days before, but this time instead of following the old foot trail to Monks Head, they skirted a marshy area, staying close to Heart Pond. Ty wondered if the "pond" name was a mistake. As they made their way around it, what appeared to be narrow and shallow at the falls turned into a three-mile-oblong lake marked by many coves and inlets. Like many places in Maine, he assumed the name once given had probably just stuck.

There was no trail to speak of, barely a narrow deer path that disappeared into the dense growth of skinny twisted trees Del called alders. They tried to move around the alders but eventually had to work their way carefully through them. The ground was spongy, knotted with roots cradling pools of water, ideal mosquito and black fly territory. The insect repellent wipes Del had packed ran out quickly. Finally, sweaty, muddy, and beating off insects, they cleared the alders and came to a wide, rutted, dirt, and gravel trail. Ty felt a welcome breeze.

He checked their position with a handheld GPS device. "We should be very close."

They followed the trail around a curve to a sign about fifty yards farther west. It marked the boundary of Granite Coast Park and explained the list of prohibitions: no motorized vehicles, no firearms, no hunting, no trapping, no fires, no overnight camping, do not remove plant or rock material, and all pets must be leashed. A few feet beyond the park sign was the first No Trespassing—Private Property sign. Ty saw similar signs repeated at intervals along the trail.

"Wilson postings," he said. "I bet that if we had a tape measure, each sign would be exactly the mandated distance."

Del pulled out a folded map. "According to Garth, we just walked past the quarry. It's supposed to be north of this trail. But that whole area is alder thicket." She slapped at a mosquito. "Shit. This is why I prefer mountaintops. I need some water."

They backtracked to where they first came out of the marsh, took off their packs, settled on a couple of stones alongside the trail, and shared a water jug. Ty's trail pants were muddy and his T-shirt was soaked with sweat. He took off the shirt and hung it on a branch to dry. The bugs seemed to prefer Del, who was still slapping but with less frequency. Ty smiled, thinking about a conversation he'd had with Gabe that morning after breakfast. Gabe had talked about how awkward he felt sometimes when he was with Evie and how he was learning to be with her. Being married to Marjorie almost fifty years, he never thought about other women. Gabe now described himself as "real gone."

Ty watched Del use handfuls of water to wipe mud splatters off her bare legs, long, fit, and firm with a few scars from what he guessed were soccer injuries, but they didn't detract from how appealing they were bare and wet. The cut he had tenderly bandaged last week was covered by a scab and healing nicely. Ty understood "real gone" without a 1950s translation guide.

"Why are you smiling?" Del asked. "So far this hike has been miserable."

"Gabe told me this morning he was 'real gone' for Evie. That's a funny expression."

"They really are cute together."

"Speaking of cute"—he reached over to wipe what looked like a bloody, flattened mosquito off her cheek—"you got this one before she could finish her meal."

"Wait. Who you calling cute—the bug or me covered in bites?"

"You, good buddy. I'm afraid there's no longer much to say about this mosquito."

"I see, Mister Private Eye, using your powers of observation …"

"Del, I was thinking—"

"Hey, don't start another thought. Did you or did you not just now call me cute?"

She wasn't making it easy for him. He looked at his hands, wondering what would happen if he just leaned over and kissed her. That might ruin a great friendship or start a beautiful romance. But he didn't know which. *What did Gabe say about learning to be with her?*

"I did. But I'm not sure this is the right place to be serious."

"Okay." She seemed to sense the change in his tone. "Are we being serious?"

"Yeah." His practiced conversations hadn't gone like this, so he felt himself stumbling. "I was hoping we would have time to talk."

"Hiking-buddy talk or who-killed-Chief-George talk or—" Del cut short her question as she used the map to swat away the mosquitoes flying around her face.

"Maybe it should wait until we're in a place with no biting insects."

"Didn't answer my question."

"Okay. What do you want to know about me? Ask something important, to seem fair."

"Ty, we're not in a contest here, tell me a secret and I'll tell you one of equal size." She was clearly irritated but he couldn't tell how much he had screwed up the conversation or whether the bugs were to blame.

"That isn't what I meant."

Del went back to her map, unfolding and refolding it so their location was in the center. "Could Garth have put his circle on the wrong side?" She stood up and took a few steps along the edge of the trail, trying to see into the forest.

"Del, look at me. Did I say something to make you mad?"

Her attention had shifted to a distant sound. From the direction of the park boundary, they heard an engine. Ty pulled his shirt from the branch, shook it, and pulled it over his head. The sound grew increasingly louder until they saw a dust cloud and the off-road ATV that was making it. It passed the boundary sign and kept coming. As it closed in, he saw it was an oversized four-seater with a driver in a full helmet with a tinted face shield and one passenger, a large German shepherd in a harness sitting alert and tall.

"What happened to no motorized vehicles?" Ty grabbed his pack.

"Rangers drive them sometimes." Del moved to the middle of the trail and waved her hands over her head. The ATV slowed and stopped a few feet from her. The driver got out cradling a rifle. He wasn't dressed like a ranger. The German shepherd watched the action with pointed ears held erect, ready for a command.

What the fuck happened to no firearms? Ty thought he recognized the rifle, a Stoner-25, a sniper rifle with night scope, semi-automatic, long-range, expensive. He was anxious that Del seemed completely at ease with being miles out in the woods meeting a strange man holding a rifle who in the last fifty yards had just broken several park rules.

"Hey, do you know about an old quarry near here?" she asked the driver as Ty moved to her side.

The driver flipped up his face shield. It was Josh Wilson. He didn't answer her right away but looked them both over. "The park service doesn't want hikers in this area," he said with calm authority. "I'm going to ask you to leave." He swung the rifle to one elbow, muzzle pointed at the dirt.

"They don't want people near Monks Head. I've got permission from the director to be here." Del showed him the map. "I'm looking for this quarry."

Wilson wasn't interested in her map. He stared at Ty and Ty stared back. It seemed like the start of an alpha dog confrontation.

Ty nodded to the rifle. "You got the right to use that here?"

"I hunt coyotes on my own land." Wilson tilted his head to indicate that his land was somewhere behind him.

"The night scope help with that?"

"We're in night hunting season."

"What size box magazine?"

"You ask a lot of questions. Who the fuck are you?" Wilson moved the rifle into both hands, to the ready-carry position. If it was meant to be threatening, Ty was not impressed. Wilson's hand was nowhere near the safety. Again, he saw a slight tremor in Wilson's left fingers.

"I'm a hiker, here with my friend who is a geologist looking for a quarry." Ty took the map from Del, who had been watching the exchange with raised eyebrows.

"You were at Settlement Creek."

Ty thought about lying, but then maybe this would play out better if he could get a reaction. "I'm doing some surveillance work for them. There's a vandal that's been destroying property."

"You're a cop."

"Private investigator."

Wilson sneered. "I heard about it. Mike Hodgkins called on me months ago. Apparently, someone at Settlement Creek thinks I'm responsible."

"We had a Bushnell wildlife camera trashed a couple of days ago."

"Expensive trail cameras can be targets for thieves. I use Browning myself."

"The vandal was bent on destruction."

Wilson lowered the gun to elbow carry and chuckled. "Good luck with your surveillance. Make sure you got one watching Pale Moon Smith." He took the folded map from Ty and studied it for a moment. "Someone marked the quarry on the wrong side. That's just an alder swamp in there." He pointed to the other side of the trail. "Go in about twenty yards past that old cedar with the busted crown."

Del took the map back. "Hey, thanks a lot."

Wilson squinted at Del with a thin smile. "But don't expect much. That quarry is filled with water this time of year. Late summer it might be dry."

Wilson climbed into his ATV, flipped down the face shield, and started the engine. He spun it in a tight turn and roared away down the trail, past the park boundary and out of sight.

"You know him?" Del asked.

"That's Josh Wilson, a former army ranger and grandson of the SOB old man."

"He acts like he's patrolling for the police." She stepped into the woods next to the cedar tree Wilson had pointed out.

Ty was right behind her. "The cops asked him to keep hikers off his property, but looks like he's extended his work into the park. Pale Moon is sure he's the vandal."

Behind the third line of trees, an oval pool appeared, one formed by a large hole cut into exposed rock. About fifty feet across the pool, an outcrop of stone rose at least twenty feet. The outcrop was stepped in four thick layers, like an amphitheater for very tall spectators.

Del stopped at the water's edge, which was ringed by broken blocks of various sizes. "Why would Josh Wilson want to vandalize their farm?" she asked, bending forward to examine the drill holes in one of the slabs.

"Maybe the same reason they think his old man was responsible for George Tozur's death."

Del stepped carefully around a heap of smaller rocks. "Grandpa said Old Man Wilson was pretty hobbled with arthritis when George was killed. How do the police think he climbed to the cave?"

"He might have had an accomplice."

That caught her attention. She turned to face Ty for the first time since she had called their conversation a contest. It gave him the chance to gaze into her hazel eyes with rays of green. He had to check his desire to touch her cheek again.

"You mean his grandson?" Del asked.

Ty shook his head. "The sheriff said Josh was stationed in Iraq when George disappeared."

"Then the police are reopening a murder investigation?"

"They never really closed it, just moved it to the cold case list. I know your project is important to you, so I hope it's not a distraction."

"How about you, Ty? What's important to you right now?"

"Well, a lot of things." Her comment was unexpected. He felt off balance again. "Finish my work for Pale Moon, hopefully catch the vandal, and …" He watched her eyes move away from him, one of her lost-in-space stares. "Celebrate the Fourth with you and Gabe and with fireworks …"

"There it is." Del rolled past his shoulder and clambered quickly to the lowest layer of the quarry wall.

"What?"

"Here, look. Where the different color granites come together, a boundary, almost textbook perfect." Running her hands over the stone, she traced a wavy line along the wall.

… and spend time with you and keep you safe and Marco out of trouble …

She pulled her phone out of a shorts pocket. "Fingers of pink squeezed into the gray. The boundary between two formations tells us a lot about how it formed, which one came later, how hot the intrusive magma was compared to the existing material. I need to follow this."

Del was entirely focused on taking photos and measurements. She climbed up and along the stepped layers of rock, following the twists and fingers where the different colors came together. With her hammer she chipped off several samples from above and below, and a couple of larger chunks that included both colors.

Settling on a flat stone in the sun at the edge of the quarry pond, Ty watched Del work. He pulled off his boots, rolled up his pants, and lowered his tired, sweaty feet into the clear, cool water. Kicking the sticks and leaves near his feet, he uncovered another stone slab about two feet underwater, like a seat in a hot tub. Only he was thinking about a cool dip. Occupied with her measurements and sampling, Del was halfway around the pond with her back to him. Ty jumped up and pulled off the rest of his clothes behind a small tree. With tiptoe stealth he lowered himself into the pool and lounged back against the rock. Using his rolled-up T-shirt as a headrest, he sank down into the delicious chill. He closed his eyes, relaxed his arms until they started to float, and imagined what it might be like if he persuaded Del to join him.

Some minutes later, the sound of another slap on skin interrupted his daydreaming. Del was crouching next to him, picking the remains of a bug off her leg.

"Hey, Ty. These shallow, stagnant quarry ponds are filled with sticks and leaves, making good habitat for leeches."

He vaulted out of the water, creating a sizeable wave that splashed everything within an arm's reach, including Del. Using his T-shirt as cover, he leapt behind the tree where his clothes were hung.

Del just about fell over in hysterics. "You need help checking for leeches? They like the tender parts, you know."

"Thanks, I'm good," he called. He really wanted to check carefully, but had never actually seen a leech before. "Ahh, about how big are Maine leeches?"

"An inch or two, dark brown or reddish brown," she said, giggling.

He found none, at least on the parts he could examine. When he stepped out from behind his privacy tree, dressed from the waist down and totally embarrassed, he asked Del to check his back.

She responded with a twinkle in her eyes. "Hold still." She slowly ran her hands over his back muscles from the shoulders down to his waist. It seemed to him to be more than a friendly check for leeches. "You're fine," she added with a final pat on his spine.

He thought about finishing the day with a nice hot shower and back scrub. Of course, that's what everyone does in tick season. He pictured it with Del helping him scrub.

Again, she slapped at something on her legs. "There are some quiet places in the park for an evening skinny-dip. Someday I'll take you. But now we're leaving before I go crazy with these bugs." She swung her pack onto her shoulders, turned away from the pond, and worked her way through the trees the way they came in. Ty was one step behind her.

Behind the trees on the left, they heard a sudden snap, another, and several thumps of footsteps moving quickly away. Someone had been watching. Ty knew that Del, raised on her toes, always curious and trusting, was about to call out. He put a firm hand on her arm and shook his head as a warning. She got it. They both froze and listened until the last few crunches were barely audible. They waited until several minutes went by with only the sounds of the forest around them.

Moving silently with cautious foot placement, he led her back to the dirt trail, taking the final step out only after ducking around branches so he could confirm there was no one in sight. Whoever it was had beaten a quick retreat.

Close behind him, Del asked softly, "Did you see someone?"

Ty shook his head, but he was making a mental list of possibilities. For one thing, Josh Wilson knew exactly where they were.

The cops may have a military record saying Wilson was stationed overseas, but Ty knew that, with a friendly commanding officer, guys sometimes get short, unofficial leaves, for morale or family problems, and if Wilson traveled by military plane, there'd be no record of a commercial ticket with any airline. A record of his coming and going at any military airport would not be easily found by state investigators.

FOURTEEN

The following day, just in time for dinner, Marco's old Volvo wagon turned onto Homestead Lane, the Corriveau family private road. Coughing and sputtering, the car clearly felt reluctant to complete the last quarter mile. Grandpa shook his head and said, "Check the injectors." Ty said, "Vacuum leak." Del said, "Find a good Volvo mechanic." Marco said he thought it should rest. He told them he had added a lot of miles to an odometer already well past two hundred thousand.

Before sunset, Grandpa left to take Evie to an outdoor concert. Del invited Marco and Ty to join her on her apartment deck, where they settled into Adirondack chairs to watch the shadows falling on Grandpa's garden-in-progress and beyond that, the last gleams of sunlight on Winter Bay. Evie had left them a small dark chocolate cake layered with cherry preserves, and their mission was to finish it. Del was sure Evie's ulterior motive was to fatten her up, so she was glad to share it.

While Del set up plates and utensils, Marco pulled a handful of papers from his courier bag. "Wait till you hear what I learned about the Wilsons and their problems with Settlement Creek. I actually had to dig through paper files at county offices because electronic records are online only for the last ten years. But my best source was a darling curator at the Pyke Island Historical Society, who invited me back anytime to join her for tea and cookies. She's a lady of advanced years, smart, organized, and can look you in the eye and size you up in about two seconds." He winked. "I've got births, deaths, marriages, and deeds. For starters, Old Man Wilson had a first name. It's Wallace."

"Old Wally Wilson." Del punctuated the syllables with swoops of the cake server she was holding. "Has a nice rhythm to it."

"Wallace left his property jointly to Charlotte and her son Josh. It includes Heart Pond, the dam at the creek, and eighty acres of woodland abutting the park and Monks Head. Wallace inherited it from *his* father, who also owned all the land now farmed by Settlement Creek, and another forty acres where the creek meets the bay, currently owned by Abby Wilson. A retired reporter who worked on this five years ago when George disappeared helped me find Abby, who is alive and pretty sharp."

"How's Abby related to Wallace?" Ty asked.

Marco raised his hand. "Hold on. Let me start at the beginning. The Wilson story starts in 1915 when Stanley Samuel Wilson, hometown Truro, England, marries Alicia Pyke here on the island and so becomes the largest landowner on the island."

"A Pyke? With a 'y'?" Del plopped a slice of cake onto a plate for Marco. "Do you want ice cream?"

"Apparently that marriage ended the surname Pyke around here. By the third generation, the descendants of the original Pyke family suffered from a string of daughters. Most were married off the island." He handed his plate to Ty, who was on ice cream duty. "Sure, one scoop."

"You want to explain that comment 'suffered from a string of daughters'? Remember, I'm holding a potentially lethal weapon." For emphasis she stabbed the air in front of Marco.

"Death by cake server?" Ty said. "I don't remember that one in my Clue set."

"Understand the historical context," Marco said. "In 1915, women couldn't vote, serve on juries, or hold public office. Keeping your maiden name would be unheard of."

Ty handed Marco his plate, now fully à la mode and melting.

"It gets more interesting." Marco balanced his plate on the arm of the chair and his notes on one knee. "Stanley and Alicia have a son Stanley Samuel Junior in 1918, and Alicia dies shortly after. Within a month, Stanley marries a woman named Mildred Theodore, from Indian Island, near Old Town, Maine. A bit of a scandal because she was a full-blooded Penobscot and his housekeeper. They had three children: Ella in 1920, Wallace in 1926, and Abby in 1934."

"Okay, Abby is Wallace's sister." Del finished cutting the last piece of cake and handed the plates to Ty for topping. "And that's the Miss Ella who Ryan talked about."

"Did they all settle here on the island?" Ty asked.

"I'm getting to that. Stanley Samuel Junior enlists in the Army in 1941, goes off to fight in World War Two, and is never heard from again. In 1955 in the village of Summer Hill Harbor, Stanley Senior builds a small house for his wife Mildred, who lives there until she dies. He deeds all his land to his three living children. He breaks up the Pyke holdings, giving the Heart Pond area to Wallace, the Settlement Creek land to Ella, and the shore land to Abby. Then he goes off to Europe to find his first son's remains, and dies of a heart attack touring in Germany.

"Mmm. Yum." Marco alternated bites of chocolate cake with sips of beer. "I should mention that, the same year, Abby is in college, only twenty-one, first in her family to attend college, has no interest in the land and never has done anything with it. I met Abby yesterday. She lives near a daughter outside Belfast and only ever had regular contact with Ella while Ella was alive. Abby couldn't 'abide by Wallace, and always felt sorry for Charlotte.' Those are her words."

"Then Ella and Wallace both lived here their whole lives?" Ty asked.

"When does Chief George show up?" Del licked the remaining cherry syrup from the cake server.

"I'm getting there. Wallace marries. Charlotte is born in 1966. Between an inheritance and exploiting his land resources, like selling both lumber and quarry stone, he's pretty rich. But his wife leaves him—abandons Charlotte when she is twelve. Abby says no one ever heard from her again."

"Wait." Del counted off imaginary numbers in the air. "That means Charlotte is not even sixty? How old is Josh?"

"Josh is forty-four, born to a fifteen-year-old Charlotte who, at the time, was attending a private, elite girls' school in New Hampshire. She dropped out and brought home a baby."

"That must have pissed off old Wally," Ty said.

"Abby said Wallace hired a lawyer to find the father but never did, and Charlotte never told. Good news: Charlotte is a caring mom and Wallace takes a liking to his grandson, becomes a strict but loving father figure. Josh attends a top-notch military high school, joins the Army, does several tours in the Middle East, and retires late last year."

"Marco, when does *Chief George* show up?" Del said. "I'd like to find out before midnight."

Marco gave her a sly look. "You need to practice your self-control."

Smart-ass. Del threw the cake server at him, which bounced off his knee and clattered to the floor. He kicked it across the deck in her direction and blew her a kiss.

"So, Ella owns the farmland the Pykes worked since the earliest settlers, but she is no farmer. She lives in an old house, raises horses, and restores antique carriages. She never marries. She does have hired help, and the earliest information I find on George Tozur is a picture that was in the local weekly on the Pyke Island Days Parade in 1980." Marco passed around a black-and-white, slightly fuzzy print showing a regal-looking woman in a high-necked, long-sleeved Victorian dress, wearing a wide-brimmed, feathered hat, sitting in an open horse-drawn carriage behind a driver in western-style clothes. The caption read, "Miss Ella Wilson in her historical barouche, driven by Mr. George Tozur, led the parade down Main Street."

Marco continued, "Abby confirmed that George worked for Ella for several years, although she doesn't know exactly when he started."

Ty scrutinized the print, holding it up to the light over the deck. "Nice work. George was the hired help? How'd he get the money to buy her property?"

"He never bought anything. But I'm pretty sure he, let's say, *influenced* Ella. Were they lovers? Who knows? In 1985, they formed a cooperative called Settlement Creek Farm with officers listing only George as president and Ella as secretary."

"If they were ever lovers, according to Ryan, that was *so* over and done by any time he can remember." Del told them about her conversation in which Ryan had described how everyone lived jammed into the farmhouse and Ella showed signs of dementia.

"Would that be enough for old Wally to want to kill George?" Ty said.

"Hard to say. There's no doubt he was extremely unhappy, because the first lawsuit was filed within a few months after the cooperative formed. Wallace claimed George swindled Ella. The case was thrown out of court. Ella died eight years later, leaving all her worldly possessions to George. The boundary and fishing disputes continued, some incredibly stupid—like if Wallace owns Heart Pond but Settlement Creek has fishing rights to the creek, who can fish at the falls. A few suits went to court, but Wallace never managed to win."

"Doesn't Settlement Creek Farm own all the land around the creek?" Del asked.

"Not exactly. I think this is tricky legal work. Ella Wilson's deed from her father covers seventy-three acres. For ten of those along both sides of the creek, she granted the farm what is called an 'affirmative agricultural easement,' restricting the use of the land. If for any reason the farming stops, I'm not sure what would happen. They also got the exclusive fishing rights to the creek."

"Easements aren't necessarily tricky," Ty said. "But someone should look into this one more."

Marco handed him several sheets of paper. "Good luck with that.

Here's the incorporation documents and the easement deed. I couldn't finish reading them without falling asleep."

Del picked up the print of the newspaper photo. "In this picture Ella seems to be very tall, big-boned, elegant, really. She might be taller than George."

Marco pulled two more photos from his courier bag. "That's typical of all Mildred Wilson's kids. Abby gave me a couple of photos that I enlarged at the local Walmart." He passed the first one to Ty and Del. "Here's the last family photo, black and white, before Stanley Senior took off for Europe. He's the short one. Wallace is six feet plus a few. Ella, Abby, and their mother are all around six feet tall. Mildred is the buxom one with the broad face in the middle. When I met Abby yesterday, she said being a tall woman was always a curse for her."

"They were just born a generation too early," Del said. "I'm looking at full athletic scholarships to any number of women's sports."

"And the second"—he said, handing them another enlargement— "is Wallace, Charlotte, and Josh, several years old, definitely before Charlotte used a wheelchair. Abby said Charlotte sent it in a Christmas card, but she doesn't remember the year."

In the photo, they were standing on both sides of the carcass of a twelve-point buck hanging from a tree branch, probably waiting for field-dressing. All three wore camouflage hunting clothes and were holding rifles. Josh is looking at the camera proudly. Charlotte is touching his arm, looking at him, not the camera, radiating a mother's love. Wallace is on the other side, standing a little crooked, slightly bent at the waist, with one shoulder higher than the other. His expression was at best a scowl, and it was easy to imagine him with a gimpy stride.

"Who's the fourth hunter?" Del asked, pointing to the edge of the photograph where there was an elbow and part of a leg and boot.

Marco took the picture back. "I didn't notice that. Looks like someone was next to Wallace, but they cut him out of the family picture."

Del suggested they move inside. A chill wind had started blowing in from the bay, and it soon would be too cool outside for them in shorts.

Ty shook his head at the photo. "When we saw Charlotte in the wheelchair on Sunday, she looked half this size."

"Sweet Jesus, yeah. I started to talk with her until guard dog Josh hustled her away." Marco started gathering up dirty plates. "She told me she never wanted to be a burden. She's suffering from a neuro-muscular disease. Good thing to stay away from."

"They're not contagious, you know." Del opened the door for him. "They're mostly genetic, either inherited or spontaneous mutations." She followed Marco inside.

"Marco, where are you going with all this?" Ty followed them, carrying empty drink glasses. "Seems like nothing you learned is surprising. Ryan implied George had a reputation with women."

"I hope to find a motive for murder. We don't know what went on between George and Ella," Marco said. "Did he trick her? Maybe. Or was he just nice to her? Abby said Ella never spoke that much about George. When asked why she granted the easement, Ella said it was the right thing to do, but she never explained it. Abby confirmed Ella was showing signs of dementia in her last couple of years. What's interesting is what's missing."

"What's missing?" Del and Ty both spoke almost on top of each other.

"At the memorial service Charlotte Wilson said, 'We have every right.' I don't understand why. Charlotte and Josh have their own lives and no contact with Settlement Creek. What 'right' was she referring to?"

"Maybe she was talking about the same rights their old man thought he was suing for?" Ty offered. "Land rights, fishing rights."

Marco shrugged.

"So that means you're not done snooping?" Del said.

"Of course not. And why would Pale Moon show such hatred toward Charlotte? After all, it was Charlotte who stopped the lawsuits." Marco placed the dishes and flatware in Del's kitchen sink and turned on the faucet. "I'm going to figure out how to get them to talk."

"Some women know how to keep secrets," Del said. "What makes you think they'll tell you?" *Is Marco actually going to do my dishes? What's up with that?*

Marco reached for a sponge and started washing. "I'll have to try turning on my charms."

"Caution," Ty said with two quick sniffs in Marco's direction. "We might be having a bullshit alert." It was one of Ty's favorite ways of teasing him.

"Not so. Charlotte already said she would give me an interview. She's going to call me as soon as Josh is out of the house for a few hours."

While Ty had his back turned putting the ice cream container in the freezer, Marco gave Del another wink. She sat down on one of the stools at her kitchen counter, pushing aside the large stack of science books. She was halfway through a summer reading list—physics, chemistry, structural geology, mineralogy, and calculus—books recommended by her advisor to help bridge the three-year gap in her education. Her thoughts replayed the image of the village at Settlement Creek.

"Where's the old farmhouse where Ella and the first families lived?" she asked. "All the buildings we saw were new."

Marco stopped washing and wiped his hands on a dish towel. "You think they tore it down?"

"There are older farm buildings in back by their fields—one house, a storage shed, and a barn," Ty said.

Marco nodded. "You think there might be something left in the old house, like a diary or photographs? That might tell us more about her and George."

"Or where he came from," she said. "With all this research, Marco, you really found almost nothing about George."

"That's the frustrating part—where's the real man? Not the one glorified at the lovefest. I searched all the online databases and a couple of genealogy sites. No mention of the Tozur family name; it must be unusual."

"Maybe he changed his name," Ty said.

"That's possible. The historical society lady said she personally interviewed George once because he was so eager to talk about the history of how the Pyke family stole native people's land. She described him as charming but shallow. He knew nothing about actual history and tried to get her to talk about what it's like to be a widow. She ended the interview. He called her a few times after that, but she never met with him again. Like I said, a smart lady."

Through the slider to the deck, they saw the headlights of Grandpa's car reflect on the driveway.

Ty started for the door. "There's Gabe. I'm going to the bunk room to pack some clothes. I'm spending the next few nights at Settlement Creek so I can manage the equipment."

"Tell him I'll be over later. I need to finish the dishes." Marco gave Del an ear-to-ear grin.

Ty stopped short in front of the door and wheeled around. "Marco, I know Pale Moon invited you to their Fourth of July picnic. She seems pleased with your article about the farm and the lovefest." He turned to Del. "You're invited too. *Ryan* wants to organize a kids' soccer game."

Del felt the dig and heard a sneer in his voice.

"I know. *Ryan's* been sending me texts all week." She tried to imitate his smug expression, but ended up laughing. "Besides, I better drive. I don't think the Volvo will make it."

She slid off the stool and hip-checked Marco away from the sink. "Grandpa is really enjoying your company. I can finish."

As Ty waved Marco over to the door, he made a final verbal jab. "Confess, Marco. How did the Wilsons get an invitation to George's memorial service? You gave him Del's invitation, didn't you?"

Marco looked surprised and shook his head.

Before they closed the door, Del opened the chemistry book on the counter, pulled out the pale-yellow printed card, and held it up to show them. "Nope, using mine as a bookmark."

FIFTEEN

While various Settlement Creek families sat in groups around folding tables and took turns grilling veggie burgers and tossing salads, Ty relaxed by himself under the shade of a maple tree at the edge of a trampled field laid out as a kid-sized, half-length soccer pitch. As forecasted, the weather for the Fourth continued a stretch of perfect sunny days, except each day was a little hotter than the one before. Today, by Pyke Island standards, everyone was expecting a scorcher. It might hit ninety degrees.

He sipped lemonade, watching Del organize a practice of goal kicks for a group of ten kids ranging in age from eight to maybe mid-teens. She lined them up in front of a net someone had made from various plastic pipes and leftover deer netting. She was demonstrating the right way to kick, reminding each kid to start with a good touch, swing your arms, bend your kicking leg, lock your ankle, keep your body straight, and follow through. Ty didn't understand what a "good touch" was at first, but realized while watching that it meant don't get too close to the ball. They took turns kicking with their shoelaces. After a couple of rounds, some of their kicks actually put the soccer ball into the net, triggering a group cheer even if it dribbled in. Ty wasn't paying attention to the lesson, but he certainly loved watching Del sprint, pivot, kick, and jump, all the time coaching, laughing, and cheering as loud as her trainees. She was definitely having a blast.

Golden. The word popped into his brain. When he first met Del in January, he judged her to be spirited, smart, but at the same time anxious and maybe even unhappy. Now he was coming to understand her differently. She wasn't a head-turner by his standards, not with her almost too-lean and muscular body, especially in places where he liked women to be a little rounded. But there was a moment at the end of last winter when they laughed together—he couldn't even remember at what—and suddenly he saw someone else. In so many ways, she was as golden as a perfect summer day.

Del had everyone sit down for a water break as she explained some basics of the game. Ty watched a bare-chested and bronzed Ryan jog across the field toward them, his ponytail flying from side to side, just like you'd expect on a horse's ass. Ty stopped paying attention completely after he heard Ryan and Del decide how they would each lead a team in a game. They were discussing half-pitch practice rules, like no goalie, taking turns on offense, and the adults don't kick goals. Ty decided to lie back on the grass and close his eyes.

Is Marco still trying to get into the old farmhouse? I should find out soon.

A rustle behind him gave away Pale Moon's approach, which made him sit up again. Gathering up her long, loose cotton dress, she lowered herself stiffly to sit cross-legged on the grass next to him. She smoothed the front of her dress and took off her wide-brimmed straw hat. Her dreadlocks were pulled back with a colorful ribbon.

Meanwhile, on the field, Del was running circles around Ryan. She passed the ball to one of her smaller teammates, who approached the goal in two kicks but was cut off by Ryan. Del stole it from him and passed it forward again.

"She's very good," Pale Moon said, leaning toward Ty. "I understand she was a serious collegiate player."

"I don't know much about it," Ty answered. He made believe he was watching the game, if that's what one would call the mayhem on the field, but he was thinking again about a possible motive for a murder, how it might benefit Settlement Creek. Marco's research had raised some interesting angles about property ownership.

Ryan was becoming flustered trying to be everywhere at once. His teammates were just standing around looking at one another in confusion. One of the smallest kids on Del's team almost scored a goal, but the ball rolled out of bounds.

"They make a beautiful couple, don't you think? Both so athletic."

"Not for me to judge."

"I heard she's finishing a bachelor's degree. Do you think she might want to coach soccer here on a regular basis?"

"You'll have to check with her."

Out on the field, Ryan had just tripped one of his own team members. Del shouted sharply for a time-out. She was vocally angry, pointing a finger at Ryan's bronzed, heaving chest, and restating the game's safety rules. All the players took a water break.

Pale Moon put on her hat and rested her hands on her knees. "It's all for the children, Ty—the farm, this village, our rules. We're trying to make the world a little better place by raising the next generation of better citizens."

Words exploded in his head. *What bullshit! You're raising better citizens by hand-picking the families, making them sign code of conduct agreements where the penalty is getting kicked off the farm. Try raising better citizens from broken homes, from drugged-up and drunk parents. Try saving kids from years of abuse and neglect.*

What he said out loud was, "We all want better citizens." Did his face reflect the moment of rage he felt? He hoped not.

On the field, the game started again. In a few quick moves, Del's team scored, and they celebrated by running around with their arms up yelling, "Goal!" Ryan gave the ball a violent punt, sending it to the sidelines, where it bounced into a group of elderly residents enjoying the shade sitting in folding lawn chairs.

"I think I'd better intervene," said Pale Moon, struggling to stand. "Uh, ugh. At my age, I'm afraid getting down is easier than getting up."

Ty got to his feet, offered her both hands, which she accepted, and pulled her up. Pale Moon smoothed the back of her dress.

"By the way," she said, "your friend Marco found all the doors locked. He should know that 'Keep Out' signs mean the old farmhouse is off limits. There's nothing to be gained from prying into the past. He's been given a warning. I expect he'll be along shortly."

"At least you didn't have him arrested."

She smiled sweetly. "No need. Our elders take care of discipline."

Pale Moon started walking to where Ryan was reclaiming the soccer ball from the lawn-chair sitters who were chewing him out. After a few steps, she turned back to Ty.

"You're a man of few words. There's nothing wrong in letting people know how you feel."

"Thanks," he said. "Part of freedom of speech is the right to remain silent."

Just past Pale Moon, Ty saw Marco being escorted by Uncle on one side and another elder, each man gripping one of Marco's arms. His friend didn't look happy.

Ty's limited interaction with Uncle had made him suspicious. Uncle seemed to be trying very hard to be spiritual, to have some otherworldly insights. Ty noticed that he preferred taking walks alone in the woods rather than working on the farm or in the village. And strangely enough, Pale Moon and the others seemed to tolerate it.

SIXTEEN

Del and the Settlement Creek kids waited in the hot sun on the soccer field while Ryan retrieved the ball. She knew the younger ones were tired, so she suggested they call the game for the day. That idea was met with a chorus of protests from some of her teammates and discouraged whines from others. She gave them the best pep talk she could remember, one out of the many that coaches had once delivered to her.

Del grabbed her water bottle from behind the goalpost and walked to where Ty was helping Pale Moon to stand. A few players wandered off in various directions, but most of her team and some of Ryan's followed her.

She saw Marco approach, flanked by two men. Something about his stiff posture made her think he was in trouble. Ty didn't look too happy himself. She was learning to recognize his degrees of annoyance by how tightly he held his shoulders. Earlier, when she had left him under the shade of the maple tree, he had been relaxed and amused by the picnic.

The man everyone called Uncle was guiding Marco by the shoulder and left him standing next to Ty. Uncle then signaled to others around the common to come and form a circle in the shade. One of the soccer players, a freckled young teen, pulled Del's arm and asked her to sit with them. "Uncle is going to tell a story," she said.

"What kind of story?"

"Ancient. With weird people like Grandmother Woodchuck and Turtle Person. Sometimes they're scary."

Del looked curiously at Ty, who remained impassive and returned the slightest shrug. She made eye contact with Marco, who frowned.

"Will it be a long story?" Del asked her freckled friend.

"You never know with Uncle."

In a few minutes, a group of more than two dozen were seated in a circle, with the smaller children on the inside. A few adults dragged over folding lawn chairs to sit on the outer ring. Del noticed Pale Moon, with Ryan in tow, heading toward the Community Center.

Uncle closed his eyes and was perfectly still for what felt like a long minute. When he opened his eyes, everyone was paying attention, and he started his story. His voice was deep and melodious, easy to listen to.

"This is the story of a boy who is trapped in a cave. Ahh, he is a very small boy, only six years old, and he will starve if he cannot escape the cave. How did he become trapped? A wicked stepfather who did not love him pushed him into the cave and then thrust a pole under a huge rock, which tumbled and covered the cave opening completely."

That caught Del's attention. A story about being trapped in a cave couldn't be a coincidence. She glanced at the children in the circle. None seemed terribly dismayed by such a scary image. For the rest of the story, Uncle seemed to be talking to her, making frequent eye contact. Del was nervous but curious.

Does he know we were the ones who found George's bones?

Uncle continued, "In the darkness of the cave, the boy saw two glowing eyes and he went toward them, trembling. The eyes grew bigger and brighter. At last, he could see they belonged to an old porcupine. 'Alas, I am too old to move this stone,' said Porcupine. The boy began to cry. 'Do not cry, my son,' said the old Porcupine, 'for I will call on the animals of the forest to help us.' He called out and many came running—Wolf, Raccoon, Caribou, Possum, Rabbit, Fox, and many birds."

Even as a kid, Del had never liked children's stories in which animals that normally prey on one another play nice together as best friends.

Tell the truth: That fox would really like to eat the rabbit, and the wolf would love to bite off a hunk of caribou.

"Each animal tried in his own way to move the stone, but none of them could. They tried very hard. Caribou broke an antler. Wolf dug at the rock until his pads were bloody. Then a new voice said, 'Kwah-ee. What is going on?' They turned and saw Mooinskw, which means 'she-bear,' who had come quietly out of the woods. Some of the smaller animals were frightened and hid, but the others told Mooinskw what happened. She embraced the boulder at the cave's mouth, and with all her strength pushed it to the side. Then out came the boy and Porcupine. They were so happy to be free." With the last word, Uncle made a wide arc with his hands. It seemed the story was finished.

Many of the children clapped. Some whispered or giggled.

Del leaned over to her freckled teammate and whispered, "Can we ask questions? I want to know if the wicked stepfather gets punished. It was his fault to begin with."

"Good point," she said. With a raised hand she called out, "Hey, Uncle. What about the stepfather? Wasn't the whole thing his fault?"

Uncle made a curious face, not quite surprised, maybe more irritated, but then he laughed. "The stepfather will be punished plenty when the boy tells his mother what happened!"

There were snickers and chuckles from the adults standing around the circle, although most of the kids didn't seem to get it.

Del said to her friend, "Hey, that was fun, but I've got to go." She stood up and started toward Marco and Ty, who were backing away from the crowd.

"Hey, guys. Having fun at the picnic?"

"I need a beer," Marco said.

"If you're thirsty, there's plenty of lemonade," Ty offered.

"My bladder is swimming in lemonade," Marco said. "What kind of Fourth of July celebration doesn't have beer?"

"Their idea of utopia. You saw the rules outside the office," Del said. "I'm ready to cut out soon and find a nice cold one, myself."

"Sweet Jesus, don't leave without me," Marco said.

"Is it my imagination, or did Uncle just turn being trapped in a cave into some kind of lesson for the kids?" Del asked. "And did you see him staring at me? Does he know?"

"He might be staring for other reasons," Ty said. "Ryan has been talking about you."

Del groaned. "I've got to leave now."

"I can't figure him out," Ty said, looking to where Uncle was still in his circle of children. "This is a small community. Everyone I've worked with tells me a little naughty gossip when I ask questions, or sometimes when I don't. Even Pale Moon has her enemies. But there's two people no one will say a bad word about—Chief George and Uncle."

"He's got a strong grip." Marco rubbed his bicep. "And knows how to sneak up behind you without making a sound."

Ty nodded toward the Community Center building. "Come check out the new security monitoring room."

Inside, the empty gymnasium was surprisingly cool. The only light came from a high row of windows along one wall, adding to the tranquil mood of the place. Their footsteps echoed as Ty led them to the far end, to a narrow door next to the stage.

"We repurposed the equipment closet," Ty explained. "With help from two members who are pretty handy, I finally got everything organized and labeled."

On the wall above a narrow shelf were three large monitors, each showing multiple images from various cameras. The monitors and the one small window in the end wall provided the only light. The room seemed to be filled by a muffled hum.

Ty pointed to a rack of electronics under the counter. "Two processors, terabytes of storage, backup, and a private network, including Wi-Fi."

"I thought the surveillance was to stop vandalism on the farm," Del said. "This looks permanent."

"It is," Ty said, swinging a keyboard out from under the counter. "Once Pale Moon and the council saw the potential, they wanted it all, not just the farm. We added the main gate, Community Center, schoolhouse, and playground."

"Sweet Jesus, look at that," Marco said, pointing to an image of a farmhouse doorway. "No wonder those guys showed up as soon as I walked around the house trying the doors. I thought I was out of sight, but as soon as I touched a door handle, they were there."

Ty was trying not to laugh. "Sorry, man. I should have warned you, but then, you were a good test of the signaling system and the remote app." He held up his phone and demonstrated how he could use it to flip through the same images on the monitors.

"Feels creepy," Del said. "Who's watching?"

"The security detail. Actually, anyone they give the remote app to." Ty ushered them out and closed the door.

"I'm with Del," Marco said. "Creepy."

Ty gave Marco a hard look. "Settlement Creek is just trying to stay safe."

"Nice little utopia they've got here, with Big Brother watching all the time."

"Welcome to the twenty-first century," Ty said with plenty of sarcasm. "What do you think your enlightened university's security looks like?"

Marco shrugged.

As they walked back to the main entrance, Del's attention was captured by the line of tables still covered with memorabilia from the memorial service—a display of posters made by children, many photos, trinkets, a couple of hats, a bandana, a set of string bolo ties with polished stones.

"Hey, is this stuff all about Chief George?" she asked. "Like a museum."

She strolled around, examining each table and looking closely at the photos. There were several group shots showing smiling, golden-hued young adults, many of whom were now the older members sitting in the folding chairs under the trees. From the dates Marco had told them last night, some would be older now by thirty years. These were photos from the very beginnings of Settlement Creek Farm.

It was easy to recognize a young Pale Moon, whose physical appearance hadn't changed much except that she hadn't been quite so tanned, and her hair was honey-colored curls, not twisted in gray dreadlocks. One photo of Pale Moon and George working in the gardens caught Del's eye, a six-by-eight in slightly faded colors. It was attached to a poster board with corner tabs, so she pulled it out to hold it up to the light. On the margin, someone had handwritten "First crop of sugar snaps," followed by a July date and year.

"Hey, Marco." Del walked over to the double doors to the entrance hall, where Ty and Marco were continuing their disagreements about security. "This is traditional film print, not from a digital camera, right?"

Marco took the photo and turned it over. "Yup. Printed on Kodak paper."

"There's a faint date on the back. How accurate were those processing dates?"

"I've never seen one wrong. The company that developed and printed the photo put the date on it."

Del took the print back and looked at it closely. "Well, something's wrong. I told you Ryan invited us to his thirtieth birthday drunk this summer."

Marco shrugged. "Okay ..."

"First of all, the date printed on the back is a year earlier than what someone wrote on the front. But you're telling me the date on the back is accurate."

Marco shrugged again. "Okay?"

"If this photo was taken in July thirty years ago, Pale Moon should be seven or eight months pregnant in the picture." Del held out the photo so they could both see. "Look. She's wearing tight jeans and a short T-shirt and her belly is flat."

"You're saying she's not that pregnant in this picture," Ty said, leaning in for a better view.

"Trust me on this. She is *not* seven months pregnant."

"She implied she was when she first became a member of Settlement Creek," Marco added.

Behind them, Del heard a soft rustle by the door, then two soft steps on the floor. Pale Moon's skinny brown arm flicked into the middle of their huddle and snatched the photo away. Tucking it into the pocket of her cotton dress, she turned and walked to her office.

Pale Moon spoke with her back to them. "The remote app works beautifully, Ty, including the audio. You do good work."

It was Del's turn to be annoyed at being spied on. Marching out the door to the parking lot with Marco and Ty trailing behind her, she said, "Including the audio? You have this place bugged, too?"

"Most security cameras come with microphones."

"Feels even more creepy," was her assessment.

"Look." Ty's voice had taken on a prickly edge. "Don't blame the equipment."

"So when *does* it turn into an invasion of privacy?" Marco asked. "Isn't this setup easy to abuse?"

"That's up to the elders," Ty answered.

When she got to her truck, Del glanced around them. "Are we being recorded here?"

"Not here," Ty said, adding almost under his breath, "but don't get twenty feet closer to the main gate."

Del waited until the three of them formed a huddle again. "Pale Moon lied to us about how and when she came to Settlement Creek. The faded print date on the back of the photo is July *thirty-one* years ago. She was growing peas with George a year before Ryan was born."

"That would also be the year before the farm was incorporated," Marco added. "And before she got her law degree."

"Interesting catch," Ty said.

"Then we have to ask whether George Tozur convinced Ella Wilson to grant the agricultural easement, or was it Pale Moon Smith, the budding lawyer?" Del asked.

"Not sure that matters much," Ty said. "She wasn't listed on the original documents."

Marco was jotting in his notebook. "She's a smart, calculating woman. There must be a legal reason she doesn't want to be associated with the establishment of this place. Why else would she lie?"

Del turned to her truck and opened the driver's door. "We can probably think of more questions over a couple of cold beers. Ty, are you coming?"

"I need to stay." Ty had turned his attention away from them toward the farm. "Hopefully, tonight we'll catch someone."

"Hey, we can probably get to a convenience store and back in forty minutes," Marco said with mischief in his eyes. "How about we sneak in with a six-pack?"

"Another time. I haven't programmed in the Marco filter yet." Ty's answer was colored with scorn.

Marco cocked his head. "My *filter*?"

"The filter that would let you roam around here but be invisible to the cameras."

"Seriously? You could do that?"

"If I could write that program, I'd sell it and never have to work again."

SEVENTEEN

The next morning Ty knocked on the door of Gabe's cottage, carrying a bag of Sally's homemade donuts, half dipped in molasses and half glazed with maple cream. He figured his news was cause for celebration, and he knew to get to Sally's early because once her donuts were sold out for the day, she closed her kitchen. At first Ty was disappointed to find only Gabe at the table, nursing a mug of coffee and reading the local weekly paper. But maybe that would work out after all.

"Is that Sally's?" Gabe asked, reaching for a donut. "Help yourself to coffee and bring a couple of plates."

"I was told these are the best. But her place is hard to find—a road with no sign and nothing on her driveway but one of the blue house numbers that the fire department volunteers give out."

"No need to advertise your product when you sell out every day."

Ty settled into a chair with a cup of coffee. "Where are Del and Marco?"

"I sent them to the Ellis Junction auto parts store with a list for the Volvo. I'm pretty sure we can fix the rough idle problem. For one thing, he can't remember the last time he changed the oil or spark plugs."

"Sounds like Marco." Ty examined the donuts, finally selecting one with maple cream. "Good of you to help him out."

"Well, we got a mutual benefit deal going. Later, he's going to help me haul my traps. My summer sternman is still up to camp with his folks, and his backup is too hung over from celebrating the Fourth."

Ty lifted his coffee cup to offer a toast. "Last night the cameras caught the vandal."

"Someone from the island? Does he know he got caught?"

"*She* lives on the island, and we definitely spooked her."

Gabe cleared his throat and pushed up his glasses. "'She?'"

Ty raised his two hands, curling them like claws, and bared his teeth, which caught Gabe by surprise. He began laughing so hard he almost choked on his donut.

"You mean all this time it *was* just a black bear?" Gabe asked once he got his breath back.

"'Just a bear?' Look at the size of her." He handed Gabe his tablet to scroll through the images. "She braved an electric fence multiple times, busted open a plywood chicken coop, tore up deer fencing, tore down welded wire fencing, and ripped open fyke nets. And was smart enough to stay in the creek coming in and out of the property so she left no tracks. She must have also figured out what wildlife cameras look like and took an extreme dislike to one."

"You sound unconvinced about the last part."

"I'm not sure. I'd like to show some of these to an expert in bear damage."

"What happens to her now?" Gabe handed him back the tablet.

Ty closed the cover with a snap. "I sent the images to the sheriff and the park. Rangers will be searching today for the den. They're talking to state wildlife biologists about relocating the family. She has three cubs."

"Hungry mouths to feed," Gabe said as he helped himself to another donut. "What's this mean for you?"

"I'm pretty much done at Settlement Creek. I'm hoping to tag along on the bear hunt so I get to talk with the experts. Then I'll have time to stick around for a week or two. Maybe do some hiking with Del."

"You're always welcome to stay here. Frankly, I feel better when she has someone to hike with. Del's been off in the woods alone many times. She's good about letting me know and never had a problem, but it still makes me nervous."

"I know what you mean. She's pretty independent."

Gabe wiped a handful of crumbs onto his plate. "Independent, headstrong, and relentlessly curious."

"Gabe, can I ask if you know if there's anything between Del and Marco? Are they more than just friends?"

"She doesn't share her love interests with me."

"Marco won't say either, but I know she stayed at his apartment a few times."

Gabe put both forearms on the table, fixed his eyes on Ty, and nodded. "That happened because of late work on campus mixed with bad driving weather. Seems his roommate is away a lot, so there was a spare bedroom. It's what friends do."

"I don't know. I'm seeing a change in Marco when he's around her."

"Okay, then." Gabe chuckled. "That kind of change is going around like a summer cold."

"What do you mean?"

"Oh, nothing." He flicked his hand in the air and sat back. "Look at me and Evie."

Ty stared at the dregs in his coffee cup, wondering whether Gabe had just confirmed Marco's feelings or not, or was just joking.

"The person to have this conversation with is Del," Gabe added.

"I know. I'm having a hard time finding just the right moment."

"Go make the right moment."

Ty sat back in the chair and tapped the table lightly with his fingertips. "Hard to do with Marco around."

"Marco is eager to get his car running so he can do more research. He was talking about checking out the Wilson property by himself. Let me know your plan, and I'm sure Evie and I can disappear for a while."

"It would be easier if I let him get arrested."

Gabe raised one eyebrow. "Tell me that's a joke. I thought you two were friends."

"We are. I think we still are," he said, swirling the dregs in his cup. "But you know Marco always takes risks when he's following a story. Checking out private property when it's posted is criminal trespass. He's been guilty of that before. One of Mike's county cops almost arrested him last winter after he was caught multiple times trespassing at Black Ledges."

EIGHTEEN

To leave the island for anywhere on the mainland, all traffic funnels through one road, which curves between walls of trees down a steep hill, crosses a causeway built on top of multiple ledges barely higher than the highest tide, and finally up and down the steep arch of the Pyke Island Bridge. It was not unusual at the height of the summer tourist season for the road to become so congested that the effective speed limit was stop-and-go, but generally not at eight in the morning. Their trip for car parts was definitely going to take longer than expected.

"Must be an accident," Del said as she applied the brakes again and came to a full stop behind the car in front of them.

Marco was hanging out the passenger window. "I can't see anything but taillights. Hold on, I think I see blue flashers."

It took fifteen minutes to advance just a few car lengths, to where they could see emergency vehicles all over the road and officers controlling traffic.

"Pull over," Marco said. "I may be able to get some pictures I can sell to the local papers. I'm in with the editor of the weekly in Ellis Junction. He always likes a good crash pic."

He jumped out of her pickup even before Del found enough room on the shoulder to park. Marco was off at a trot. She decided to get out and follow him.

As she got closer, Del saw a medical transport van almost completely across the road with its rear doors open near the end of the guardrail.

Brown-and-white county sheriff cars were on both sides of the transport. Two officers were stopping traffic in both directions. Others were standing next to the guardrail, looking into the ravine where a creek went under the road. Del recognized Sheriff Mike's unmarked truck on the opposite side of the road, along with a couple of white cars used by park personnel. Del knew the sheriff's truck well enough after spending several hours in it last winter. Marco was nowhere to be seen.

Her first thought was that someone had gone off the road into the ravine. Grandpa had complained that the guardrail here didn't extend far enough. He had pointed it out to her with a stern warning when she first moved in with her grandparents on Pyke Island.

Well outside the circle of activity, anxiously and on tiptoes, she watched as a team of rescuers appeared just below the roadbed carrying a stretcher with someone strapped on. Struggling with footing on the steep, rocky surface, they were trying to keep the stretcher as horizontal as possible. Del's anxiety turned into alarm when she caught a glimpse of spiky orange hair.

Lucy?

Del took off in a sprint toward the rescuers, but after five steps her arm was hooked and her waist encircled by a force stronger than her panic.

"Whoa," said Sheriff Mike. "Let them do their work."

"Is that Lucy Irwin?"

He unwrapped his arms and held her by the shoulders. "Come with me."

Sheriff Mike walked Del around the side of his truck to where Granite Coast Park Director Colleen Foster was holding a phone to her ear. Del had met the director twice, once when she'd applied for and received her permit to remove rocks, and again last Sunday when she volunteered at the park information desk. She was only in her second year as a park director, but Del found her a natural manager and good listener, deliberate in her responses.

"Lucy's car went off the road and into the ravine." Sheriff Mike was using his I'm-here-for-you voice.

"Is she …?"

"She's unconscious but alive. They'll have her in the ER at Ellis Junction soon."

When Director Foster saw Del, she whispered "Hello, Del," signaled that Del should stand by, then ended the call with a curt "I'm on it."

"Del, what can you tell us about the earthquake report?" the director asked, slipping her phone into a pocket. "How'd you know about it?"

"Why are we talking about the report?" Del asked, looking back and forth between the sheriff and the director. They regarded one another for several seconds.

"The accident appears suspicious," the sheriff said.

"Wait. Are you saying Lucy's accident is linked to the earthquake report?"

"The investigating officer is documenting another set of tire marks. Lucy may have been forced off the road." Sheriff Mike leaned against his truck, stretching his shoulders. "No one cared about the report until Lucy took one out and put your name on it. Now someone cares. We just don't know why yet."

Del told them how she had first exchanged email with Lucy and then went to the office to pick up a copy. "It's only one copy," Del added. "Why would anyone care?"

The director looked grim. "All the copies from the files are missing."

"I made a digital copy," Del said. "And Ty has the paper copy Lucy gave me."

"I have that copy and made one for Director Foster," Sheriff Mike said. "But don't mention to anyone that you have or know about copies. It might be dangerous."

Del took a sharp breath. "Lucy said she would confront everyone who was in the office that morning."

They heard a siren start and watched the transport van slowly make a three-point turn.

"When she found all the copies missing, she went through the roof," the director said. "Lucy's a sweetheart, but she knows how to intimidate, the experience of twenty-five years of teaching math to eighth graders." She checked her watch.

"I know this might just be a random act, a coincidence that it happened to Lucy," Sheriff Mike said. "But we need to start an investigation assuming she scared someone. I've been doing this a long time, and coincidences just don't happen."

The director opened a car door and reached for a notebook. "I hope you're wrong. Nothing I saw in the report would make someone turn violent."

"I'll need a list of everyone who contributed to it and had access to the office area," the sheriff said. "You said Kay Levant was the editor?"

"She's our best writer and computer savvy." The director started writing. "I've got eight full-time rangers, a dozen part-timers, a biologist, and I don't even know how many volunteers, between the information desk and the gift shop, not to mention the vendors who are here once or twice a week."

"Let's work on what we want to say about Lucy to your staff," he said. "Nothing about our suspicions."

"And you"—he pointed a finger at Del—"say nothing to anyone about any possible link between Lucy's accident and the report. Well, except for Ty Holden. He knows how to stay quiet."

"I gotta tell you." With a hint of reluctance, Del pointed over her shoulder to the road. "Marco is over there somewhere taking pictures for the newspaper."

"Now everyone with a smartphone takes pictures for the media." The sheriff nodded toward the road where several people were milling around. It seemed like more of the car-crash-curious were stopping to gawk, and the sheriff's officers were trying just as fast to disperse them. Marco's curly-haired head was at the front of the crowd.

"Before you go," Del said to Foster, "when can I hike the Monks Head area again?"

"I'm sorry, Del. Even though we should have the cave openings secured by next week, Monks Head and the area around it will be closed for the foreseeable future."

"How do you secure a cave opening? It's not like it's framed for a door you can buy at the home center," Del said.

"Something like a big heavy metal door and giant padlock. You create a custom frame and bolt it to the stone. I don't know the details. It's still considered a crime scene, but soon a state archeologist will be assigned as principal investigator who will oversee all the work at the site."

"Then the park owns it?"

"I believe so. We won't know for certain until the survey is complete."

"Which will bring even more attention to Monks Head," the sheriff added.

"But necessary. The old deeds describe monument stones, line of sight, and compass information that is often imperfect when it comes to the side of mountains."

The sheriff nodded. "I saw the hand-drawn Pyke-to-Wilson property maps. Pencil sketches, not even to scale."

"When we get to the office, I'll give you a list of volunteers." Foster tore the handwritten sheet from her notebook and handed it to the sheriff. "The cave is an important find, probably the most important in Maine in many years. To keep it secure, we must keep it secret for now."

"Too late for that. Your rangers know. All my staff, state investigators, Settlement Creek's council—they all know. Del and friends know. Josh Wilson knows something's up."

The director's expression slowly changed to that deer-in-the-headlights look. "Sheriff, that's already over a hundred."

"Next week, even more—surveyors, the crew securing the openings." Foster shook her head.

He continued, "Then triple it by the weekend. Someone mentions it to a spouse who mentions it to a friend who … you know. We've got signs posted saying the Monks Head area is closed, but every day we catch a few more folks trying to find some trail to the peak. Might as well be advertising it on the internet."

NINETEEN

"**M**arco, you ready with the bait bag yet? We got a trap waiting." Gabe had to shout over the rumble and chug of his rebuilt six-cylinder, four-stroke diesel Cummins. He was trying to be patient, but it was getting close to supper time and they still had five traps to pull. Marco certainly knew the routine when he put his mind to it, but in the last hour, he'd been spending more time staring at the clouds over the island than baiting traps and banding lobsters. Granted, after replacing ignition parts on Marco's old Volvo, they got a late start. But it was time well spent. When they were done, the Volvo almost purred. Gabe thought there would still be plenty of time to haul his meager allotment of seventy-five traps—just the right number of tags for a retired guy. He and Del would have got it done in less than three hours. Something was needed to speed up Marco, only Gabe didn't know what kind of new ignition parts that would take.

Gabe spun the wheel and circled back to the general area where he had gaffed the last buoy. Marco inserted the bait bag and balanced the trap on the edge of the boat. When Gabe nodded, Marco let the trap drop overboard with a splash and watched the line play out.

Marco leaned into the wheelhouse. "Gabe, do you know if there's anything between Del and Ty? Are they more than just friends?" His voice was raised to near-shouting even though he was only two feet away.

Gabe cleared his throat not once but twice. With his eyes fixed on the water, he finally said, "Del doesn't share her love interests with me." Hopefully, Marco wouldn't see how hard he was working to hold back a laugh.

"There's something going on. I'm seeing a change in him when he's around her."

"Okay, then." Gabe coughed over a chuckle. "That kind of change is going around like a summer cold."

"What do you mean?"

"Oh, nothing, I guess." He increased the throttle and steered the boat along the coast. "Look at me and Evie," he said after he lowered the throttle and drifted toward another of his buoys.

"You saw how eager he was to go to the university with Del next week, even though he said his work here was done."

"Maybe he just had free time. Have you asked Ty directly?"

"You know he never talks about himself."

"Then the person to have this conversation with is Del," Gabe said.

"I know. I'm having a hard time. And whenever I'm ready, he seems to show up."

"You got to make the right time. You ready with the gaff? We're coming up."

The trap brought up four keepers for the box, nice-sized early shedders. Gabe threw back two V-notched females and one short. He waited while Marco sleepwalked another bait bag over to him.

"Four more to go."

TWENTY

On Sunday, Del put in her second volunteer day at the park informa-tion desk. Working with two others, she organized piles of hand-outs, maps, and the park information brochure in the public area while waiting for the doors to be opened at nine. Everyone spoke in hushed tones, and the mood was somber. There was no booming Lucy voice asking the volunteers to listen up.

The weather continued its perfect run of sunny days and cool nights, exactly the kind of weather that drives people from the sweltering, oppressive cities of the urban east to the coast of Downeast Maine.

Lucy was still in the hospital. The prognosis was good. She had regained consciousness and was able to speak and move, but was confused about what had happened. Park Director Colleen Foster told the staff that doctors were limiting Lucy's visitors for the next few weeks. One of her sisters had flown in from New York City and was taking charge.

Once the initial burst of tourists thinned, Del took her break in the office area, intending to up her coffee intake. She noticed a small clutch of park personnel hovering around the closed door to the director's office. All of a sudden, the office door burst open, and Kay Levant rushed out, stopping short when she came face-to-face with her coworkers. Without a word, she walked purposefully past them, down the aisle to the rear entrance, and disappeared. Del saw Sheriff Mike just inside the office. He stepped out and asked another employee to come inside and have a seat. The door to the office closed.

"What's going on?" Del asked one of the waiting groups.

"Interviews," he answered. "Sheriff wants to know where everyone was Friday morning and what they were driving."

"You think it's connected to Lucy?"

"Seems obvious. Though they said it was an accident."

"Kay looked really upset."

"She's been inside more than once. I think she's got something to hide." Another coworker asked him a question and he turned away.

Del filled a paper cup from the coffee station and checked the time. She still had a few minutes of her break left. She wandered along the nest of cubicles in the back of the office area. Kay's chair was empty. She continued to the rear entrance, which led to a stairway. Del thought she heard a soft voice on the other side of the door, so she did what Marco would do. She opened it.

Kay Levant was squatting against a wall, talking on a phone. When she saw Del, she swiped it with her thumb and put the phone face down on the floor. As she looked up, Del saw Kay's cheeks were streaked with old tears.

"What do you want?" Kay asked as she wiped her cheeks with the back of a trembling hand. Her voice wasn't angry but scared.

"Uh, I'm sorry, Kay." Del's words stumbled out. "I didn't know anyone was here."

"Don't lie. I saw you in the office."

Del felt a twinge of guilt. "You're right. I wanted to make sure you were okay."

"As you can see, no, I am not 'okay.'"

"Anything I can help with?" Del sat down on the floor beside her.

"Not unless you can find out who is trying to screw me."

"What do you mean?" Del asked.

"Seems they found a paint scratch on Lucy's car that appears to match damage on my car. Only I didn't go anywhere that morning. I was here at my apartment with a friend."

"Then you have an alibi," Del said.

Kay slid the rest of the way down the wall with a plop and straightened her legs. "Shit. Maybe," she said. "The friend I was with is married to someone else, and if this gets out, even more people will be *not okay*."

Del was surprised Kay would reveal that to her, but then Kay knew that she was only a volunteer and probably wouldn't be back in the office the rest of the summer.

"I know Sheriff Mike," Del said. "Be honest with him and he'll do his best to keep it quiet."

Kay looked completely defeated. "Everyone suspects me, like I've got something to hide, even when Hiram was director."

"That's Hiram Lemuel, the director before Colleen Foster, right?"

Kay nodded. "They say I sucked up to him."

"My grandfather liked him a lot, and he was here a long time."

"I never sucked up to anyone. That's what you get for trying to do your best."

Del finished her coffee with a long swallow. "Hey, Lucy's accident has everyone scared. Don't take it personally."

"Oh, it's personal all right." Kay spit out the words. "You saw them huddled together staring at me."

"No, that wasn't what I saw. They were huddled together trying to make sense of what was happening."

"Well, their making sense of it means I'm going to be the scapegoat." She pointed a thumb at her throat. "Time for me to ask for a transfer."

Del felt she wasn't making any headway. Kay was already convinced she was a victim.

"I think my break is over."

As Del rose, Kay gave her a deadpan stare. "Thanks for the pep talk."

"If someone here wanted to hurt Lucy, I think we all want that person found," Del said. "If you have any suspicion of who that might be, tell the sheriff. Don't share it with anyone else."

"Another goddamn secret."

TWENTY-ONE

Garth was everything Del had described, not just a tall man, but powerful enough that you could imagine him as an old-time blacksmith, lifting and hammering with heavy iron tools. Although in *this* century, Ty was pretty sure his occupation would be football tight end.

It was early morning when he found Garth and two other rangers at a parking area off one of the dirt access roads about three miles from Monks Head. They were waiting for the arrival of state wildlife biologists who called themselves the "bear crew." After Ty introduced himself, Garth narrowed his eyes and gave him a thorough look over. Not a very polite welcome.

"You're the fellow that's putting the cameras all over Settlement Creek."

"That's me," Ty said. "How'd you hear about it?"

"It's a small island." Garth sniffed once and turned to watch the road.

Ty wasn't done with the conversation. "With the cameras, we identified the bear and how she got into the farm, so I'd say they were pretty effective."

"Waste of money," Garth growled. "I told them early on it was probably a bear."

"Really? When was that?" Ty was surprised. No one had told him that Garth had been consulted.

"Sheriff came to talk in April. I told him it was the time for bears to come out of hibernation. If they asked me, I would've tracked it."

"But no one believed you?"

"Sheriff said those folks were sure it was a person or a gang. Someone was convinced it was that Wilson fellow."

"Then you never actually talked to the Settlement Creek members about it?"

"Never heard from them. Wasn't my business."

Ty pulled out his tablet and handed it to Garth. "Take a look at some of the pictures of the damage. You think the bear did all this?"

Clearly having no idea how to scroll, Garth at first held the tablet with both hands and blinked. After Ty demonstrated how to move his finger to the next image, Garth got the hang of it. He went through several pictures, backward and forward.

"Bear … bear … bear … that's a human. Too clean a cut." Garth identified each with confidence. "Bear. But that last one is a bad imitation of bear marks on a tree." He handed the tablet back with a smirk. "You caught a bear, but your search for a vandal ain't done yet."

A van pulled into the lot. Garth waved them into a spot where four park-owned off-road vehicles were waiting. Three biologists dressed for fieldwork climbed out of the van. After introductions, Garth handed out maps and described where they were headed, a dirt trail that went part of the way, and the final two miles of terrain they needed to hike. He had located the den under a rocky outcrop just south of Monks Head in an area designated as wilderness. Normally, the bear family would have been left alone, but because this female had become a "nuisance" (the term the wildlife biologist used; Pale Moon called the female "vicious and deadly"), the crew intended to trap and relocate the mother and cubs. They explained that there was a helicopter waiting at the airport in Ellis Junction, which would airlift the bears as soon as they radioed for it. They were all hoping everything would go according to plan. They showed Garth the gun and tranquilizer darts they would be using. The darts looked like a cross between a hypodermic needle and a badminton shuttlecock with pink feathers. In case the darts weren't effective, they were also carrying two high-powered .30-caliber rifles.

The bear crew began to unpack gear from the van and reorganize it on the ATVs. Ty was instantly impressed with their preparation and professionalism. Unfortunately, he also learned he wasn't going to be tagging along to see the capture. Garth said Ty could ride with him to the trailhead, but he wasn't welcome on the hike.

"She's a fighter," Garth said. "She'll think we're threatening her cubs, and she'll attack with two hundred and fifty pounds of muscle and claws that will rip you open like a stuffed toy. If we miss with a dart or it doesn't take her down, it will be dangerous for anyone not armed."

Ty wanted to offer that he could be armed if the park let him. He had his 9mm Glock G19 handgun and a .270 Winchester rifle locked under the back seat of his Lexus. But he knew that wasn't going to happen.

"What if they're not in the den?" Ty asked.

"They'll be there. She's used to hunting at night and likes to sleep in the morning."

Ty stood next to Garth as they quietly watched the bear crew finish moving equipment and packing.

"Why did you give my friend the wrong location of the quarry near Wilson's land?" he asked after a pause.

"You mean the girl geologist?" Garth scoffed. "I put some circles on a map."

"And you knew the one near the Wilson property was wrong, wrong side of the dirt road, wrong distance from the boundary."

"I guess I haven't been there in a while. Did the girly find it?"

"Her name is Del," Ty said. "Yes, we found it."

"Then all's good."

"All's not good if your intent was to get us lost."

"Just an honest mistake." Garth's face was completely expressionless as he opened the storage compartment of his utility vehicle and pulled out two helmets. He held a helmet out to Ty. "You coming?"

Ty shook his head, turned, and walked away. He was chewing over Rubin Garth, trying to see through his stony but apparently sincere attitude. The man was being nothing more than a professional ranger, at least around the bear crew. One by one, the crew started the ATVs, and the roar of two-stroke engines filled the air along with a blue haze of exhaust. Ty also thought about a second vandal, someone who wanted the Settlement elders to think they were being threatened whenever it seemed that the bear was foraging somewhere else. He decided to discuss that with Mike Hodgkins.

Ty drove the long, circuitous public road back to Settlement Creek village imagining how frightened and fierce the mother bear would be. *Totally outnumbered.* He'd read somewhere that often a female will run away from a serious threat and abandon her cubs. Sometimes fighting is just too overwhelming. *But this one will fight.*

A few hours later, as he was giving final instructions to the Settlement Creek members he had been training on the security equipment, he heard the helicopter. Looking out a window, Ty watched it fly from the north toward Monks Head and then disappear behind it. In the electronics room, he posted the backup schedule, picked up his personal notes, and shook hands with his helpers. As he turned to leave the room, he saw that Uncle had placed himself just outside the doorway and was listening to the end of their conversation and goodbyes.

Ty stepped out and paused in front of him. "Do you have any questions?"

Uncle flicked his glance to the electronics and back to Ty. "We're expecting the next bill to be your final one."

Ty nodded once. "Except for the maintenance retainer, if you decide to use me. I've already given a bill and quote for maintenance to Pale Moon."

Uncle glanced at the sheet of paper in his hand. "How do we know you're not taking confidential information?"

Ty handed him the paper. "This is an equipment diagram. I keep it in case you have a problem and I'm remote, which I will be most of the time. It's part of our warranty agreement."

Uncle narrowed his eyes until they looked like shiny black beads almost disappearing above his broad cheekbones. "Tell me what you think about a farm co-op with security cameras."

"Uncle, is there a problem?"

He relaxed his face. There was still a coal fire shining in his eyes. "Better yet, tell me what the sheriff thinks."

Ty pulled the paper from his hands. "Ask him yourself. Call his office on the island. He's usually here once a week."

"I know—not your job," Uncle said with a hint of a smile. "But you are good friends with him."

"I wouldn't describe us as good friends. We've got a professional working relationship."

"Ahh." Uncle turned toward the electronics room. "And how much about your time at Settlement Creek did you share with him?"

"Why do you ask?" Ty felt himself tighten and worked to keep an impassive face.

Uncle stared at him for a long moment. "Questions answered by questions are always reason for suspicion."

"If you're accusing me of something, just say it."

Uncle took a step toward the entrance to the gym, then turned as he asked, "Is the sheriff still looking for Chief George's murderer?"

"The case is open."

"And you're, ahh, part of the team?"

"No. What makes you think that?" In silence, Ty stared just as hard as Uncle was staring at him. For a long minute, it seemed to be a contest of sorts to see who would flinch first. It ended when the sound of chopper blades reverberated through the Community Center building. From the volume, Ty knew it was flying low.

The sound echoed a different time and place for Ty, when choppers coming and going, coming and going, raised dust in the desert. He walked past Uncle and stepped outside the building to track the chopper on its way north until it was finally just a tiny speck in the sky.

Ty thought about the images he'd taken of this female bear and her three cubs. She might have been dangerous to Settlement Creek, but she wanted nothing more than food, a safe shelter, and to raise her cubs in peace. She wasn't the first mother to tear down fences for her family.

TWENTY-TWO

Monday morning, Del pulled into a spot near the university's Geosciences Building, gave Ty the keys to her pickup, and told him she would probably be in her meeting for at least a half hour, maybe longer. Because it was cloudy and looked like rain any minute, she pointed out the general direction of the campus center and cafeteria, thinking it wasn't the best day for a stroll around the grounds, even though that'd normally be her suggestion. Uphill from the river, the clusters of university buildings were surrounded by tree-lined green spaces. Del grabbed a box of rock samples and a folder of papers from behind the seat. She said she'd call him as soon as she was done.

On her way into the building, Del once again rehearsed the story the park director had suggested and everyone had agreed on: Monks Head had recently experienced an unusual rockfall and was considered too unstable and dangerous to climb. Her discussion with her thesis advisor would determine if she would be able to submit what she had as an independent study project, or if she would have to pick another geological feature and start over. He would be pleased with her best find—the boundary between the pink and gray granites by the old quarry, which clearly showed a later intrusion of the Monks Head formation. What bugged Del was that, if she could actually report on discovering the most valuable archeological site on Maine's coast, he would probably give her an A and suggest they publish a paper on it together. Park Director Foster had hinted that, as soon as a principal archeologist was actively in charge, Del could reveal her role to the university. But she couldn't guarantee that would happen this summer.

Ninety minutes later, Del left the building almost dancing down the front stairs with the rock samples bouncing up and down in her box. She was relieved. Her advisor was pleased with her handling and identification of the samples and impressed by her photographs and lab work on mineralogy. Her analysis showed internal consistency, measurement-to-measurement, and established the chemical composition of the Monks Head granite. He suggested that she spend more time around the base of Monks Head looking for other areas where the different granites came together in order to complete the mapping, but only if it could be done safely.

Ty met her by the truck and they stowed her boxes and papers. Proposing a walk to a scenic spot he had found, he led her along a green, dewy slope, toward silvery glimmers of the river between tree branches. Del wasn't sure whether this was part of the university grounds or a town park. She saw benches and picnic tables near the water's edge.

"It's misting, almost rain," Del said. "We didn't bring rain gear. Which is so *not* like you, as someone who is always well prepared." She pulled up the hood on her summer sweatshirt.

Ty smiled. "It's not that far. Besides, after all that hot, sunny weather we just had, this feels nice."

"Grandpa said this morning the weather experts were almost ready to call a drought."

"You Mainers have no idea what a drought is."

"Okay, so tell me about your experiences with droughts."

"Weeks and weeks of oven-baking heat. Everywhere you look the only color is brown."

"Where was this?"

"Somewhere a long way from here."

Del stopped and faced him. "You don't have to be so mysterious. Just tell me."

His eyes searched her face before he said, "I did a couple tours in the Middle East."

"Doing what?"

"I flew unmanned aerial vehicles, UAVs."

"You mean drones?" she asked, as they continued the stroll toward the picnic area.

"Yup, drones operated from a bunker complex a thousand miles from the targets."

"But in the desert?"

"The desert is all there is. When you fly in, there's these sprawling, air-conditioned military air bases surrounded by sand and scrub."

Del sighed. "You know, the wars in the Middle East have been in the news since I can remember, at least as far back as kindergarten."

"The Pentagon calls it a 'complex set of overlapping conflicts.'"

"Conflicts. Factions. Warring ethnicities. Warring religions. Power grabs. And no end in sight. It's depressing."

He let out an extra-long sarcastic *right.* "That's one word for it."

They stopped when they reached the edge of the river. Del saw a scatter of concentric ripples in the water from the first sprinkles of rain. A few drops landed on her cheeks.

"It must have been hard, dropping bombs from the drones," she said.

"With the right mindset, it was surprisingly easy. Your view of the world consists of pixels on a monitor. I wasn't responsible for much of anything—an officer gave the order, another confirmed the order, the grunts on the ground dealt with the aftermath. I didn't have to be brave or strong or fast. Just excellent eye-hand coordination."

"Something tells me there's more to it."

He didn't tell her—not then, anyway. Instead, Ty quickly stepped forward, placed his hands on her back, pulled her in gently, and kissed her on the lips. It wasn't a long kiss, but it wasn't a peck, either. It felt very warm compared to the cool, misty air. But the quickness surprised her.

Del slapped her palms against his chest and pushed him one step away. "What the hell was that?"

"I'd like to call it a kiss."

"Don't you know anything about first kisses?" She jabbed a finger into his ribs.

"I guess not."

"Where are the 'may-I' moves?"

He dropped his arms, his look curious but somewhat befuddled. "I'm not sure I understand."

"Women do not like to be grabbed and kissed. You need to establish consent." She reached for his hand, tugged him over to a park bench, and pressed him down onto the seat. "Else it's disrespectful," she said.

"I certainly didn't mean that."

Del sat down close beside him. "Of course you didn't, which is why I need to do some coaching here."

"Okay …"

"May-I move number one: You start by putting your arm around my shoulders," she said. "And if I don't pull away, you *may* go on to move number two."

He wrapped his arm over her shoulders and snugged her closer. She didn't pull away. But she did inhale his scent, which reminded her of the polished leather interior of his car and something new, fresh, like rain.

After a pause, he asked, "Do you think I'm ready for the next move?"

She pushed back the hood of her sweatshirt. "Yes, lean in toward my ear with a little kiss, like on the earlobe or neck. No slurping. If I don't turn my head away, you *may* go on to move number three."

Ty ran his warm lips from her earlobe down her neck. She didn't turn away.

"Do you think I'm getting it?" he asked.

"Well, later you might need to practice that move some more." She snuggled into his side and raised her face toward his. "Now move number three is the first kiss … should be a bit tentative, 'cuz you don't know whether I'll like it or not." She closed her eyes.

With his free hand, Ty delicately lifted her chin and held it while he kissed her long and sweet. It wasn't tentative at all. Del liked it. A lot.

She opened her eyes, feeling little droplets of mist on her eyelashes as she blinked. "You might have to try that move again."

This time he put both arms around her and she folded hers around his neck. Del closed her eyes and lost herself in the kiss. She moved her hands along his neck and ran her fingers over his damp hair and across his ears, outlining the lobes. Her index finger found the thin scar at the hairline in front of his left ear. She traced it with a fingertip to where it ended in his beard.

She felt his body stiffen and pull away.

Del opened her eyes. "I'm sorry," she whispered.

Ty slid away from her on the bench. He leaned forward, rested his forearms on his thighs, and stared at the flowing river.

After a long silence he said, "Not your fault. I lost the moment. Something I need to deal with."

"Would it help if you talked about it?" The first big drops of rain splattered on her hair and cheeks. She pulled up her hood.

"No, we're not doing the therapist bit together."

"I'm not offering therapy."

"Then what?" He stood up so abruptly that beads of water shook off his windbreaker.

"Suppose I just listen."

Still staring in silence at the river, he stuffed his hands into his jean pockets.

Del rose slowly from the bench and stood beside him, contemplating the trillions and trillions of vibrating molecules rushing past them every millisecond. And yet, at that moment, the river as a whole was serene and the flow of water caressed the bank with a soft breath. So much like a silent man.

She tugged his right hand out of a pocket and held it in both of hers.

"Let's go before we get soaked," she said.

He didn't pull away.

TWENTY-THREE

A set of headlights coming down Homestead Lane toward Grandpa's cottage broke the quiet spell of a rainy summer evening indoors. Del was curled up on the couch with a book. Ty was at the dining table scrolling through information on his computer. They were waiting for Marco, who said he was catching a private dinner with Charlotte Wilson at her home on Heart Pond.

Grandpa got up from his favorite easy chair to look out the window. It was still pouring outside. "Evie's here," he said. "She didn't call. Something must be up."

With water dripping from her yellow slicker and slouched hat, Evie stepped into the cottage, put both hands on her hips, and announced, "Everyone knows. Everyone."

She slipped out of her slicker, pulled off the hat, and handed them to Grandpa. Del thought for a second she was going to give him a peck on the cheek, but then she didn't. Evie was rounder than Del's Grandma Marjorie, right on the edge of plump. She wore her champagne-from-a-bottle-colored hair short. Her bangle earrings made her crinkly eyes sparkle, and her wide mouth was perpetually smiling.

"Everyone knows what?" Grandpa asked.

"Don't you fool with me, Gabe," she said. "Everyone knows about the cave and the art. Here I am, supposedly friends with the people who found it, and I'm the last to hear?"

Ty came over to the couch and sat next to Del. They shared a half smile and a look that said "uh-oh." For the last couple of days things had been pretty subdued between them, so Del was pleased.

"Have a seat, Evie," Grandpa said. "You'd better tell us what you heard and how."

"First, offer me a drink," she said. "Have you learned to make a Manhattan yet, or do I need to do it myself?"

Grandpa tilted his head toward the kitchen. "Come and we'll make two. I finally got the right sweet vermouth. Anyone else?"

Del and Ty both declined with some version of "no, thanks" as Grandpa and Evie disappeared around the corner. Del leaned over the back of the couch. She watched Evie and Grandpa exchange a quick kiss when they thought no one was looking.

"Everyone knows?" Del said, turning back to Ty. "Are we in deep shit with Sheriff Mike now?"

"Probably not," Ty answered. "I have a meeting with him on Friday. I'm sure he knows that the island's rumor mill is working overtime."

Grandpa and Evie returned with cocktails in hand. Evie wiggled her way in between Del and Ty on the couch. Grandpa settled into his favorite chair and swiveled it to face them.

"Now, let's start again," Grandpa said. "What did you hear?"

"I just came from the market outside Summer Hill," Evie said. "The cashier was talking to the man in front of me at the checkout. They said there's a cave somewhere on Monks Head with prehistoric art. They said it was where Chief George's bones were found, and that he was murdered by some cult that worshipped there and was trying to keep it secret."

Del leaned back behind Evie to flash an eyebrow arch at Ty. He gave her his familiar "don't" signal—a tight-lipped frown and almost imperceptible shake of the head.

Evie took a long sip of her drink. "And I put two and two together. I know you kids found that cave. That's why you were so late after your hike there." She turned her head back and forth between them. "Tell me, what do you know about the cult?"

Ty had on his patient, slightly lopsided smile. "Sorry, Evie. We didn't meet any cult."

"That doesn't mean there isn't one," she retorted. "They just weren't there when you found it."

"I got the impression no one had been in the cave recently," Del said.

"Then where did the cult come from?"

"You should've asked at the checkout counter," Grandpa said with a chuckle.

"Don't laugh." Evie said, waving a finger at him. "This is serious. We could have a murderous cult on this island, right under our noses."

"The cops aren't even saying that George was murdered," Ty said.

Evie eyed him over the rim of her glass. "But what do *you* think?"

"The medical examiner said he died from a puncture to the back of the skull."

"Baloney! I know an evasive answer when I hear one," Evie said.

"They're the facts we have," Ty countered.

"You should've been a lawyer or a politician." Evie took another long sip of her drink. "And I know what they're like. My ex is both up in Aroostook County. I spent enough years as his legal aide while we were raising our boys to know prevaricating when I hear it. My ex is a very good lawyer and a fine probate judge, but he *sucks* at fudging about his extramarital sex life without perjuring himself." She rocked back, put a hand on Ty's arm, and filled the room with an explosive cackle. "And I've got the alimony to prove it!"

Del exchanged a smile with Grandpa, who was hiding a grin behind his glass. He obviously thought Evie was a hoot, and who wouldn't? Her firecracker personality lit up every conversation. Even Ty couldn't help but laugh with her.

"Evie, you lived on Pyke Island when Chief George was alive, right?" Del asked. "Did you know him? What was your impression?"

"I can't say I really knew him, but he was a handsome devil." Evie punctuated her assessment by raising her glass in a mock toast. "One of my friends in garden club thought he was so wonderful because he spoke up for native people at some meeting. She went up to him afterward and introduced herself. Next thing, she's inviting him to her house for coffee and they're discussing gardening. She told us how sweet and thoughtful he was. I think they may have had a fling and *she's almost eighty*! Anyway, then George disappears off the face of the earth and she starts keeping house with Murray Rice, the retired harbormaster. A year later, he's dead of a heart attack." Another burst of cackling. "Isn't that the damnedest!"

Everyone's attention turned to the front door as Marco clomped in and shook himself like a big brown dog. He pulled off a soaked hoodie. His hair hung to his shoulders in soggy ringlets. A puddle was beginning to form on the flooring around his feet.

"Did you *walk* back from Heart Pond?" Grandpa growled.

Marco pointed over his shoulder. "Left the Volvo by the garage. This happened on the quarter-mile length of your drive."

Grandpa actually sent Marco upstairs for a change of clothes, making everyone wait to hear his report on dinner with Charlotte Wilson. Before he came back down, they brought Evie up to date with the history of the Wilsons and the feud with Settlement Creek.

"You mean they did an agricultural easement?" Evie exclaimed. "A sorry way to make your heirs suffer for not wanting to be farmers. Basically, you're restricting the use of the land in perpetuity."

"In a way it makes sense," Del said. "Generations of Pykes farmed the basin around the creek. It honors that tradition."

"Baloney!" was Evie's reply.

After bouncing down the stairs wearing dry sweats, Marco pulled up a chair from the dining area. "In the last three hours, I learned one thing over and over: Charlotte Wilson never wanted to be a burden to anyone. That was her only message. She repeated it as an answer to almost all my questions, completely ignoring their intent. Even the cook was rolling her eyes after a while. At least the food was great."

"A cook?" Ty asked.

"Charlotte has a cook for lunch and dinner, a live-in personal nurse and assistant named Marissa, and there's Bruce, the property manager, who manages the house and grounds. He let me in at the gate."

"There must be money behind that," Ty said.

"You bet. The house is magnificent. A huge, classic log home perched at the edge of the pond, with a great view of the peaks of Granite Coast Park. Charlotte said the house was designed by her father and constructed using white pine harvested on the property. As the quarry stone business dried up, he kept his best men working another decade by building the house."

"Sounds like a nice gesture," Del said. "Not something you'd expect from mean Old Man Wilson."

"But talk about a fortress. The whole place is gated and fenced off."

"And where was Josh?" Ty asked.

"The guard dog is visiting the VA and a specialist in Boston."

"The guard dog?" Evie asked.

"Not to be confused with Marshmallow, their monster German shepherd," Marco answered.

Ty shook his head. "Right. They named the shepherd Marshmallow."

"No, his real name is Spike or Killer or something like that, but I call him Marshmallow. After sniffing my crotch, he sat by me the whole time and even slept with his head on my foot. Charlotte said normally he hates visitors and Bruce has to put him in the kennel."

"Do I detect bullshit?" Ty asked, punctuating his question with a couple of sniffs.

Marco crossed his heart. "Honest to God!"

"Then the interview was a bust," Ty said.

"Yes and no. I learned a lot by being left alone in the family room waiting for Charlotte to roll in. They have a wall of photos and memorabilia, mostly of Josh's service. He's a decorated war veteran. There was one framed list of citations of his service. And a number of photos of Charlotte growing up. She was the epitome of a tomboy."

"Like how?" Del asked.

"Riding horseback, hunting, fishing, skeet shooting. The Wilsons have an extensive gun collection and their own firing range. And you two should talk geology. Several photos showed her in the quarries posing with the workers. She was very interested in stonework, told me they took the last monument granite out of a quarry about fifteen years ago. Now it's all shut down. Except for some logging, I think they're living on investments."

"Any help in tracking down a murderer?" Ty said.

"Ha!" Evie jumped up and pointed at Ty. "I knew you would admit it eventually."

Grandpa joined Del in laughing out loud at Ty's annoyed expression.

"What's this?" Marco asked.

Evie stood tall to explain. "This young man was trying to avoid telling me the truth that everyone's talking about. These two found a cave somewhere on Monks Head with prehistoric art and Chief George's bones. Everyone says he was murdered by some cult that worshipped there and was trying to keep it secret." She sat back down.

"Evie, there's no cult," Ty said.

"I heard the cult thing today at the gas station," Marco said. "Maybe there is something to it. How do you explain that the cave was a secret for years?"

Ty put his hands on his thighs and stared at Marco. Del thought he might just stand up and walk out of the room, but instead he just shook his head and mumbled about another "bullshit alert." While that was usually one of Ty's amiable ways of teasing Marco, this time Del heard some anger in it.

"Let's see," she offered. "One: It was a couple hundred feet up a rockfall in an area with no hiking trails. Two: The opening is barely large enough for an adult to get through. Three: Except for the log that fell in the chimney hole and George's remains, there was no other evidence that people had regularly been inside in, like, a few thousand years."

Marco was nodding along with Del's list. "Okay, but hear me out. Motive and opportunity, right? That's what you look for in solving a murder. Suppose you were standing next to George, looking at the petroglyphs, and suppose you thought the cave was on George's land and you knew he had no will and no heirs. Who would take possession of the land if he died?"

"The state," Evie answered without hesitation.

"Who would the state give the land to?"

"The park," was the consensus around the room.

"So, if you were an over-the-top lover of the park, would George be worth more dead, or alive?"

"That's simple," said Evie. "Dead. But how do you know he doesn't— or didn't—have a will?"

"Because Pale Moon implied that when I first met her," Marco sat back in his chair and folded his arms across his chest. "And I'm just saying *if*."

"There are always heirs, even if they only find cousins," Evie countered. "He came from somewhere."

"I've done a lot of searching. No spouse, no children, no birth certificate, no background."

"You just don't have the right tools," Evie said. "Probate will assign a personal representative to the estate who will have access to his social security number and legal papers. It's the personal rep's job to advertise and track down relatives. Once word gets out that he owns a nice chunk of Pyke Island, the heirs will turn up, you'll see."

Ty was beyond exasperation. "Stop it, Marco. You're speculating. You have no evidence of any of this. This is worse than the nonexistent cult."

"There *could* be a cult in the park organization," Marco said. "A cult of silence."

"You're implying that there are a number of park staff who knew about the cave?" Del said. "And when George found it, someone had to kill him to keep it quiet? Sorry, that doesn't work. Now it's being put under a state archeologist to research."

"By a new park director, and how long has she been here?" Marco asked.

"Two years or so," Del answered.

Marco held up his palms in the hello-it-must-be-obvious sign.

"She hasn't been here long enough to be part of the cult," Evie concluded. She pushed herself up and handed Grandpa her empty glass. "This has been fun, kids, but I have groceries in my car and need to get home." Grandpa went to get her slicker from the bathroom, where he'd hung it to dry.

"I forgot something upstairs." Marco jumped up.

Ty got up, walked around the couch, and leaned over Del to say, "I wish you wouldn't encourage him."

"I know," she said. "But everyone has always suspected the Wilsons because the old man was sure that George had swindled Ella out of everything. Remember, Ryan implied that George played around with other women. You told us once you have suspicions about some Settlement Creek elders who've always worked hard on the farm while George was slacking off and causing trouble. You thought some of them could be jealous enough to want him gone. Well? Why not someone with the park?"

"We can speculate all we want. It's gossip, not progress," Ty said. "Not until we can tie someone to the cave."

Marco came back downstairs as Grandpa and Del were waving goodbye to Evie. He handed Del a map. "Here is my biggest win from the interview."

She recognized Heart Pond and the dirt trail where she had met Josh Wilson. There were at least a half dozen crisscrossing trails and three other circular markings in a ring well southeast of Monks Head. "Is this a map of the Wilson land?" she asked.

"Yup. Look at the miles of private roads. The circles are three old quarries where Charlotte says there's pink granite. She said we should check them out on Friday when the rain is supposed to stop. She said you can take samples."

Del gave Marco a high five. "Yahoo! This could clinch it. Maybe there'll be more exposure of the boundary between the two granite bodies."

"We can all go Friday morning. But we have to hike in from the other side of the pond," Marco said. "Charlotte doesn't want us parking or walking down her driveway. She wants to keep it from her staff and Josh."

"Hold on." Ty scowled and his cheeks colored. "No one should be roaming around the Wilson's land without Josh knowing."

"No worries. Josh should be away until Friday night."

"'Should be'? Last time we saw him on patrol he was carrying a high-powered rifle."

"As he's been doing for months," Del said. "So far he hasn't shot any hikers."

"Something's not right," Ty said, looking hard at Marco. "If Charlotte gave you permission, why does she want to keep it quiet?"

Marco shrugged.

"This is a big break for my research project. I'm willing to risk meeting Josh Wilson again." Del caught Grandpa's eye, and he looked curious but not concerned.

"Something's not right," Ty repeated.

"We don't need your approval," Del said softly as she started putting on her own slicker. She still had reading to do and was heading for her apartment over the garage.

"Right." Ty moved away toward the kitchen. "Anyway, I can't join you. I've got an appointment with the sheriff Friday morning."

Ty was being stone-faced, but Del saw something deeply worried behind his eyes.

"Hey, guys, don't forget I'm meeting Ryan for drinks tomorrow night," Del said. "He's been texting me all week. Are you both coming?"

"Sure." Ty nodded.

Marco pulled another crumpled scrap of paper out of his pocket. "Sounds like fun, but first we need to pay a visit to Marissa Fairlie on her afternoon off tomorrow. As she wheeled Charlotte away, she pressed this note into my palm." He handed the paper to Ty.

"'You need to know the real George story,'" Ty read. "With a phone number. What story?"

"My mission since the lovefest: the real George story." Marco started gathering up empty glasses from the living room. "That's what we're going to find out tomorrow at three at her family compound outside Ellis Junction."

Marco called out from the kitchen as Del started for the door, "We'll leave at two for the Fairlie place, catch dinner somewhere after, and then meet Ryan in Summer Hill. Forecast is for showers off and on all day, so keep the slicker handy."

Del called over her shoulder, "Okay, Mom!"

TWENTY-FOUR

The family compound where Charlotte's nurse Marissa lived, when she wasn't living at Heart Pond, was a private dirt road labeled with her family name: Fairlieville Lane. Del surveyed the compound through the gate of the five-foot chain-link fencing. Underneath a canopy of shade trees were about a half dozen clean and well-kept single-wide trailers, evenly spaced and surrounded by lawn. At the end of the lane, she saw a large backyard playset that any community would be proud of and a small but overflowing vegetable garden.

In front of the gate where Fairlieville Lane met the paved public road was a sturdy, three-sided wooden shelter. Marco said this was where the Fairlie kids waited for the bus that took them to a summer day camp. Marissa wanted to meet there so that the dogs inside the compound were not alerted. Ty and Del made themselves comfortable on a bench seat on the inside wall of the bus stop. Marco waited outside until he saw Marissa approach on the other side of the gate.

Charlotte's nurse was tall and square, forty-something, with thick hair that fell almost over her eyes as bangs and hung loose around her shoulders. Her hair color was layered starting with black at the roots, then dark purple, and ending in bright pink tips. It cried out, *It's my hair, so quit staring!* Dressed in jeans and a linen T-shirt, her stride was quick and confident.

After Marco made introductions, he also settled onto the bench. Marissa remained standing by the opening. "I'm going to start by saying that, whatever you've heard about Mister Wilson, Charlotte's father, is probably wrong. He was a good man, tough if you were a screw-up, but if you worked hard and showed him loyalty, he would return that in droves."

"Some people said he was hypercritical and held grudges," Marco said.

"I'm sure those people were the kind that did shoddy work for him." She tossed a pink lock of hair off her neck and crossed her arms. "Everything he touched he made better, including being a single parent for his daughter and grandson."

"Then you knew him a long time?" Ty asked.

"Personally, I've only been with Charlotte for four years, but my family has worked for the Wilsons since the early eighties—Gramps did some carpentry, Dad did tree work. Before they built the Pyke Island Bridge, we owned land on the east side of Summer Hill, on the road to Heart Pond. Gramps was sure the bridge would ruin the island, so he sold to a developer. Ha!" Her laugh was abrupt. "I pass that property every week, and it's now a big fancy hotel."

"One person's idea of ruin is another's idea of progress," Del murmured.

"Oh, yeah." Marissa rolled her eyes. "You got that right."

"So, tell us the *real* story about George," Marco said.

"My Aunt Lillian, my father's sister, was Ella Wilson's best friend and significant other for almost twenty-five years. She started as a house-keeper, but Ella came to love her and pretty soon they were an item."

"What kind of item?" Ty asked.

Marissa leaned forward and gave him a piercing look. "The kind that today would be a marriage, now that we recognize same-sex rela-tionships." Her look said, *I dare you.* Ty's look said, *Not intimidated.*

"Lillian Fairlie? That's a new name to me," Marco said. "What happened?"

"George Tozur happened. He wormed his way into Ella's home and heart. Ella stopped being social with Lillian and started treating her like a housekeeper again. Finally, she was given the boot and told to move out. She was heartbroken. She expected more."

"Like an inheritance?" Del asked.

Marissa dropped her arms. "Damn right. You give someone that many years, let go of your own future, share a house and responsibilities, be a nursemaid through sickness. Lillian should have been recognized as Ella's common-law wife."

"And you're sure George took Lillian's place as a lover?" Del said.

"Never as a lover, but as a son, a sweet and doting son, one whose company she liked better than Lillian's." Marissa tossed her hair again. "You know how mothers can be when it comes to sons. And how some sons can stoke that love fire so it never goes out."

"You said Lillian expected more. Did George get Ella to change her will?" Marco asked.

"Lillian told me she asked Ella several times to make a will, but she didn't, kept putting it off—until that hippie bitch, Pale Moon, showed up. After that, they kept the lawyers busy with a will and the farm and everything else they stole from Lillian."

"Do you know what year that was?" Del asked.

"Not exactly. Lillian wasn't too good about remembering dates, but she knew trouble when she saw it."

"You mean Pale Moon?"

Marissa glanced over her shoulder. "You got that right. Lillian saw that bitch as an expert at manipulating others without getting her own delicate hands dirty."

"Is Lillian still alive?" Marco asked.

"Too late for that," Marissa said. "She died a few months before Mister Wilson, but over the years I heard the whole story. After I got my degree, we shared that last trailer." Marissa nodded her head in the general direction of the compound. "And my dad confirmed much of it."

Del saw Marco start to open his mouth but she beat him to it. "How did she die? Was she, um, physically active, I mean, pretty healthy, five years ago?"

Marissa was silent, looking at her feet for a few seconds. "A bad liver killed her, but it's not what you think. She caught a virus that destroyed her liver fairly quickly. Never even got a chance for a transplant." She glanced over her shoulder again. "She was working as a cleaning woman in the hospital up to six months before the end."

"Did you tell the police any of this when George disappeared?" Ty asked.

Marissa shrugged. "My dad told me not to. At first a lot of people said the police were considering murder. My dad didn't want us to get caught up in that. But now …"

Marco stopped taking notes. "Now what?"

"Now that they say his death was an accident." Marissa narrowed her eyes, perhaps sensing a problem. "At least that's what I heard."

They watched a school bus come around the corner. "Okay, the kids are home from camp and I need to go," she said, waving at the bus.

They all stood and moved out of the shelter.

"Can I call you with follow-up questions?" Marco asked.

The bus squealed to a stop, and a small team of elementary school children carrying backpacks and gym bags tumbled out. Herding them to the metal gate, Marissa nodded in Marco's direction.

After the gate clanked shut and the school bus roared off, Del peered again through the opening to watch Marissa and the children greet three big, sleek mongrels, dogs of no recognizable pedigree but with large jaws and bobbed tails, wagging their hindquarters. Marissa and what looked like the oldest boy, still a head shorter than her, hugged and walked away with arms around each other. The rest of the Fairlie crew dispersed with shouts and laughter, some running to the playground and others disappearing into a trailer.

She turned back to Ty and Marco. "Do you guys believe her?"

Ty gave her a slight nod. With lips tight, Marco wagged his head as if he wasn't sure.

"Would Lillian want revenge? Five years ago, it seems she was healthy enough to climb Monks Head," she said.

"If we were looking for a Wilson accomplice," Ty offered, "either Lillian or Marissa might be on the short list."

"Not Marissa." Del swung around for one more look at the Fairlie compound. "Makes no sense that she would expose herself by talking to us if she were guilty."

"Unless it was to deflect," Ty said. "Still no link to the cave."

Marco was already halfway to the car, with Ty and Del lagging behind him.

"If there's no physical evidence, how can anyone ever be linked to the cave?" she asked.

"Motive. Someday the murderer will reveal himself by telling someone why," Ty said.

"That's my point. All the murderer needs to do is shut up."

"And so far that's been working."

Marco was waiting for them by Ty's SUV. "That was a whole other angle. But not enough to work with. Sweet Jesus, why wasn't the bus a half-hour late?"

"Quit complaining, Marco," Ty said. "Marissa just solved one of your mysteries—Ella Wilson gave everything to George because he became her son."

Across the roof of the car Marco sighed in frustration. "I know you're going to tell the sheriff, but I'd like to get another interview with Marissa to verify some of this first. Once the cops come knocking on her door, she won't talk to me again."

"So work fast," Ty said, climbing into the driver's seat. "You know I've got an appointment with him tomorrow."

Marco got in the passenger seat, slammed the door, and slumped down with hunched shoulders. Del could almost smell him fuming.

She saw Ty bristle in response. Since they had kissed on the park bench by the river, he didn't seem to be enjoying much of anything the three of them were doing together. So much for the trio enjoying some time off together.

TWENTY-FIVE

Ty felt lucky to find a parking space only a couple of blocks away from the waterfront. It was high tourist season on Pyke Island, and the bars in Summer Hill Harbor were perpetually crowded and boisterous, even on a Thursday night. They met Ryan at the smallest place Del knew of, tucked in the basement of a building next to the town pier. Down a narrow stone stairway, it consisted of a short bar on one wall, two dimly lit booths, a handful of small round tables, and a scatter of chairs. To make the best of its tiny size, the hovel called itself an English-style pub.

Ryan was saving one of the circular booths. Ty wasn't disappointed with Ryan's let-down expression when he saw that Del had come with two friends. Ryan got up to let Del slip into the middle of the bench seat and then slid in beside her. After an awkward hesitation, Ty sat next to Del, and Marco opposite him next to Ryan.

Marco was still acting prickly, even though they'd talked over dinner through some of their disagreements about the murder and Marco's research. Del had gotten them to both laugh it off by describing the hijinks of two tom turkeys who frequented the Corriveau property. The toms seemed to be browsing buddies, until early May, when they moved to opposite sides of the yard and started a mating season gobbling contest, loud enough that Gabe threatened to turn them into dinner. That was followed by a fully puffed-up strutting competition. A few weeks later, the two toms were back together, browsing the scrub like old friends. Marco got his own dig in by pointing out that, for humans, mating season had no regular timeframe.

Ryan perked up when Ty offered to buy. He pushed away his empty glass and ordered a double shot of bourbon and water while the others ordered beer. He started the conversation by telling them everything he knew about the slab cave and the petroglyphs, which turned out to be slightly less than the three of them already knew. "I had a wicked fight with Pale Moon. She finally had to admit that she didn't want me to find out. But it's all good now. I'm going to take a leave from Wisconsin and start research as soon as I can get in."

"Did you hear from a state archeologist?" Del asked.

"No," Ryan answered. "We don't think there's going to be a state anything. It's on George's land—uh, I mean, *our* land."

"Director Colleen Foster is paying for a survey. The state is pretty sure it's theirs," Ty said.

Ryan waved his hand. "Probably wrong. We've got the old Pyke-to-Wilson deeds and surveys, and they show that George inherited half of Monks Head."

"But who are *his* heirs?" Del asked.

"Settlement Creek Farm, of course, his one and only love." Ryan smiled and puffed up his chest. "My mother and our lawyer filed with probate last week."

"I wouldn't get too excited," Ty said. "There's still an unsolved murder hanging over the place."

"Feels like old news already, doesn't it, that someone found George's bones?" Ryan chugged the rest of his drink.

Ty flagged down the waitress and ordered Ryan a refill. "Did Uncle's 'find peace in the wind' sermon help you through?" he asked.

"Uncle? That dickhead. I don't take him seriously," Ryan answered.

"How long have you known him?" Ty drew back in his seat, moving out of the pale-yellow cone of light over the table.

"He showed up, I don't know exactly, some months before George disappeared."

"Where did he come from?" Del asked.

Ryan slid closer to her so that their upper arms were touching "I'm thinking Colorado." Now, he and Del were directly in the spotlight and he seemed to have lost interest in Ty and Marco.

Del continued her questions. "Did someone recommend him? What's his connection?"

"I don't know." Ryan licked a drop off his lips. He laid a hand over her forearm. "Maybe if you came over, we could look through the membership files together."

Del deftly moved her arm away from Ryan's touch as she smiled warmly at him. "Uncle doesn't seem to be into farming like the others. Do you know why?"

Ty watched her hazel eyes sparkle. *Nice move—keep him talking.* She might be studying science, but she was a crime snoop at heart.

Ryan snorted. "He says he's the medicine man, the healer."

"You forgot storyteller," she added. "We heard him on the Fourth tell about the bear who moved the large stone to let the boy out of the cave. What was that about?"

"I haven't a clue," Ryan said. "It's a traditional Wabanaki tale. You can find it on the internet. Only, Uncle got the ending wrong. Shows you what a phony he is."

"What's the real ending?"

"The boy doesn't go back to his mother and make trouble for his stepfather. He's adopted by the she-bear and raised like a cub," Ryan explained, while downing more bourbon. "When he grows up, he repays the bear's kindness by protecting the family from human hunters."

"At least that version has a moral," Del said. "Was Uncle trying to hint that he knew about the cave?"

Ryan shook his head slowly, leaning even closer to Del as if he wanted to lick her ear. He seemed to be having trouble finding his center of gravity. "You know, pretty soon I can show it to you. When're we going?"

Marco had been quietly sipping his beer and watching Ryan. That last come-on must have crossed a line. "What about the cult?" he demanded as he moved into the light. "You're a member too, aren't you?"

Ryan weaved back and forth trying to focus on Marco. "What?"

"I thought so," Marco said. "The farming thing is a cover, isn't it?"

"What're you saying?" Ryan sloshed his drink as it banged on the table.

On her other side, Ty put his hand on Del's shoulder and guided her out of the light. "Lean back," he whispered. "Let's watch Marco have some fun."

The gleam in the reporter's eyes would have started a fire. "Tell us, why does a farming community need steel gates and security systems?"

"Don't ask me."

It was as if a shark had smelled blood. Marco didn't let up. After a few more "What?" answers, a few "You!" accusations, and one "You're cra-crazy," Ryan was sputtering in a state of inebriated confusion.

Other patrons were starting to notice. Ty leaned into the circle of light and said to his friend, "Counselor, you are browbeating this witness."

Marco laughed and beat a short drumroll on the table. He called for the waitress to bring Ryan another bourbon. "Dude, you did great," he said, slapping Ryan on the back. "You held up under cross-examination. A toast?"

Gradually, Ryan seemed to find some fun in it. With one closed eye and the open one focused on his hand, he held up his glass without spilling any contents.

"To George Tozur! May he rest in peace," Marco said.

Ty and Del repeated, "To George Tozur."

"To shlief George," Ryan added and finished his drink in a few gulps once the glass found his mouth.

Ty and Marco had to support a swaying and stumbling Ryan as they climbed the stairs to street level. Del went through his pockets and found a key fob. They searched the lot near the town dock until they found the car that answered the call with a flash of headlights. After being shoved into the back seat, Ryan curled into a fetal position and instantly went to sleep. Ty made sure he was breathing.

"This man should not be driving," Marco announced and tossed Ryan's key fob high over his shoulder. They heard it land in the harbor with a *plunk*. "That was for the good citizens of Summer Hill Harbor."

Ty was enjoying Marco's game. When Marco went rogue, sometimes he was annoying, but just as often entertaining. They shared a couple of *attaboy* snickers.

Del seemed amused but added a note of sympathy. "Come on, guys. He may be a fool, but that was kinda mean."

"And, for the good constable, a text concerning a drunk sleeping in his car near the town pier. You know how the tourists hate that. Gives the village a bad name." Ty finished typing on his phone and gave them his best imitation of an innocent smile. "We are *not* being mean."

Like a best bud, Marco clapped his hand on Ty's shoulder. "Not at all. We're being responsible."

TWENTY-SIX

Late Friday morning, as Ty was waved into Sheriff Mike Hodgkins's office at the county headquarters in Ellis Junction, he saw the earthquake report on the edge of the sheriff's desk. By the staple and the way it was folded, he recognized it as the copy he had given the sheriff weeks ago. Mike excused himself to refill his coffee cup with a flavor he called "barely brown."

Originally, Ty had made the appointment to ask Mike about how the vandalism started and about suspicions he had concerning Settlement Creek's finances. As neither of these was directly related to the ongoing investigation into George Tozur's remains, he hoped the sheriff would share some history with him. There were many aspects of his work at the farm co-op that troubled him, not the least of which was Uncle's hostile behavior. There was no doubt that he and Del had been followed and spied on when they were at the quarry near the park boundary. Who was the target, Ty or Del, or both? And why— because they'd found the cave, which almost no one was supposed to know, or because of the security work he was doing? Or did someone see Del's ongoing exploration of the Monks Head area as a threat for a completely different reason? Seeing the report brought back a nagging, frustrating feeling they were missing something key, and it was hidden somewhere in that handful of pages.

When the sheriff returned, Ty gave him a very brief summary of what Evie and Marco had heard about the cult. Mike was definitely amused by the gossip, although he didn't laugh out loud and playacted that he was taking the information seriously. He made a note for his staff to come up with a respectful response whenever a conscientious citizen of the county called to report the rumor. Explaining that Marco was on the hunt for material for a story on the real George Tozur, Ty summarized what they had heard from Marissa. Mike jotted more notes in between sips of coffee.

"I'm pretty sure the Fairlie name came up in the initial investigation, but I'll pass it on," he said.

Ty gave him a brief summary of his conversation with Garth.

Mike nodded when he heard the part about Garth saying he knew all along it was a bear. "Sure, Garth would say that now," Mike said. "At the time, it was just another idea. I told that to Pale Moon."

"Garth is also sure that at least two of the vandalism acts were done by human hands." Ty showed Mike the specific images Garth had identified. "The first while you were investigating and one while I was still installing cameras. Both of them happened several days after the last actual bear visit."

Looking through the images, Mike frowned. "We thought the vandal wanted us to think it was a bear, but Garth is probably right."

"I'm sure Pale Moon was looking for an excuse to install some high-tech security," Ty said. "You know, the system I set up for them is permanent, latest technology, on a private network, and covers all of the village and the farm."

"Maybe she saw an opportunity," Mike acknowledged. "She's got to get approval from her council for expenses like that."

"They invited me to the part of the meeting where they approved expanding the security work, and oddly enough, cost wasn't even a concern. The guy they call Uncle was already convinced, and he bullied a couple of others. It was approved by a slim majority."

"Then you think the vandalism is over?"

Ty nodded. "I'd be surprised if anything happens now. I'm betting that Uncle had a hand in keeping up the fear factor, which brought the council around to spending more than they originally planned."

Mike arched back in his chair with his hands behind his head. "Just curious. What did it cost them?"

"About eight grand, and most of that is my consulting fee."

Mike whistled softly.

"Right. They farm about four acres of vegetables, plus a few chickens for eggs and goats for milk. I see them deliver daily to various grocery stores and they work two farmer's markets in the area, but I'm wondering how they support eighteen families year-round. The research I did shows a small vegetable farm can support about four workers per acre. Well, they have twice that per acre, more if you add in a handful of perpetual students like Ryan Smith who get money for education expenses."

Mike leaned forward, reaching for his coffee cup. "I know most farms that size aren't making much income per acre. Settlement Creek harvests elvers, the baby eels, every year. That's making them fifty or sixty thousand."

"There's a buy-in cost for new members," Ty added. "They use those funds to build new houses."

Mike nodded. "That's something like group equity. Outgoing members sell their shares to incoming members, so they can't use that for operating costs."

"There's been some turnover. Mostly, membership has been increasing, especially in the last five years." Ty was typing on his phone. "Doing the math on our estimates, the farming is supporting eighteen families on about a hundred and forty thousand. That's less than eight thousand per year per family."

Mike ran his hands through his hair. "Christ, how do you even pay for utilities and health care?"

"How do they pay for that large greenhouse they're building?"

"Chief George did get some inheritance from Ella Wilson," Mike noted.

"Why aren't there questions about his inheriting everything?" Ty asked. "Several people told me she showed signs of dementia before she died."

"Her will was written about the same time she created the farm, well before dementia became a problem. The courts found her sound enough when Wallace Wilson tried to sue."

"Then there's no way to understand how the co-op supports that number of families."

Mike drained the liquid in his cup. "I'll give your thoughts to the state detectives working the case. Maybe they already looked at Settlement Creek's finances. Nothing they've shared with me."

"The one to watch is Pale Moon. She's like the puppet master of Settlement Creek Farm. She knows how to make things legal, ironclad, and permanent. We've learned that it was Pale Moon who influenced the creation of the farm co-op, even though her name never appears on the original deeds." A restlessness came over Ty and he stood up, but with no intention of leaving.

"So she avoids any legal fallout," Mike said.

"And the security system has the same feel. If you read the minutes of that council meeting, you would not know her opinion. She chaired the meeting but she never spoke in favor or against and never voted."

"You're accusing her of faking vandalism and filing a false report," Mike said, tapping the desktop lightly.

"Not by her hands, anyway. Like I said, she's too smart to put herself in jeopardy. But I'm pretty sure she got someone else to do it."

"That alone would be a crime. A false report could be a felony. My officers spent a lot of time there." Mike jotted a few more notes. "Thanks for this information. We'll take it from here."

"Mike, is anyone actually working the Chief George case?"

The sheriff sat back in his chair. "The state's pushed it to the back burner. They're done with interviews. No evidence was found in the cave that they can work with. We're just going to have to wait until something develops." He leaned forward again and looked over his notes.

Standing in front of the desk, Ty knew he was being dismissed and that Mike wasn't about to share anything else he knew. The paper report caught his eye and he picked it up. "You read it?" He placed it back on the desk directly in front of the sheriff.

"Several times." Mike laid a hand on the report to flatten the fold in the middle. "Monks Head is barely two lines on a list of minor rockslides, ones that they felt caused no risk to visitors."

"Can we talk to the author of the report?"

"Kay Levant wrote the final document. What would you ask her?"

"How was the information gathered?"

"She'd tell you that, after the quake, the ranger staff explored all the trails looking for damage."

Ty crossed his arms. "Then why is there a list of rockslides in areas where there are no trails?"

"Hmm." Mike picked up his phone and punched the buttons. "Kay's been with this park for almost ten years. She should know every inch."

"I'd guess you could say that about any of the long-term rangers," Ty said. "Then why is it no one ever reported finding the cave?"

The sheriff acknowledged his point with a lift of his finger. It seemed like a long time before his call was answered. Mike asked whoever he was talking to if he could speak with Kay and broached the idea of looking at background information she'd received from other staff. Ty couldn't hear the answer, but there was another pause. Finally, the sheriff said, "Tell her we'll see her at two. Yes, at her residence, not your office." He put down the phone.

"Kay is supervising some tree work in the campgrounds, clearing a blowdown from the storm. She's expected to check in after. The director says to meet Kay at the ranger's housing unit."

"Sounds fine. I'd like to be back on the island by then anyway. Del and Marco are exploring old quarries on Wilson land."

"With their approval?"

"Marco said Charlotte herself gave him a map." Ty turned to leave.

"That's surprising. I know a number of folks who were chased off their land. Never anyone who was invited in."

Ty stopped at the door. "Has Josh Wilson ever shot at anyone?"

"Nah, not even Uncle, who he's caught poaching wild ducks at the pond." The sheriff folded the report and put it in his pocket.

"Uncle hunts? Firearms are on Pale Moon's forbidden list."

Mike shrugged. "I hear Uncle ignores a lot of rules. What makes you concerned about Josh? He wouldn't shoot at Del and Marco if Charlotte gave them permission."

"Because I suspect Marco lifted the map and lied about it."

TWENTY-SEVEN

When Ty first drove up to the park's residence building, he thought it might be a repurposed, old-fashioned motel—one long, low structure with a substantial roof overhang several evenly spaced doors, and small picture windows. The parking area out front could have been a paved-over swimming pool. Mike had told him that, while some of the year-round staff with families had private housing on the island, the park offered these tiny apartments to seasonal staff, interns, or anyone who might tolerate living in one. By the looks of things, Ty thought the rent must be really cheap.

Kay Levant's door was number four. It was opened by Mike just as Ty was making a fist to knock. Apparently, the sheriff and the park director had already been talking to Kay for several minutes. She was sitting hunched on a stool in front of a small kitchen counter with a look that said *Why me?* She pushed the folded copy of the earthquake report away from her.

"I didn't keep a copy," she said in a curt voice.

Mike made the introductions and settled himself in the only upholstered chair. He identified Ty as a private investigator for Settlement Creek, which was only a small twist on the truth.

Park Director Colleen Foster was sitting at the only other seat at the counter. "Kay, we're just trying to find out if or how the report is tied to Lucy's accident."

"How should I know? Five and a half years ago my job was to

compile the information and make it look professional. Once we got the grant for the rerouting and repair of trails and bridges, it just collected dust in the files."

Foster put her hand lightly on Kay's shoulder. "Now, I thought you also kept track of the expenses and wrote the final completion report on the damage. The park received two million dollars on top of the normal operating budget."

"It should be in your files," Kay said. "I wrote it with Hiram."

"It's missing too. I called Hiram in Augusta to see if he would send me a copy. He said when he took over as commissioner, they gave him a new laptop, and he doesn't have any files from when he was director."

Kay shrugged. "I don't know what he did with the report."

The director smiled, removing her hand. "He speaks highly of you, Kay. He told me he depended on you and you never let him down."

The ranger blinked and fidgeted.

"Tell us how the staff was organized to assess the damage," Ty said. He remained standing, as there was nowhere else to sit.

Kay lifted the cover page between two fingers as if it was contaminated. "It's explained in the introduction. We made a map and assigned sections. Each person assigned came back with a report."

"How long did it take?" Ty asked.

"Most were done within a few days, maybe a week."

"Where are those reports?"

She narrowed her eyes, clearly annoyed. "*I* didn't keep them."

"What did they look for when they surveyed the damage?" Ty asked.

"Besides obvious damage to trails, they looked for new slides that might threaten a trail in the future."

"Not in the wilderness areas?"

"No." With her fingernail Kay picked at a dried bit of something on the countertop.

"But there's a list of other slides in places like Monks Head with no official trails?"

"Oh, yeah, Garth did that. He went out of his way to check the backcountry."

Ty picked up the report and flipped to a back page, pointing to the one line mentioning Monks Head. "Is this all he reported?"

"I guess."

"Are you saying he wasn't thorough?"

"Oh, you don't know Garth. He planned on hiking with a crowbar. It sounded like he was going to check every inch for loose boulders. Like, on Monks Head, he knows people climb the rockslides all the time, particularly the locals on that side of the island."

"And what if he found a loose boulder?"

"Garth would stabilize it, jam another in, or move it. He's an expert. With cables, pulleys, and crowbars, he can move and place a rock that weighs hundreds of pounds," Kay explained. "You know, every spring, Garth and his crew work for weeks to repair winter damage to the stones lining our trails. There's always a few dislodged by frost or erosion."

Ty exchanged a slight nod with Mike. "Thanks for your time," Ty said, offering the report to Kay, who made no effort to take it from him. He placed it on the counter.

Mike stood, and said to Colleen Foster, "We should talk to Garth next."

She leaned forward and sighed audibly. "That will have to wait about ten days. I granted his request for vacation time this morning. He said there was some problem at his camp."

"A camp here?" Ty asked.

"Somewhere up north on a lake. He doesn't spend much time there in the summer, but it's important to him."

TWENTY-EIGHT

Del and Marco broke clear of the tall pine woods by late Friday morning. Because of the prior days of rain, they had to skirt standing water in the alder thicket. At least it was somewhat cooler than when Del had first trekked to this location with Ty. To limit the number of bug bites on this trip, she wore long hiking pants and a shirt with sleeves she could roll down. Her daypack contained mostly geology gear. Marco's backpack held the drinking water, ponchos in case of showers, peanut butter sandwiches and fruit for lunch, a first aid kit, and a flashlight. Apparently, Ty helped him organize before he left for his appointment with the sheriff. They brought their phones just to take pictures. Heart Pond was the deadest dead zone on the island.

They walked along the trail where Del had first seen Josh Wilson on his ATV. Past the park boundary sign, they were on Wilson land. Marco was in a mood to explore, taking note of how the landscape had changed from almost virgin forest with little undergrowth to an area of scrub, saplings, and slash piles, a sure sign it had been logged within the last ten years. Del insisted their late start meant no side trips if they were going to find the quarries and be back home by four. Marco stopped to take pictures of Monks Head behind them.

They continued straight, to the four-way intersection where the dirt trail widened, making enough room for a truck. They turned to follow the road that went due south.

Marco stopped when he heard the long, low *coo-OO-oo* of a

mourning dove. "Listen. Doesn't that just break your heart?" he asked, turning his head to hear the same call from another direction.

"You are a romantic," she said with a smile. "Let's keep going."

"What do you think they're mourning?"

"It's the males, and they're not mourning anything. They're saying stay away from my female."

He threw back his head and cooed, "Coo-OO-oo." It was a pretty good imitation. He stepped to her side, kissed her on the cheek, and cooed again.

She had to laugh. "Okay, I get it, but I'm not *your female* and we're wasting time."

"Sweet Jesus. A male's got a right to try."

Del trekked on with a goal of making time while Marco alternated between stopping to take pictures and jogging to catch up with her. She admired his boyish, freewheeling style, so different from Ty's uptight and totally self-controlled companionship. A month or so ago, she had actually entertained the idea that Marco might be "the right one."

The first time just felt right, almost innocent. She hadn't planned to stay on campus, but it was already after seven, with a hammering April rain and sleet storm outside, and she had a class the following morning at nine. Marco had made the couch in his off-campus apartment a standard offer anytime she wanted to skip the ninety-minute drive to Pyke Island.

He was delighted when she rang his bell. His roommate was away. Del would get a bed instead of the couch. They opened a bottle of wine and shared some leftover spaghetti. They talked for two more hours. They told each other funny stories about other grad students and faculty. It was all good.

He offered her one of his undershirts to sleep in, one of the cheap, tight-fitting white cotton tanks he always wore under his flannel shirts, the kind that made Del smile because they were so old-fashioned, so uncool unless you were thinking of a young Marlon Brando in *On the*

Waterfront. Marco's waist was more on the beefy side than Brando's, but he liked to show his muscular shoulders and let you think he was just a working-class guy.

She wondered later if he knew the undershirt was a trap. It smelled like Marco. She couldn't sleep in it. She tossed it off and tried sleeping in her underwear, but after an hour still felt restless and awake. She took off everything and tried to sleep cocooned in the fleece blanket. No luck. Finally, she knew what she wanted. She grabbed his shirt from the floor and, completely naked, padded to Marco's door, which was open an inch. He wasn't asleep either.

In the light of morning, they had agreed to stay focused on their current priority—Marco to finish his PhD thesis and Del to finish her bachelor's and master's degrees. They were being practical because, at some point, maybe a year or eighteen months out, career decisions could take either one of them somewhere else.

The second time, in May, she called and asked if she might sleep over. She made no pretexts and he didn't ask for any. She met his roommate, Lilly, who was dating a student named Ada with a foreign accent Del couldn't place, maybe Russian. The four of them ate Chinese takeout. With winks and grins, each couple retreated to their respective bedrooms. Lilly and Ada were noisy lovers, their headboard beat dull thumps for a long time. Marco had no headboard on his queen-sized bed. He was nervous, more than before, but after her second orgasm, he almost burst with his own pleasure. Marco stretched out flat on his back and noisily exhaled "Arrrhhh" like a bad imitation of a pirate. Del broke into laughter. He gave her an evil one-eyed squint, then tossed his long locks out of his eyes, and they laughed together. It was a laugh like kids running around the playground, like the laugh you couldn't stop when the teacher told you to stop but your friend was making a fish face behind the teacher's back. Lilly yelled across the hall to ask what they were smoking and was there any left. That made them laugh more. They both got a good night's sleep.

After that night, they renewed their agreement. They would only have those *benefits* whenever both felt they needed some—no commitments, no strings attached. Over the next few weeks, Del began to see new facets of Marco. For all his apparent ego and sometimes impulsive, self-serving behavior, he was also sensitive, caring, and loyal, generous with his time and anything else he could spare, even if he didn't have enough money to pay his rent on time.

But then there was Ty and the unexpected moment on a park bench when she really wanted him to kiss her. And more. Maybe she was just being what college kids called "thirsty" and it might be time to calm down. Over the last couple of days, Del had felt like she was bumbling around, trying hard to bring back the "hiking buddy" relationship. It felt awkward, not to mention that Ty himself seemed more uptight than usual. He was a mystery, but what bugged her now was that she really wanted to turn over the rock he lived under.

Following the Wilson gravel roads, Del and Marco hiked about a mile to where she expected to see a fork that led southwest to the quarries. Near the fork, they saw a dark-green pickup truck with an extended cab. As they got closer, a man got out of the truck. Del recognized him.

"Hey, it's Ranger Garth." She waved. "I wonder if we took a wrong turn and are back in the park." She picked up her pace.

Garth didn't say anything or wave back. He waited by the open door of the pickup while they approached.

"Hi, are we in the park?" Del pulled the map out of her back pocket.

"Where's your other friend?" he asked.

"If you mean Ty, he's busy today." Del hesitated. "Why?"

Garth stared at Marco. "Nothing."

Del held the map out to Garth. "Can you show me where we are?"

"Open it here," he said motioning to the front seat.

Slipping out of his backpack, Marco strolled away to take more pictures.

Del spread the map on the seat. She glanced over the front seat and noticed the shotgun propped up in the passenger foot well. Garth leaned over her shoulder. Del ran her finger over the map pointing to the intersection they had just passed. "I think we should be just north of this fork."

"That'd be about right," Garth answered as he leaned in further.

"Then we're on Wilson property, right?"

Garth didn't answer. Del felt his breath on her neck. It made her nervous and she tried to back away. In an instant, she felt a painful bite on her outer thigh and a burning sensation around it. She tried to jump back but she bumped against Garth's massive body.

"Hey!" Del glanced down at the source of the pain and saw what looked like pink feathers attached to a cylinder with a needle in her right thigh. "You stuck me!"

Marco must have heard her yell. She heard him walking toward them. "What's up? Did you find where we are?" he called out.

Del craned her neck to look at Garth's face, which loomed over her. His lips were pressed together in serious concentration. Without warning she felt nauseated, and gagged. Garth reached up to put his hand over her mouth, but she ducked and twisted away under his arm. She managed to limp three steps away from him before what should have been a straight road started sidewinding like a snake in front of her eyes.

"Run! Run!" With shaking hands, Del pulled the needle out of her thigh. She gulped in air. "Run now!"

Instead, Marco froze. Through a gathering black veil, Del turned to see Garth holding the shotgun low on his shoulder, aimed squarely at Marco. They were less than twenty feet apart.

"The girly said run," Garth growled.

"Let him go!" she screamed, swaying as though she was on a pitching boat. Her right leg was going numb. She was fighting the urge to lie down in the dirt.

"What do you want?" Marco shouted. "I won't let you hurt her, if that's it."

"The girly said run," Garth growled again. His expression was focused, his eyes fixed on Marco's chest.

Somehow, Del became aware she had fallen. Feeling the pebbles and grit of the road, she knew she was on her hands and knees. She had to close her eyes. She was so very tired.

As she sank deeper into a black void, time lost its grip. Del wasn't able to grasp if everything was happening in slow motion or if there was a long standoff with both men immobile. She heard a *chick-click* from the rifle. There were crunching sounds. Something moved past her, a swish in the air, maybe an object being thrown, a series of grunts, shouts, the rapid beat of footsteps, and the explosive crack of a shotgun.

Marco! The scream was still forming in her brain when someone abruptly hit the stop button and the lights went out.

It was the bouncing and jerking from side to side that brought her back to some level of consciousness. Del became aware of engine noise and then the sound of a man's deep, soothing voice saying gentle words. Garth was speaking to someone, someone he cared enough about not to growl. Del couldn't move, her muscles and bones seeming to be missing in action, but she could hear, and so she focused on every syllable, unable to understand their meaning but working to memorize them. After a while, her world stopped bouncing and jerking. The engine roared on, but the voice stopped. Del slipped back into the void.

TWENTY-NINE

The meeting with Kay Levant convinced Ty that there was something very troubling about Garth. Ty explained his gut feeling to Mike as they stood in the parking lot in front of the ranger apartments. Mike wasn't buying it.

"He must have found the cave opening," Ty insisted. "Doesn't that tie him to Chief George's murder?"

Mike leaned against his pickup truck and crossed his arms. "Maybe he did, but it doesn't tie him to murder. There's no motive. Don't jump to conclusions."

"He had plenty of opportunity to take the copies of the report. He might have driven Lucy Irwin's car off the road."

"Why would he do that?"

"Because he feels cornered."

Shaking his head, Mike said, "Garth's not a man who's easily threatened."

"Can you find out where this camp of his is?" Ty asked. "I'd like to ask him some questions."

"No. It can wait until he gets back. And you know that this is not your job anymore, so don't try to track him down." The sheriff turned away and opened the driver's door. "I'll get this information to the state cops."

"Ten days is a lot of time." Ty glared at the sheriff, who was dismissing him by climbing into the driver's seat. "Who knows what can happen?"

Mike grabbed the steering wheel with both hands. Ty saw in his profile that Mike was working his jaw, the sheriff's way of carefully choosing words. He turned deliberately to Ty with a stern look. "What I know is that Rubin Garth has given most of his adult life and energy to this park and Pyke Island. We depend on him to be here for every emergency in any weather, not just search and rescues, but flooded roads, moose accidents, fires, you name it."

Ty wanted the last word. "If he loves the park so much, maybe he would kill for it." He ended the stare-off by pivoting to where his car was parked.

"Let it go, Ty." Mike slammed the door and started the engine.

Ty steered his SUV to the right turn out of park headquarters, which would take him to Ferry Landing and the Corriveaus' private road. It was just after four, and the hikers should be on their way home. On his hands-free system, he connected with Gabe's phone. "Are they back yet?" he asked.

"They're late," Gabe answered. "Haven't heard from them."

"I know where they parked. I'll meet them there."

"Okay, then."

He made a U-turn and headed for the road to Settlement Creek. He had circumnavigated the island this way so many times in the past four weeks he was sure he could do it with his eyes closed. With little traffic, it would take about thirty-five minutes, time that his mind fixed on worry and regret. All week it had gnawed at him—he'd really blown his opportunity with Del. Their first kiss had been so perfect. But now she probably thought he was a mental case. His thinking at the moment was a tangle of how, if, when he should approach her again—all questions, no answers.

He pulled into the parking area near the falls by the mouth of Heart Pond. Marco's old faded blue Volvo sat alone near the far side. There was no one around. Ty contemplated going into the woods on the trail that Del had used the first day they found the cave on Monks Head, but he wasn't sure Del and Marco would come that way. In fact, because the trail was not marked except by the faintest areas where moss was scraped off rocks and roots, he wasn't sure he could follow it by himself. It was likely they were just delayed. After all, Marco was tagging along, and that often meant distractions. The sun was still high, and it wouldn't be really dark until after nine-thirty.

Ty decided on plan B, which was locked in a special suitcase in the back of his SUV—his unmanned aerial vehicle, a handy quadcopter that he had used to follow the mama bear and her cubs into the park. He was certified and registered to operate the drone, having finished the course in the spring, and he knew well that he'd be breaking the rules by flying over private land and the park without permission. If he got caught, he'd have to deal with that later. By flying the drone from the edge of Heart Pond, he hoped to be able to keep the device in his visual line of sight while searching the trails for Del and Marco. If not, he was prepared to break that rule, too.

With the drone launched and flying at around one hundred feet, he followed the video image on the remote control. He had the drone hug the edge of the pond, watching for any movement under the trees. *No one.*

Once he saw the trail where they had first met Josh, he changed the direction to follow the line of dirt toward the Wilson property. Soon it widened into a road, wide enough for larger trucks to use. He hovered over the first four-way intersection, not sure which way they would have gone. He brought the drone up to two hundred feet so he could see the layout of the roads better. There was some movement on a road to the south, and he brought the drone down for a closer look. It was a doe and a fawn browsing at the edge of some scrubby trees. When the drone got below one hundred feet, their white tails shot up and they bounded away. The drone made an audible buzzing sound at that height.

With the drone at two hundred feet again, he slowly followed the road going south, scanning every foot until it ended in the pit of an old quarry.

No one.

He backtracked to the intersection and followed the road heading around Heart Pond to the south and east. After several minutes, he caught motion under the afternoon shadows of the trees. He gradually brought the drone down lower. The shadow stepped out into the sun.

Marco!

Marco was swaying, standing with his weight on one leg, holding his other bent at the knee, and using a tree branch for balance. He squinted up at the drone, but didn't seem to understand what it was. Marco hobbled—or more like hopped—a few steps, stopped, and looked up again.

Where's Del?

Ty buzzed the drone back and forth over the area to find her, but he saw no one else.

Then Marco dropped down onto his hands and one knee and sat on the road as if he wanted to write something using his tree branch. Ty brought the drone down within fifty feet. He watched Marco scratch a *D* in the dirt.

D for Del?

Marco scratched out the letters *T A K E* and stopped after making two lines that might have been the start of an *N* or an *M*. He turned his upper body toward the right and swung his hands over his head, in a signal to mean "over here."

Ty quickly adjusted the controls to raise the drone to see a wider area. At around one hundred fifty feet, the screen went blank. A message appeared on the information bar. *Contact lost with device.* It was known as a "flyaway," but Ty was dead sure his drone had not malfunctioned. He ran to his car, slapped the control unit onto the passenger's seat, started the engine, and gunned it for the Wilson's driveway.

THIRTY

Groggy and limp, Del woke feeling a slight tickle across her cheek. *Marco's hair? He must be okay if he was bending over her.* She wrinkled her nose and sneezed. The tickle stopped. She opened her eyes, blinking to focus in the dusky light. She was lying on her side, with her cheek on a cool surface that smelled like dirt. About six inches from her nose was the largest house spider she had ever seen, with a body almost an inch wide and long, arched legs. This close, Del could make out the covering of short hairs and count the segments of exoskeleton on its legs. It was checking out her scent by waving its short, arm-like pedipalps.

Del blew air toward the spider. It scuttled back a yard.

Slowly becoming aware of her surroundings, she felt her hands tied in front of her with what looked like cotton clothesline. Her bare feet were tied the same way at the ankle. Leaning on one elbow, twisting, and pushing with her feet, she managed to sit up. As she struggled, she caught more movement in the shadowy ring around her. A dozen or more, a whole community, of house spiders were checking her out. She was in the four-foot crawl space of a cabin-sized building held up by a fieldstone foundation. The only light was from hundreds of little openings where the rocks of various sizes didn't quite meet. The little points of light were filtered even further by the spider webs covering them. It was as if the entire wall of stone was draped in dirty gauze.

"I'm not dead yet," she whispered to the spiders. They were cautious, but by turns one or two tried to approach. Any movement made them scuttle a safe distance away. Del knew these spiders were quite harmless. At least as long as she stayed alive. She had read recently that spiders were known to eat dead meat, especially when there was an overpopulation, and this crawl space definitely suffered that condition. The image of the skeleton on Monks Head popped into her brain, and she shook if off.

Ignoring the back and forth of the spiders, Del examined the ropes on her wrists while she listened for any sound from, or movement on, the floor above her head. It was perfectly quiet. The knots were not particularly tight, and after a few minutes she was able to free her hands. She began thinking about Marco again, imagining him lying on a dirt road, injured, bleeding, or worse. She clawed at the ropes around her ankles and hurriedly untied them.

Crawling on her hands and knees, she found a trapdoor next to a segment of tree trunk that was almost in the center of the structure, acting like a support column. Again, she paused to listen but heard nothing on the floorboards above her. Kneeling, she put her hands on the trapdoor and cautiously pushed. The door seemed unusually heavy, but it opened a crack. Del was relieved. At least it wasn't locked. She moved into a crouch. Leaning her upper back and one shoulder against the door, she strained hard, thrusting with her legs. The door lifted about six inches before she saw there was a rug of some kind over it. She stuck her arm out and attempted to push the rug up and get the weight off the door. It took a few tries but it worked. With one more big thrust, Del lifted the door so that it was vertical and held in place by the rug tented over it. She could stand upright in the opening and was excited to see daylight where the edge of the rug had lifted. Bracing her feet against the support column, Del hauled herself out of the crawl space. With a big exhale, she rolled out from under the rug onto the wood floor of a large one-room cabin. Looking back at the trapdoor, Del saw a couple of spiders had followed her. She swept them back into the crawl space and closed the trapdoor. She pulled the bump out of the rug so that it was perfectly flat.

Del stood up and looked around the cabin. It was made entirely of rough logs, skillfully caulked and chinked so there were no gaps. There was a fieldstone fireplace centered on one wall; on the opposite wall, a row of windows and a door to a porch with a view of water through a scatter of trees. The cabin was clean, neat, and sparsely furnished with handmade wooden pieces, except for a metal bed frame topped by a bare mattress. The hand-braided rug that Del had struggled with covered most of the center of the room. When she noticed a kitchen area on the side wall with a sink and a hand pump, she rushed to get a drink of water. She was incredibly thirsty and gulped down as much as her stomach would hold. That also brought on hunger pains. She opened cabinets on either side of the sink, but the shelves were empty. One cabinet was built as a gun locker, also empty.

She splashed cool water on her face and wiped it with her sleeves. Del would have loved to explore the cabin more, but her alarm was ringing louder with each passing minute. She had to get out of there to find help.

Garth brought me here, dumped me in the crawl space. So where is here? She knew this wasn't Pyke Island, because it smelled different.
Get moving. Marco might be dying.

Del stepped out onto the porch. Curiously, there were several cardboard boxes and an empty canvas duffel bag next to the screen door. Digging into them, she found sheets, towels, dishes, an oil lantern, books, and framed photographs. It was as if someone was moving in or moving out. A large-framed photo sat on top of the items in one box. She recognized it, at least the part she had seen before—a picture of a happy hunting party.

Seeing the photo raised her level of alarm. Bare feet or not, she needed to find help. She trotted out of the cabin and down a grassy slope to the gravel and stone shore. To one side was an empty wooden dock about the right size to tie up a small powerboat. Kneeling on the dock, she scooped water with her hands for a taste. That confirmed it—fresh water with a typical lake shoreline, boulders of different sizes, and pockets of gravel, all overhung by the black forest of spruce and fir. Across the lake the sun hung well above the treetops—a few hours after noon, she figured. She scanned up and down the shore and across the mile or so to the other side. Nothing but trees and boulders. To the north was a cluster of particularly prominent boulders standing high out of the water, definitely glacial erratics dropped by the last melting glacier. The largest was as big as a school bus.

Del chose to go south, working her way through the forest close to the shore and trying to step only on the layer of moss and dried needles to avoid impaling her feet on twigs and rocks. She wasn't entirely successful.

She kept going, expecting any minute to see a change in the angle of the shoreline, but instead it kept falling away to the southeast. After several more minutes, Del realized the sun that had been over her right shoulder was now over her left shoulder.

Fucking Garth. This is a peninsula, and I started in the wrong direction.

She picked up her pace, ignoring the stab wounds on her feet. When she came to a tumble of boulders at the water's edge, she scrambled up the largest one. Looking out from shore, she recognized the cluster of particularly big glacial erratics.

Fucking Garth. This is an island!

The next decision was easy. She would have to swim.

THIRTY-ONE

Ty powered his Lexus onto the Wilson's paved but unmarked driveway and screeched to a halt in front of a gated steel fence with a call box that said VISITORS BY APPOINTMENT ONLY. He jammed the call button several times. A male voice came on after the fifth time. "Identify yourself."

"This is an emergency. Let me in."

After a pause, "What kind of emergency?"

"My friends are seriously injured on one of your roads."

"Identify your friends and yourself."

"One is Marco Avila. Charlotte Wilson knows him. I'm Ty Holden. Don't waste time." With each sentence, Ty's voice grew louder.

There was a murmur of voices and then Ty heard a click and hum. Slowly the gate swung open. The calm, authoritative voice said, "Proceed to the parking area by the house. I'll meet you there. Keep your speed down. We have pets."

Ty exhaled and waited for the mechanism to open the gate fully. He exhaled again trying to control the urge to gun the engine.

The driveway was almost a mile long. It wound through a thick forest ending in an opening where a massive dark-brown house stood. A large deck on one side of the house perched on the edge of Heart Pond. Ty saw Charlotte standing on the deck holding on to the railing, an empty wheelchair behind her. She watched his car approach. By her side, a regal German shepherd stood alert and ready. A man wearing dark overalls waved him over to the front of a garage at the other end of the house. He introduced himself as Bruce, the property manager.

Ty showed him the last video from the drone, where Marco sat down to scratch letters in the dirt. Bruce walked him around the outside of the house to a grassy area near the other end of the deck. Charlotte was back in her chair, and she wheeled herself over to them. She was sitting tall, with her black wig on straighter than when Ty had last seen her. Wearing a cream-colored, long-sleeved silk shirt and dark slacks, she seemed elegant from a distance. Up close, he could see the points of knobby joints through her clothes. Her hands quivered any time they were not grasping something. Somewhere inside the house, their shepherd was barking away.

There were no introductions.

"What is it?" she demanded of Bruce.

"Fellow here has pictures of that reporter. He's injured himself. Looks like he's near the birch spring area," Bruce explained without a shred of urgency, as if he was talking about a mowing schedule.

"Take him," Charlotte said with a nod to Ty. "Take Josh's four-seater."

Bruce hesitated.

It was clear who was giving the orders. "Don't waste time, Bruce."

"I'm the only one here, ma'am," he said.

"I know that," Charlotte insisted. "I won't die in the next hour. Go now. Josh will be home soon anyway."

Bruce turned smartly and Ty followed him back to the oversized garage. He disappeared through one door and when another overhead rolled open, he pulled out driving the four-seat off-road vehicle Ty had seen Josh Wilson use. Ty climbed in. Bruce handed him a helmet, and they left the paved area and turned onto a dirt road.

The road Bruce followed pulled away from the shore of Heart Pond and they were quickly swallowed by forest. There were many twists and turns as Bruce avoided potholes and tentatively crossed one washout. He drove straight through two intersections where the trees had been thinned. Ty was trying to picture where they were going from what he had seen from the drone but was completely disoriented. And it was all taking too long. Ty thought Bruce wasn't driving as fast as he should be. Where was Marco heading? Why didn't the drone see Del?

"Are you sure we're going the right way?" Ty shouted over the engine roar.

Bruce nodded deliberately, once.

Finally, they saw Marco in the distance, hopping along with his tree branch crutch and holding something in his free hand. He stopped and waited when he saw them approaching. Bruce slowed down. Ty jumped out before the vehicle came to a full stop.

He tore off the helmet and raced the last thirty feet shouting, "What happened? Where's Del?"

With an unsteady hand, Marco held out the remnant of Ty's quadcopter. "A big redheaded guy. She called him Ranger Garth. He drugged her and took her away in his truck."

Ty grabbed Marco by the shirtfront and shook him, making his neck snap back and forth. "You let him take her!"

"You think I didn't try to stop him?" Marco stared at him in shock. "You think I wouldn't have died first? If I had a chance?"

With a shove, Ty let go of Marco's shirt so that his friend fell flat on his back with a loud grunt. He grabbed what was left of the quadcopter and savagely heaved it into the woods. He wouldn't look at Marco, even as he heard him gasping in pain. He couldn't think, couldn't move. He was afraid he might kill Marco with his bare hands.

Bruce stepped between them and said evenly, "Hold on, now." He helped Marco to stand, pulling his arm over a shoulder. "Let's get this guy in a seat. We'll call an ambulance when we get back to the house."

They hobbled a few steps. Marco's breathing was ragged. Ty heard the anguish, something more than just physical pain. He saw tears on Marco's cheeks and a layer of caked blood on the side of his head, down his neck and shoulder. Ty stepped over, put his arm around Marco's waist, and carried most of his weight the last few feet. Together, they lifted him into a back seat and Bruce buckled him in. Ty retrieved his helmet from the dirt and snugged it over Marco's head. He said to Bruce, "I'll sit in back so we can talk."

Bruce started the engine, did a three-point turn, and drove back, again with an incredibly irritating overabundance of caution. Leaning close so he could be heard over the engine, Marco described Garth holding a shotgun, how he threw his backpack and rushed Garth, how Garth smashed the gun stock into his head, how Marco staggered and fell into a ditch. Then Garth actually did fire the gun, but Marco managed to scramble into the woods first. There was a second shot, and he dove behind some trees where he caught his foot in roots and wrenched his knee. He was sure it was dislocated. Marco heard the pickup truck drive off. He crawled out of the woods and started hopping. Their backpacks were gone. He assumed Garth had taken them.

"Can you describe the pickup?" Ty was counting the seconds until they got back to the Wilson house.

Marco fished in his cargo shorts and pulled out his phone. "Better. I got pictures of Del and Garth by the truck just before he stuck her with something with pink feathers."

"Shit, Marco. Why didn't you show me right away?" Ty grabbed the phone and flipped through the photos. "As soon as you get service, send them to me and to the sheriff's office."

"I'm not thinking right. Feeling kinda sick." Marco wiped the sweat from his forehead and crusted cheek.

"Sorry, man. What happened to the drone?"

"I finally figured out it had to be you. Did you see me writing in the dirt?"

"The first few letters but then what happened?"

"A man stepped out of the woods. I thought it was someone to help me. Next thing, he raises a rifle and *bang!* the drone falls. Practically on my head. By the time I stood up, he's gone."

"Who was it?"

"I'm pretty sure it was Uncle. And I know he saw me."

Ty hunched his shoulders and brooded until they reached the Wilson garage and came to a stop. He jumped out of his seat.

"Bruce, is there another entrance to your road network?"

Bruce nodded. "There's a back gate that the logging trucks use."

"And it's not locked?"

"Combination lock. Our contractors all know it." Bruce shifted his eyes to the now empty deck. Charlotte was nowhere in sight. "I told her it wasn't a good idea."

Ty put his hand lightly on Marco's shoulder. "Bruce will call an ambulance. Call the sheriff and then Gabe as soon as you can." He took off at a jog.

"Where are you going?" Marco called.

"I need to find a camp," Ty yelled over his shoulder.

THIRTY-TWO

Del waded into the lake gingerly. It was colder than she expected. She focused on the shore to the north, partly tucked behind those huge boulders, because from her perch on the rock, she thought she'd seen a glint of silver. She hoped it was the reflection of an aluminum dock. It was at least a mile away.

She swam steadily, her hands and feet growing numb in the cold water. The lake was calm enough, and she made good progress until she came to the boulder-strewn area. She scraped her hand on the first rock she hit just beneath the surface. The entire area was shallow, sometimes only knee-deep. She tried to walk, but underwater the rocks were slick with algae. She slipped, splashed face first, and banged a knee. She tried again, slipped, and fell on her hip. Finally, she resorted to floating in the water while trying to pull herself from rock to rock. Then, just as quickly, the lake bottom dropped away, and she was able to swim again. Steadily, she gained on her target and her view of the shoreline improved. Thankfully, it *was* a long aluminum dock—with a boat tied to it—and she could make out two people. They were turned away from her, but she saw a woman stretched out in a chair wearing a billowing bright-yellow dress and large sun hat. Another was a boxy man in oversized shorts who walked to the end of the dock to throw something in the water. She thought about shouting for help but decided it was just as easy to swim the short distance to a small opening at the forest edge not far from them.

As she reached the cut of sand and gravel, the dock was out of her vision, behind dense undergrowth hanging over the lake, but she could hear voices. Del crawled out of the water on her hands and knees. Exhausted and still fiercely angry at Garth, she hung her head and tried to calm her breathing when a long, deep-throated growl came from the shadowed undergrowth nearby. Del gasped and rose on her knees with her palms out in front of her, afraid the creature might attack.

"Please?" she said, not knowing what, or who, she was talking to.

A man's voice called from the woods on her right. "Janie? Dickens is stalking that muskrat again!"

A woman's voice on the other side. "Go find him! I don't want him dragging home another carcass."

"Dickens?" Del asked in a whisper and was answered with a soft whine, but she still couldn't see who made it.

From the forest came sounds of branches swishing and twigs snapping. The man's voice said, "Dickens, come?" It was more of a question than a command. Then, "Janie? Are you there?"

The woman's voice, much closer, "Over here, Jules. I hear him."

Del sat back on her heels. "Good boy, Dickens," she breathed.

Silently, Dickens stepped out into the opening. He was a stately, sleek, all-black Rottweiler with tan paws. He approached Del with caution, sniffed her feet and knees, and acknowledged her with a single low *wuff* and a jerky wag of the stump that a veterinarian had left for a tail.

"Let's not drag home another carcass," Del said, reaching out cautiously to stroke his head, which was level with hers. Dickens might have easily ripped off her arm if he'd wanted to.

At that moment, pushing aside a wall of spruce branches, the two people she saw on the dock appeared.

"Oh, my god!" said the man's voice, only it came from the woman in the yellow dress. The arm keeping his sun hat on his head was covered in curly black hair, and several days of salt-and-pepper stubble framed his very surprised expression.

"You poor thing," said the woman's voice, coming from the stocky man in the baggy shorts, sporting sunbaked skin, deep wrinkles, broad shoulders, and a faux-hawk hairstyle buzz-cut on the sides. "Where did you swim from?" She stepped over the last branches in her way, put her arm around Del's waist, and helped her to stand. "You look positively exhausted. Let's get you inside. Jules, hold these branches so they don't slap us."

"I, ahem"—pointing over her shoulder, Del cleared her throat and said—"I swam from that island."

Janie, who had helped Del stand, surveyed the water. "Was there a boating accident? Are there others?"

"No, not a boating accident," Del answered. "A man named Garth drugged me and I woke up under a cabin. I can't explain it all now. Can I use your phone?"

"Rubin Garth! Why am I not surprised?" said the one named Jules. He motioned them to follow as he pushed and stomped through the underbrush, holding the yellow dress up over his knees so it wouldn't get snagged. "Didn't I tell you, Janie? There is definitely something weird about that man."

After a few more steps, they came to a worn path under towering spruce trees. Dickens appeared as if by magic and was now leading the way.

"No phone, I'm afraid. We're completely off-grid," Janie explained. "But we'll take you to Buck's. As far as I know, he has the only phone service on the lake."

A short distance away was their cabin, a modern A-frame, lots of glass and vinyl siding, the polar opposite of Garth's primitive log cabin. Inside this cabin, the sparkling white walls were accented with furniture in bright orange and deep blue. Janie led her to a chair in the kitchen area that was occupied by gray fluff balls. They turned out to be cats once Janie swiped at them. "Keats and Shelley!" she hissed. "Off the furniture!" The two sauntered into another room.

"Jules, go put on pants. And bring the first aid kit." Janie helped Del into a chair. "He's a cross-dresser," she said in a low voice. "Don't worry. Jules is a wonderful partner and father. We summer here so he can enjoy his silk dresses in peace."

"Really, I'm fine," Del said. "Can we go now?"

Jules handed Janie a blue box labeled FIRST AID. Dickens settled down out of the way but where he could watch everyone.

"This will only take a minute," Janie said as she wiped blood from Del's wrist and feet. "Roll up this pant leg. It looks like your knee is bleeding." Janie opened several adhesive bandage wrappers with her teeth and snugged them over each cut she found.

Reappearing in hip-hugging jeans and an open-throated white shirt, Jules looked not just manly, but quite attractive, with a distinguished sweep of gray in his wavy black hair. He stood in front of the windows surveying the lake. "Garth! Ugh! We saw him in his bass boat pass by going toward his island, and a while later heading back up the lake."

"How long ago was that?" Del asked.

"About three hours ago."

"What time is it? I'm hoping it's still Friday."

"Almost five and my god, yes, it's still Friday."

Janie put both hands on Del's cheeks, turning her head slightly to examine her face and scalp. "No concussion or other injuries, I think." Janie ran her hands over Del's arms down to her hands. "Your skin is cold. Hands like ice. I'll get you some dry clothes."

"Please, I'm fine," Del insisted and stood up with a wobble. "They'll be starting to search for us now."

Janie stepped back with her hands on her hips. "When was the last time you ate?"

"I had an orange and toast for breakfast," Del said. "Please, I need to get to a phone."

"Jules, get some of those oatmeal cookies we made yesterday," Janie said as she reached inside a closet and pulled out a sweatshirt. "At least put this on." Del accepted it gratefully. Janie went into another room and came back with a pair of bright magenta flip-flops. "One of the kids left these last week. I think they'll fit you."

Del squeezed the thongs between her bandaged toes and gave Janie a grateful smile. Dickens raised himself and padded over to smell her feet. He snorted once and moved away.

"Dickens made up his mind about you right away," Janie said. "He usually barks his head off at strangers or anyone he doesn't like."

Jules handed Del a cookie as he started filling a paper bag from a container on the kitchen table. It was probably the sweetest, most delicious thing she had ever tasted. They walked downhill toward the dock where an open-seated Boston Whaler with a center console and big Mercury outboard was tied up. Janie started taking off mooring lines while Jules helped Del onto a bench seat. He was just getting ready to start the motor when they heard an engine in the distance.

"That sounds like Garth," Jules said. "He must be on his way back."

Del jumped out of the boat. "He can't see me. When he finds I'm gone, he'll search the island first. If he finds me with you, I don't know what he'll do."

Janie swept her hand toward their cabin. "Everyone in the house."

The throaty two-stroke engine sound grew louder. Peeking from the edge of the windows, they watched Garth's hulk of a silhouette as his boat cruised by, staying close to the opposite shore. He disappeared behind the giant boulders.

"We can't drive to the phone place?" Del asked.

Jules smiled. "No roads here, I'm afraid."

Janie scanned their living area. "We need to give her a disguise in case he catches us between here and Buck's."

Jules snapped his fingers. "I know. One of our trash bags. We say that we're taking our trash in." He reached under the sink and pulled out an extra-large black plastic bag.

Janie gave him a one-arm hug and a wet smack on the cheek.

"Genius." She turned to Del. "Don't worry; we won't close it tight. You just have to not move at all."

"We better go now, while he's still figuring out why I'm not spider food," Del said, heading back out to the dock.

Janie, Jules, and Dickens were right behind her. Dickens hopped into the bow. On the floor between the console and the engine, Jules held open the bag while Del, hugging her cache of cookies, climbed in and made herself as small as possible. They tore a couple of small holes in the bag so she could breathe. She felt him apply a twist tie. She couldn't see anything, but at least for the first time all day she felt warm.

After a couple of coughs, the engine roared to life. The boat rocked and moved slowly through the water. A few minutes later, the RPMs increased to a smooth, steady cruising speed. Munching on another cookie, Del had just begun to relax when the engine speed suddenly dropped down to an idle. Dickens started to bark furiously. Del froze. Small waves slapped against the sides of the boat.

She heard Garth's angry growl call out. "You headed to the marina?"

"Afternoon, Rubin," Janie said. "It's not hunting season now, is it?"

"I'm looking for someone who broke into my camp." Garth had to shout over Dickens, who was alternating between deep growls and sharp barks.

Janie shouted, "Dickens! Quiet!" And instantly he was.

"When did that happen?" she asked.

"Today. Have you seen anyone on my island?"

Both Jules and Janie at the same time said variations of "No" and "No one" and "Nothing."

"Did you report it to the police?" Jules asked.

"I'll get to it once I'm done searching." Garth's voice was farther off.

"We didn't see any boats coming or going except yours, Rubin," Janie hollered. "Now, you wouldn't try to shoot anyone today, would you?"

Del heard Garth start his outboard.

The Whaler went back to a cruising speed. Del felt the surge of water against the hull. She counted the minutes. It seemed like a long way to Buck's, wherever that was.

173

THIRTY-THREE

Ty banged on door number four at the ranger's residence building. Kay Levant was slow to open it.

"Oh, you," she said with one hand on the doorjamb and the other holding a tumbler of amber liquid. She saw him eyeballing her drink. "What? It's after work on a Friday and I'm not on duty this weekend."

"I need to find out where Garth has his camp."

"You'll have to check with Human Resources on Monday." She tried to close the door, but Ty held it open.

"It can't wait," he said. "It's an emergency."

Kay rolled her eyes and sighed. "Then call our twenty-four-hour emergency number."

Ty stepped into the doorway. There was no way she could slam it without damaging his face. "I need your help," he pleaded. "Garth drugged and kidnapped Del Corriveau. I'm betting the only place he would have taken her is his camp."

"What?" Kay said. "Garth is a weird guy, but kidnapping?"

"Do you know the location of his camp?"

Kay narrowed her eyes, and for a moment stared through him. "He's mentioned it, but I really don't remember." Then she quickly gulped down her drink, opened a kitchen drawer, and rummaged through a mess of tools and kitchen junk. Finally, her hand came out with a small key ring. "Come with me."

Ty followed her around to the other side of the building, where a row of identical sets of doors and windows looked much like the front except the door numbers started with eleven. She stopped at number fifteen and started sorting through the keys on her ring. Ty scanned the other apartment doors and the walkway. They seemed to be alone.

"This is Garth's apartment," she said

"You have keys to them all?"

"Not all. Over the years, I've moved up from these smaller apartments to the nicer ones on the other side. The property manager is not so good about us turning in keys."

Kay tried one key, but it didn't fit. She tried another that slid in but wouldn't turn the lock mechanism. The third one she tried worked after some jiggling. She opened the door.

The "apartment" was little more than a bedroom with a bed, stuffed chair, TV, wooden chair and desk, closet, and dresser, piled with magazines and books. Kay closed the door softly behind them.

"I'm guessing what we're doing isn't legal, even if I did have the key," she said.

Ty went first to the desk to examine a blank notepad and paper scraps laying on top.

"What are you looking for?" Kay asked. "Maybe I can help?"

"Anything that might have an address of where his camp is, maybe a utility bill or statement."

"That won't work," Kay said, sifting through the pile of magazines. "His place is primitive, off the grid."

Ty started going through desk drawers. "How about a mortgage statement?"

Kay opened and closed each drawer in the dresser next to the bed. "Probably not. I think Garth has owned the land forever and built the cabin by himself."

"A letter, correspondence from a neighbor?"

"I'd be surprised if Garth had any neighbors that he'd correspond with," she said, slamming the last drawer. "This is almost empty. I thought he had more stuff than this."

Ty found the desk drawers were also empty. He looked around frantically.

Kay poked inside the closet. "Really strange. The only thing in here are his uniforms and some trash on the floor. I wonder where his stuff is."

On the open closet door, Ty noticed a wall calendar with several months torn off. The top half was a picture of a smiling, happy family—blonde wife with a fresh-from-the-hairdresser look, handsome husband, and two adorable kids—in an open powerboat on a sapphire-blue lake.

He read the ad out loud: "Buck's Village. Lake Awasosee, Maine. Full-service marina, general store, lunch counter, cottages for rent."

Kay jerked her head out of the closet. "That's it! I remember he said that he had to leave his boat at Buck's because his place was on an island in the lake. It was one of those things he grumbles about because Buck charges him a monthly rental for what used to be free."

Ty took a picture with this phone and was typing in *Lake Awasosee* as he bolted out the door. Kay would have to figure out on her own that she probably should tell the cops what they found without exactly telling them how.

THIRTY-FOUR

Tucked inside the black, plastic garbage bag, Del was beginning to overheat. Her hair had stopped dripping but had made the back of the sweatshirt wet. Her damp skin stuck to her hiking pants. She was bone-tired but at least not hungry anymore. The bag of oatmeal cookies was empty. After what felt like many more minutes, she heard the engine slow to an idle, felt a bump, and then another, followed by a creaking sound. They must be at the marina. Jules and Janie were whispering and taking their sweet time. There were other voices. Finally, Jules opened the bag, reached in to help Del stand, and pulled her onto a floating platform.

"Quickly, now," he said. "Follow Janie to the store. There were some kids fishing from the dock, and we had to bribe them with ice cream money to get them to leave before letting you out. No need to raise any eyebrows."

Del hurried down the main dock, one of two in the marina. At the gated end, where she stepped onto the shore, a large sign in red with white and blue lettering said: BUCK'S MARINA. FUEL DOCK. BOATS FOR HIRE. A boxy, fairly new three-story structure dominated the clearing in front of the marina. An oversized sign, also red, white, and blue, stretched across the entire front of the building above the porch: BUCK'S VILLAGE STORE. WELCOME TO LAKE AWASOSEE. She was sure it could be seen from miles away on the lake. Another sign on the paved side of the building was a large red arrow with white-and-blue lettering that read: This Way to Buck's Rental Cottages.

Janie was waiting on the porch with Dickens. As she ushered Del inside, two laughing kids ran out past them holding ice cream cones.

The store was the entire first floor of the building, one long room with goods on shelves taking up most of the space. Along a side wall was a plywood counter with fixed stools. Above the counter was a red, white, and blue sign: Buck's Café. Breakfast and Lunch.

At first, they saw no one inside. With a few "yoo-hoos," Janie searched and ducked around the rows, looking for Buck. She found him in the back corner loading bags of frozen vegetables into a freezer chest. With a deep, melodious voice and just a hint of a southern drawl, he greeted Janie like an old friend and stood up. Buck was at least a head taller than the racks of shelves, which were taller than Del. He had broad shoulders, copper skin, anthracite eyes, and a bald head in contrast to a full black beard, making his white smile dazzling.

"Buck, this is …" Janie turned to Del. "Oh, I don't think we ever asked your name."

"Del Corriveau. Nice to meet you," Del said, nodding to Buck. "I don't want to be rude, but I really need to use a phone to call the police on Pyke Island."

Buck raised his eyebrows. "We're a long way from Pyke Island."

"Garth drugged and kidnapped her, and she escaped by swimming to our shore," Janie explained.

"That's why you came up the lake with Jules and Janie when I never saw you go down the lake." He tossed a box into the freezer, closed the lid, and walked directly to the lunch counter. "Everyone on the lake comes through here," he said with a wave of a large brown hand with long, graceful fingers. "It's where the road ends."

"Did you see Garth today?" Del asked.

"He came about one-thirty or two. Loaded his boat with a duffel bag and some boxes." Buck's face registered a surprising thought. "Was that you in the duffel?"

"Probably," Del said. "Not that I remember."

"We got another problem," Janie said as she followed Buck's long strides that already had him at the lunch counter. "We just saw Garth patrolling in his boat. He was carrying a rifle and a sidearm. If he shows up here, you might want to close the store."

"Rubin Garth's always been an odd duck, but it sounds like he's snapped completely," Buck said. Stopping in front of a bulletin board, he pulled off a card. "Here's the number of the Maine game warden for this area. He's the closest law enforcement and a friend of mine. Tell him what happened, and he'll contact the state and county law."

"Thank you," Del said. "If I stay out of sight until the police come, I don't think Garth will do anything. It's me he wants."

"Janie, take her up to my apartment and use my personal line," he said. "Stay there until we say the police are here. You'll be fine."

Jules had entered the store and heard most of the conversation. "Buck and I will keep an eye on things," he said. "Come, Dickens." Dickens ignored him.

Del followed Janie to a door in the back of the store. Dickens was right on their heels until Janie widened her eyes and gave him the slightest toss of her head. He turned and strolled back to Jules.

With a smile, Buck clapped a hand on Jules's shoulder. "As long as you're not looking for employee wages, Jules."

"And take away one of your revenue streams?" Jules responded with an exaggerated eye roll. "I wouldn't dream of it."

Dickens added a *woof.*

Next to the door was a booth with an old-fashioned pay phone. A sign on it read: To Make a Call, See Buck for Exact Change. Janie led Del to an enclosed stairway, and they climbed to the third floor.

THIRTY-FIVE

"Ty, stop the car! Stop and listen to me!" Del cut his questions short. "I told you, I'm fine. I'm safe. I called the police. They're on their way. I talked to Grandpa, who was at the hospital in Ellis Junction. Marco is going into surgery for a torn meniscus in his knee. Grandpa is coming to get me. He said he'd check in with Sheriff Mike and he's probably on his way now. You need to turn around and go back." She was relieved to have caught him. She had to leave messages the first three times she had tried his number. At any moment he might lose service again.

"What?" Ty was shouting into his hands-free phone. "I'll be there in an hour."

"No! You need to go back to Pyke Island and stop her!"

Janie looked up sharply from where she was sitting on Buck's couch. Del covered the mouthpiece with her hand and whispered. "We're okay. We're friends."

The line went dead. "I lost him," she said as she set the cordless handset back into its charging cradle. "Hopefully, he's turning around to backtrack to a signal."

Standing in front of the open windows, Del became aware of the lakeshore breeze smelling of balsam and sweet water. It was a bright-blue, cloudless summer day. Near the cottages, a handful of children were splashing in the water and playing on a beach made from almost-white sand, definitely man-made. Two men were pulling into the marina in a small rowing skiff. A few people strolled along the path near the cottages. Buck's Village had all the makings of a perfect lakeside vacation.

Del changed her focus to the wall next to the windows, where she saw a map of the lake. Awasosee was a three-lobed lake, shaped like a lopsided snowman. Buck's was on the northernmost end, the head. Del found Garth's island, shaped like a teardrop, near the middle of the southernmost and fattest lobe, the belly. The boulder field she had swum across was charted as a field of asterisks above his island.

The rest of the wall was covered in framed photographs, the largest of a group of graduates in caps and gowns in front of a stately brick building. The caption said HOWARD UNIVERSITY CLASS OF 1982. It was easy to identify Buck in the back row among the beaming brown and black faces. There were many other photos crowded close together—elderly relatives on unpainted porches, outings, picnics, a clunker station wagon, church weddings, a young man in uniform, and a young woman being awarded a master's degree—each one a memory of a moment in time. This was the collection of a family man who was proud of his heritage.

"What brought him here?" Del asked. "Based on his accent, I take it he's not originally from Maine."

Janie laughed. "It's a long story, but this is his retirement plan after teaching high school science and raising three kids, one who still needs help with tuition. Before he bought it, this was a rundown, mostly abandoned hunting camp."

The phone rang and Del jumped to get it. The caller ID displayed Ty's number.

"Ty! Stop. The. Car. I don't want to lose you again. You need to go back."

"What? What did you say?"

"I'm not going to say another thing until I hear the engine shut off!" With the handset held slightly away from her ear, Del paced around the three walls of open windows in Buck's third-floor apartment. Below her, the whole marina was visible, and both shorelines stretched into the distance. She saw the access road approaching from one side and the parking lot wrapped around the other. From here, Buck perched like an eagle lording over his territory.

After a pause, Ty's voice, still loud but without the background hum of the engine, said, "What're you saying? Stop who?"

"Charlotte. She's going to do something; I'm not sure what, but it's bad."

"What's that got to do with Garth kidnapping you?"

"Everything!" Del slapped her free hand against her thigh. "I saw him point a gun at Marco's chest. Marco should be dead, but he's not, because Garth never meant to hurt him. Marco was supposed to raise the alarm, sending *you* and maybe the entire sheriff's department off the island to find me."

"That makes no sense."

"Yes, it does. Ty, I'm the diversion, not the main event."

"How's any of that lead to Charlotte?"

His voice sounded completely unconvinced, but at least he wasn't shouting anymore.

"Think about it. Who knew we would be on the Wilsons' dirt roads looking for quarries?"

"So, Charlotte did give Marco the map."

"And she told him to come through the park, not by her driveway, because she didn't want to alert her staff to us being there." Del stopped pacing as her attention was drawn to a familiar silhouette in the distance in an open boat heading toward the marina. Pointing out at the lake, she exchanged a glance with Janie, who went to the windows.

"That still doesn't make them conspirators. I think he's been stalking you," Ty said.

"There's more. Remember the Wilson family hunting photo that Marco had, the one with a fourth person cut off? There's an enlargement in Garth's cabin. He's the fourth person."

"Okay, we already heard he was once a guide. So, they know each other."

"More than just 'know.' The enlargement was a gift from Charlotte. She wrote a sweet note on it thanking him, signed 'with love' and a date. A date in November only a few weeks before Chief George disappeared. Think about it: Charlotte was standing strong in the picture. Strong enough to climb Monks Head."

"You're saying Charlotte and Garth are murderers? I still don't get the connection to you."

"I also heard him talking to her."

"Why didn't you say that before?" He was becoming annoyed.

Del began pacing again. "Because it's kind of fuzzy, just coming back to me. I was drugged and lying in his truck. I couldn't move at first, but I could still hear. I'm guessing he was on the phone."

"Tell me what you remember."

"He said, 'It's done. I've got her and the other one will come running. It should give you enough time.' Then he said something like, 'I don't like it, but I never could talk you out of something you already decided.'"

"Did he ever call her by name? How do you know he was talking to Charlotte?"

Del watched as Janie started lowering the wooden-slated blinds over the windows facing the lake.

"It had to be Charlotte," Del insisted. "She planned it and set us up. He was *waiting* for me and Marco."

Del lifted the edge of one of the lowered blinds to spy on the marina activity. At the floating dock, Garth was pushing his boat between a hard-sided rowboat and an inflatable. He grabbed a line and hopped onto the dock to tie it off. Janie was watching from behind the blinds of another window. She gave Del a shrug.

"Even so, she's in a wheelchair now. What would she do?" Ty asked.

"She could harm herself. Garth also said, 'I guess this is the only way. Take the eighteen-inch double-barrel. It's easier for you to hold steady.'"

There was a long silence on the phone line. Finally, he said, "That makes no sense. Suicide takes just minutes. She doesn't need a diversion for that."

"Let me think. Wait. It was specifically to get rid of *you*. The Wilsons know you're connected with me. And they know you're a private investigator and the guy installing security cameras at—"

"Settlement Creek Farm." Ty finished Del's sentence in a monotone.

"Please go back and stop her," Del pleaded.

Del again peered through the blinds. She followed Garth's movements as he walked up one dock and then down the one where Jules and Janie had tied up their boat. He stopped abruptly by their Whaler and reached behind the center console. He held up the empty garbage bag. Janie said, "Shit," and Del jumped back as if the blinds had burst into flames.

"You're sure you're safe?" Ty asked.

"Yes. I'm in Buck's apartment. Garth doesn't know where I am, and the police should be here any minute."

Was my voice convincing enough? She heard Ty's engine start up.

"I'll contact Mike's office as soon as I can get through," he said. "There's no service coming through the mountains, but I should pick it up by the time I get back to the Ellis Junction area."

"I don't know how long I'll be at this number. I'll leave you messages if I'm not with Grandpa after that."

"I'll do my best. I saw Charlotte on her deck over an hour ago. Lots can happen in that time, and it may already be too late. Call the local cops back and tell them to contact the Prescott County sheriff with what you know about Charlotte. They can get there faster."

"You're right. I should have thought of that." Del picked up the card Buck had given her.

"Stay safe."

"You too."

The call ended. Del turned her attention to where Janie was still watching the marina through the blinds. "What's going on?"

"He went back to his boat to get the rifle," Janie said. "He's coming straight for the store. I better warn the guys." With that, she galloped down the stairs.

Then Garth was still after her. Del did a fast survey in case she needed to hide somewhere. It was a modest apartment. There was one bath and one closet, both too obvious, neither with a door that locked. Hiding in either would make her feel more trapped than safe.

Wild barking and shrill voices exploded from the first floor. Del noted a small deck off the kitchen with external stairs that led down to the parking area. Leaning against the wall next to the sliding glass door to the deck, Del listened to the commotion in the store. She didn't understand the words, but she identified Janie's yell and Buck's bass turned up to a feverish pitch.

Someone is going to get hurt.

Near the door to the interior stairs were hooks with key rings. Del grabbed the key fob attached to a Ram truck insignia and flew out onto the deck. It was easy to spot the truck, the biggest, newest BAT, big ass truck, in the lot—bright red, with white-and-blue detailing. Large lettering on the door said: Buck's Village. With the key fob, she unlocked the doors and started the engine as she raced down the stairs with one thought in her head: *Distract him.*

Del jumped into the truck and drove around the building to where she could see the front porch. She leaned on the horn. Garth, carrying his rifle in both hands, was the first out of the store's front door, followed closely by Buck and then Janie, struggling to hang onto Dickens's collar. Garth jumped out to run toward her but was pulled up short when Buck put both arms around his chest. Del steered the pickup toward the access road and floored it.

She had understood Buck to say there was only one road that led to Lake Awasosee. Her plan was to meet the police along the way.

THIRTY-SIX

The asphalt pavement leading from Buck's Village ended after a short distance, becoming a roadway of "improved" gravel, the standard for private roads in the north woods of Maine, where you were just as likely to pass a logging truck as a moose. The road builders had more or less leveled out a rough path by dumping truckloads of crushed rock, sand, and gravel that left the roadbed in many places several feet higher than the surrounding forest floor. Without regular maintenance, the surface became a washboard of ripples and a minefield of potholes.

After throwing off the sweatshirt and struggling to clip the seat belt, Del drove as fast as she dared, often slowing down for the bumps and washouts. Even though Buck's pickup and suspension were new, the truck lurched and rocked. She maintained a tight-fisted hold with both hands on the wheel and kept her eyes on the utility poles. They would lead to civilization. Unfortunately, about two miles out, as the road curved sharply to the right, the power lines and the utility poles went straight into a swath of clear-cut.

She stopped at the first Y intersection, a choice between two gravel roads with nothing but forest on all sides. Buck hadn't mentioned there were multiple roads leading to the village. Del craned her neck out the driver's window hoping to catch a glimpse of the power lines but couldn't see into the dense forest. Finally, she decided on the left fork, as the power lines should be in that direction.

She drove several more miles. At one point, the road crossed under the power lines. After that, it curved sharply and just ended in a clear-cut area overgrown with waist-high vegetation. *Dead end!* She cursed her luck. Del turned the truck around and headed back to the Y intersection, hoping she wouldn't meet Garth on the way.

The right fork turned out to be slightly wider than the one that came to a dead end. She should have paid more attention to the condition of the road when making her choice. Whenever she could take one hand off the steering wheel, Del poked at the truck's electronic navigation hoping for an area map. After a delay, the miniature image of a truck, appeared on the display exactly in the middle of nowhere, not one line indicating a known road, only the blue lobe of a lake getting farther away. Del checked her rearview mirror but didn't see anything but the cloud of dust the pickup was raising.

Her plan for meeting the police partway might be in trouble.

Another intersection appeared, this one more in the shape of a *T*, a hand-painted wooden sign on the right pointing to WAPATON.

A town, or a camp name?

Del stopped the pickup and leaned out the window to listen. She was hoping to hear an engine sound or the crunch of tires, but heard nothing but the drumming tattoo of a woodpecker. She checked the time. Twenty-five minutes since she'd left Buck's Village. She decided to go right, to Wapaton, wherever that was.

The road curved, dipped, and rose again in rapid succession, narrowing at every turn. Del was keeping one eye on the odometer. Twelve miles had ticked off since she'd left Buck's Village. The navigation display now showed her traveling somewhere between two lobes of blue. There must be multiple lakes in this area. She realized she hadn't seen anything but forest interrupted by a few crossing trails, about the size used by snowmobiles. There had been no cabins, utility poles, or even a handwritten sign since the last intersection. Here and there, the underbelly of the truck scraped on low woody growth as the roadbed deteriorated.

Del was pretty sure she was lost.
Go on to Wapaton, or turn back?

THIRTY-SEVEN

Ty pushed the Lexus hard through the mountains, making good time by passing on every straightaway or riding someone's bumper until he got to one. The final miles through Ellis Junction and south to Pyke Island were painfully slow due to the number of locals and tourists on the roads. As soon as he got service, he called Mike's personal number and left a message. He called the sheriff's office on Pyke Island and also left a message. Finally, he called 9-1-1, only to hear from the operator that his suspicion was not an emergency, as he wasn't sure if anyone was in imminent danger. She transferred his call to the Prescott County sheriff's main number, where an operator calmly took the information and said he would pass it on to the officer in charge—who was out of the office.

Where the fuck is everyone?

After he crossed the bridge to Pyke Island, he was able to speed up again. It was dinnertime for most people, and the roads seemed to clear off. He skidded into the Wilsons' driveway, stopped just short of the closed gate, and started jamming the button on the call box. There was no answer. Ty jumped out. He grabbed the bars of the gate and shook with all his might, but the gate didn't budge. He went to the back seat of his car, opened the storage compartment, and reached for his rifle with the intention of blowing away the locking mechanism. Just then, he heard the roar of an ATV. It was Josh Wilson approaching the gate from inside and going much faster than Bruce would have liked. The off-road vehicle's wheels skipped sideways as he braked to a stop.

"Where's your mother?" Ty shouted before Josh even flipped up his face shield.

Josh stared at him for several seconds.

"Where is she?" Ty couldn't take the silence, not even a second.

"We can't find her. Her personal four-wheeler is gone, but she's not on any of the trails."

"Are any of your weapons missing?"

"A shotgun she uses for birding."

"Get in." Ty slammed down the back seat over his weapons.

Josh punched in a code on his side that opened the gate. He hesitated. "What do you know?"

"There's reason to believe Charlotte plans to harm someone at Settlement Creek. Get in." Ty jumped into the driver's seat and started the engine.

Josh dropped his helmet on the pavement and climbed into the passenger seat.

As Ty sped toward Settlement Creek, he asked, "Tell me, is the wheelchair thing a cover? How is it that your mother drives a four-wheeler and still hunts?"

Josh was stone-faced, eventually saying, "She has a few good days after her injections of a muscle protein. She got her shot day before yesterday."

"What's a good day?"

"She can ride but can't walk more than fifty feet without resting. She fatigues fast."

"You talked to Bruce?"

Josh nodded. "I heard about the reporter and your friend Del. Mother ordered Bruce to accompany the ambulance. I got here not long after, and she was gone. Bruce and I have been searching the trails for the last hour."

"She planned this, didn't she? Even you being away?"

"Looks like it." Josh's expression was still immobile, but Ty felt for the first time that they were both on the same side.

"Did she go by the public road?"

"Probably not. There's an old carriage trail from Aunt Ella's farm that connects with our roads."

"Allowing her to bypass their security gate," Ty noted.

When they arrived at Settlement Creek, the security gate was open. There was a county car partway across the entrance instead. A sheriff's officer got out and waved them to a stop.

"We have a situation here, and no one's allowed inside," the cop said.

Josh identified himself and Ty explained his ability to access the security cameras. After a few short words on her radio, she let them pass with instructions to proceed as far as the sheriff's vehicle.

Charlotte's ATV was parked on the lawn right in front of the double doors of the Community Center. Four county cars made a barrier between the Center and the parking lot, with officers guarding a perimeter around the lot. Outside the perimeter, people were watching from their porches or windows. The only Settlement Creek members inside the perimeter were Uncle and another elder. They were pointing to a phone, showing Mike, who was holding a bullhorn, the display from the security cameras. Ty grabbed his tablet. He signed into the app and waited for a connection.

"Is my mother inside?" Josh demanded. "Let me talk to her."

Uncle pushed his way past the sheriff to confront Josh. "You've already been told you're not welcome."

Ty jumped between them and Uncle took a step back. "Where do you get off? You owe *me* an explanation! Not only did you shoot down my drone, you then walked away from my injured friend. Who the hell are you?"

There was fire in Uncle's eyes. But he held his tongue.

Ty wasn't done. "What's your game here? Why did you abandon him? Why're you trespassing on Wilson land? To spy on Del, or me?"

Uncle flashed a look at Josh as he moved to box him in on one side. "Those are good questions," Josh said. "You ready to answer?"

It was Mike's turn to take control. "Enough." He put his hand on Uncle's arm. "Go back to your house, Uncle. That's an order." Uncle walked back several feet and stared in silence.

Mike motioned Ty and Josh several feet in the opposite direction. "We're still assessing the situation," he told them. "Pale Moon opened the door a while ago to tell us that Charlotte was holding her and Ryan hostage. She said Charlotte intends to negotiate when she's ready. Then she went back inside. We tried to connect with her phone, but no luck."

Showing his tablet to the sheriff, Ty said, "This is a better view, and I opened the audio channel."

Although curved by a fish-eye lens that took in the entire gym, they could assess the tense scene at the far end. Charlotte, in camo-colored riding gear, was seated on a chair in front of the stage. She was slightly hunched over, holding a shotgun tight to her ribs, one hand under the stock and two fingers of the other on the triggers. The barrel, resting on her thighs, was pointed directly at Ryan, who was sitting on the floor in front of her. At that distance, the buckshot would just about cut him in half. They saw Pale Moon working nervously to take down the posters and photos from the tables that displayed Chief George's memorabilia. She was making a pile in the middle of the room. The microphone wasn't picking up the voices clearly, but at one point they heard Charlotte order Pale Moon to hurry up.

"Do we know what she wants to do?" Josh asked. His attention shifted back and forth from the tablet to the Community Center.

Ty handed the device to the sheriff. "Maybe she plans on blasting that pile."

Josh was insistent. "Sheriff, let me go in. She won't shoot."

"I can't do that," Mike said. "She might not shoot you, but there's the others. I'd like you to talk to her. I've got a script for talking down hostage takers. We'll start there while we're waiting for the state police hostage expert."

"By the way, that microphone is also a speaker," Ty added. "It sounds like someone turned it way down. If I get into the security room from the back window, I can zoom and focus the camera in for a better view and up the volume."

"Without being seen or heard?" Mike asked.

"Yes." Ty pointed to one side of the stage. "The door to the equipment is closed."

Mike paused while watching the action on the tablet. "I don't want her to know we're watching and listening. Not yet, anyway." He narrowed his eyes at Ty and waved over another officer. "Duerr, go with Holden and make sure it can be done without creating any noise. Meantime, Wilson and I will try to get her attention."

With one eye on Ty's tablet, Mike turned to an open notebook on the hood of a car. He pointed the bullhorn toward the building. "Charlotte Wilson, this is Sheriff Mike Hodgkins." His amplified voice echoed and reverberated against the steel siding. "Your son is here with me. He wants to talk to you. Are you listening? We need to talk. Come to the door and tell me everyone inside is all right."

Ty led Officer Duerr around the back of the building. They moved silently through the grass and shrubs until they came to the small window to the control room. It was higher off the ground than Ty expected. The window was open a few inches. With a boost from Duerr, Ty was able to remove the screen and raise the sash the rest of the way. He climbed in carefully. With a few clicks at the main computer, he zoomed the camera closer to where Charlotte was sitting, while still being able to watch Pale Moon's movements. He slowly increased the volume on the microphone, making sure there was no feedback or echo from the bullhorn.

From the security closet, Ty watched the action for several minutes. The questions and assurances from the bullhorn were loud enough.

Charlotte completely ignored it. It wasn't long before Pale Moon finished piling George's memorabilia on the floor. Ryan was frozen, immobile except for moving his head just enough to keep an eye on his mother.

There was a dull smack followed by a grunt outside the window. Ty was surprised to see Josh climbing in.

"Sheriff let you come?" Ty whispered. "What happened to Duerr?"

Josh flexed and rubbed the knuckles on his right hand. "His way wasn't working. I slipped away when the guy with the braids started making a stink again. Duerr will be all right in a while." Josh walked directly to the door and opened it a crack. "Mother! I'm coming in! Don't shoot. We need to talk." As he cautiously opened the door wider, it was abruptly pulled out of his hands.

THIRTY-EIGHT

Del braked to a stop when she saw an old log bridge over a small river. The navigation display showed a thin line of blue connecting two lakes. But what she saw downstream of the bridge wasn't an actual lake, but a broad wetland where the river split into several channels separated by islands of tall grasses and shrubs and dotted with collection pools. A small hand-painted sign nailed to a tree trunk next to the road read WAPATON, and nearby a family of crows complained loudly and flew off when she opened the truck door.

Del climbed out to look closely at the bridge, which spanned a twenty-foot-wide stream of swift-flowing water. The bridge was just wide enough for one vehicle, built from long sections of split logs supported at the ends and in the middle by pilings anchored in the stream. There was no guardrail. The bridging itself was only two courses of logs, each slightly wider than truck tires. She took a few steps to where she could see water running beneath the crossing members. She jumped up and down to see if it would give. It seemed solid. She would have to steer perfectly straight to stay on the logs. The gap between them was large enough for a person to fall through.

Go on to Wapaton, or turn back?

Del looked back along the gravel road she had just crossed. A whisp of dust lingered in the air. If Garth was following her dust trail, he might lose it here once she crossed the bridge. There were still a few hours of daylight. If she didn't find civilization in two more miles, she would turn back. By now the police must be looking for her.

"Hey, we're going to Wapaton," she announced to Buck's pickup as she climbed back inside.

She shifted to a low gear. The pickup inched along. Staying on the logs wasn't a problem until about halfway across, when something unexpectedly shifted. Del hit the brake and opened the driver's door to see where the wheels were. The next jolt made her realize that the problem was the bridge, not her driving. The center was collapsing. Del slammed the door and stepped on the gas pedal, hoping to fly across. She gained less than a car length before a series of loud cracks sharply dropped the driver's side of the truck, suspending it over the stream at about a thirty-degree angle. Del crawled uphill to the passenger door. Before she could reach the door handle, several more cracks echoed from under the bridge. In what felt like slow motion punctuated with a long squeal, the pickup plunged into the water and landed on its side. Del was thrown against the driver's door, her head hitting the glass and the armrest cracking into her spine. Instantly, she found herself sitting in water. Around the truck, the river was at least five feet deep, but not quite up to the passenger door, which, like a trapdoor, was now over her head. Water poured in from every direction. Within seconds it was a foot deep.

Bracing her feet against the center console and pushing with all her might, Del tried to open the passenger door. It didn't budge.

Of course! The doors were locked.

There should still be power from the battery. Del had to put her head underwater to find the controls on the driver's armrest. She pressed the open window button. The passenger's window groaned but didn't open more than an inch. She tried it again and it just groaned. The accident must have jammed the mechanism.

Wait!

But the water wasn't waiting. She went back underwater and hit the unlock door button. Again, she braced herself and tried to lift the passenger door. Still wouldn't budge. Hunched on the edge of the center console with her head touching the driver's door, Del sat still and took a long breath.

Time to think.

The water was up to her chest.

Shit! The doors won't unlock with the transmission in drive.

Del ducked back underwater. She swung the shift lever into park and unlocked the doors. This time, still bracing her feet against the center console, she felt the door open. She was able to force the heavy door upwards, but because of the angle, it wouldn't stay open on its own. She couldn't get her torso out while carrying its weight and there was nowhere else to put her feet. The door slammed shut. She looked around the cab for something she could use to prop it open. Del groped through the center console filled with tie-downs and tools and found, at last, one really large screwdriver. Once again, she forced the passenger door up, enough to jam the screwdriver in place, when the door flew wide open by itself.

Well, not exactly by itself; it was being held open by Rubin Garth.

THIRTY-NINE

A visibly trembling Pale Moon was holding open the door to the equipment room. Ty thought she might faint, but she managed to say, "She says get in here."

"There's two of them?" Charlotte called out. "This is all going to shit." She motioned to Ty and Josh with the gun barrel. "Sit down against the wall where I can see you. You," she said to Pale Moon. "Tell the sheriff now I've got four hostages and I need a little more time to figure this out before we start talking. Come back right away or I shoot your boy."

Josh and Ty squatted against the wall. They were about twenty feet behind Ryan and to one side. Ty thought that staying close to Josh was probably best at this point, even though Charlotte barely glanced at him. She was wigless for once. Her patchy dark hair, liberally streaked with white, was in long thin braids circling her head like a crown.

"Josh, you're a damn fool," she said.

"This needs to stop." Josh's voice was calm and firm.

"It stops when I'm done talking or I pull the trigger," Charlotte answered without taking her eyes off Ryan.

Between his shoulder blades, Ryan's shirt had a long, dark, wet *V*.

Pale Moon left by the double doors and was back in less than a minute. She started, "The sheriff said—"

"Shut up! I don't care what the sheriff says." Charlotte motioned to a spot on the floor next to Ryan. "Sit there." Charlotte straightened her shoulders but without changing her grip on the shotgun. "Now that we're all comfortable, we can finish the conversation we started. Then we'll have a bonfire. My lawyer told me you filed for probate. I've seen the filing."

"We are George's rightful heirs." Pale Moon precisely measured each word.

"*We?* Tell him the truth!" Charlotte barked.

Ryan wasn't following and just gaped at his mother.

"Yes." Pale Moon was looking at Charlotte, not her son. "George is Ryan's father."

Ryan dropped his head and closed his eyes.

"He was sweet and sexy, wasn't he, when he seduced you?" Charlotte leaned forward to examine Pale Moon's expression.

Pale Moon was silent, her gaze fixed on her son.

"Answer me!" Charlotte screamed.

"Yes."

"He said not to worry, he was sterile. There was no risk."

"Yes."

Charlotte inched forward in her chair. "And when you told him you were pregnant, he called you a slut and accused you of sleeping around."

"Y-yes." Pale Moon's voice cracked.

"And when the boy was born, George treated him like a sack of flour."

Pale Moon took a deep breath. She put her hand on Ryan's arm. He lifted his head and regarded his mother's face with horror.

"He did, didn't he?" Charlotte demanded.

Ryan looked at Charlotte and rasped, "He always hated me."

Josh stood slowly. "Mother," he said, "you've done enough."

Ty thought about scooting away, as his role was being a fly on the wall, but Charlotte was still in control. Barely in control. He could see that her bony, blue-veined fingers were shiny from sweat. And there was a hint of twitching in her left hand, the one on the trigger.

"How do you know?" Pale Moon breathed. "How did you …?"

Charlotte laughed a short, sharp, deep-throated bellow. "Josh, say hello to your half-brother!"

No one laughed with her. No one moved except Ryan, who slowly swung his head around to stare at Josh.

"I'm coming to take the gun," Josh said with a slow step forward. "You're not going to kill anyone today."

"Stop!" Charlotte snapped. "If you value your brother's life. Of course, you shouldn't care, really, because once I kill him, you'll be the only heir and we can make the Wilson land whole."

Josh froze. "Is that why you're doing this? For the land?"

"I'm doing this for the *truth*." Charlotte spit the words at Pale Moon. "I thought it would end when I smashed the back of his sorry skull. You made him a chief and he was nothing but a sexual predator. Ryan, stand up!"

Shaking off his mother's hand, Ryan pushed himself off the floor, gradually standing but in slow motion, as if he wasn't sure what Charlotte wanted.

"No!" Pale Moon reached out for him again, but he moved an arm's length away from her. She attempted to stand herself.

"Sit! I'm not going to shoot the boy. *You're* the guilty one. You, Pale Moon, are the worst kind of enabler. You covered for him at every turn. Because of your deceit this community still honors him. I almost threw up when I read the disgusting newspaper article where you called him our most respected Native American. And a bronze plaque? So future generations will honor him?" Charlotte cleared her throat and spit on the floor.

Pale Moon shook her head. "You don't understand. I had to make it work. There was no place else for us to go."

"Ryan, come here!" Charlotte leaned to one side. "Reach into the side pocket and take out the lighter."

Ryan stood upright and did exactly as she asked. Standing next to

Charlotte, he could have easily knocked the gun away, but instead he flicked the lighter, mesmerized by the flame. Then he walked directly toward the pile on the floor and waited for Charlotte's final word.

"Where's that reporter?" Charlotte called out. "I want that reporter here so he can write a better story—one that tells the truth about Pale Moon. Josh, go get him."

Josh said, "Forget that. The reporter is in the hospital. I'm not going anywhere."

Pale Moon seemed to be unable to choke back a flood of tears. She was frightened and trembling but at the same time defiant. "Yes, I covered for him. But I also watched over him. *I* kept him away from underage girls. He knew I would expose him if I chose to. We had an agreement. He got Ella's wealth and I got a farming co-op."

Charlotte seemed disgusted with all the tears. "And all along, you knew that someday Ryan would take over."

"At least I didn't hide in a fine, safe home behind a rich father."

"I was protecting my son. And waiting for the right time."

"At least I gave mine the education he deserved to honor his Native blood."

For a brief second, the image of two mother bears flashed in Ty's imagination. He had no doubt both of them would fight to save their cubs, the only difference being what they were using for claws.

"Stop it!" Ryan yelled at this mother. "It's all a lie!"

"Ryan?" his mother whimpered. "Why? Even if you didn't know who your father is till now, you were once proud when I told you he was a full-blooded Cherokee."

"Full-blooded joke!" Ryan mocked. "George was a full-blooded liar. Last year I took a DNA test, *Mother*. You know how they work. And you know what I am? One. Half. Italian. And it's not from your English gene—"

Charlotte forced out a laugh that sounded like metal grinding against metal.

Pale Moon struggled to her hands and knees. "No. That can't be right," she said.

"There's no mistake. I've been holding my tongue ever since because I thought my father had abandoned us, and it didn't matter who he was. The whole 'aren't we nice little Indians' was your masquerade."

Pale Moon labored to her knees. "You don't know his story. George was an orphan in Oklahoma, raised in a home where many of the children were Cherokee. To him, it was an identity, and he believed it."

"Was that the sob story he told you—the story you wanted to hear? How could you be such a fool?" Charlotte hissed. "He told me he was a cowboy raised on a ranch in Montana. He was my riding instructor. The difference is that I was fourteen years old when he had me in the back of the hayloft. And that's why he wanted *you*—because you looked fourteen when you were what, twenty-four?"

Pale Moon wiped her cheeks with her hands. "Then we were both fools, weren't we?"

"Too late to talk about foolishness. Ryan—"

"What did you think when he showed up working for Ella?" Kneeling, Pale Moon was almost as tall as the seated, hunched Charlotte. They were eye level with each other with nothing between them but a few feet of air and a double-barreled shotgun. "Did you imagine that he had come back for you? That he still wanted you?" For the first time, her voice didn't waver.

Charlotte's face darkened. "I'm the one asking the questions." The slightest tremor showed itself as a twinge in her neck. She jerked her shoulders.

Pale Moon flinched and shut her eyes tight but opened them as soon as she realized Charlotte hadn't pulled the trigger. "You must have been livid when it was apparent that he had seduced your Aunt Ella."

"I will tell you this to set the record straight," Charlotte said with a note of calm. "I tried to warn her, but it was already too late. That old fool, she found her heir in the only person who ever shared her passion for antique carriages. At least it's what she believed. Ella loved George. He made himself fit to her needs—the way he did with us all. At first. Before he discarded us like trash."

Meanwhile, Josh had stealthily moved closer to the women even as Ty wormed himself farther off to the side.

Charlotte nodded to Ryan. "Go on. You know what needs to be done."

Pale Moon shut her eyes again and broke out in the sobs that must have been hammering her insides.

Pulling himself a little taller, Ryan turned and lit the pile of photos and cardboard. The fire took quickly. They watched the flames leap high. Josh flicked a glance at Ty. In one movement, he shoved Pale Moon aside and lunged for Charlotte. Ty dove forward and pulled Pale Moon sideways, pushing her flat at the same time he flattened himself on the floor and covered his head with his arms.

The explosive sound of both barrels going off was deafening. Sharp bits splattered against their bodies.

There was a second of silence before the smoke detectors started screeching.

FORTY

Garth was straddling the pickup's frame and holding out a hand to her. Del hesitated, but the cold water, now up to her armpits, changed her mind. She reached out to him. Garth yanked her out and guided her along the outside of the truck bed which was submerged ankle-deep. From the rear wheel, Garth leapt a short distance to a section of bridge that hadn't collapsed. Again, he held out his hand and she accepted. From there it was a long leap to another solid section and finally the road surface.

Garth retreated to an ATV parked on the gravel. Del wiped her hands over her clothes to squeegee off the cold water. She had lost one of the flip-flops Janie had given her. She felt resigned to whatever would happen next.

"Well?" she asked. "Do I get tied up again? You don't need to drug me this time."

Without a word, Garth opened a rear compartment on his vehicle and pulled out her hiking boots with socks stuffed in them. He walked them over to her and set them down at her feet. He stepped back and stood with his arms at his side.

Frustrated and angry, Del plopped down on the riverbank. Most of the bandages Janie had applied to the cuts on her feet had come loose or were missing. Del pulled off any that were partially stuck before putting on her socks and boots. She pitched the one flip-flop. It bounced once and disappeared.

"How'd you find me?" she asked, struggling to pull socks over her wet feet.

"Saw the truck go by from the side trail where I was loading up," Garth answered in his usual growl. "You took the wrong turn. No one comes here except to fish."

"I wanted to find Wapaton." Del was in no mood to be reminded about how stupid she had been to think she could find her way on unmarked gravel roads in the wilderness.

Garth cocked his head. "Then you found it."

"What?"

He nodded to the river. "This is the Wapaton. It drains Lake Awasosee."

Del stood, brushing off the pebbles stuck to the back of her soaked pants. She looked behind her, to the collapsed bridge and Buck's pickup lying on its side and creating a partial dam. Water was surging around and over the upstream side. "Shit," she mumbled.

"I never did want anyone to get hurt."

"You expect me to believe that? What was that scene at Buck's? Why were you riding around the lake with a gun?"

"I was supposed to hold you until six. Just so you couldn't tell anyone until she was done." He gave her a small thin smile. "We're past that now. I would've come back to set you free."

"And then what?"

"Go live in the woods like I used to," Garth said as he headed back to the ATV.

"The police know about Charlotte going to Settlement Creek," she called out to him.

Garth stopped walking. He stared at the scrubby roadbed. "They'll be searching for you, probably pull in volunteers."

Del realized he intended to leave her there. "You must really love her."

"From the first day I met her. We were on a hunting trip with the old man and the boy. He was about ten years old then." Garth contorted his face in pain. "I knew right away. Charlotte is one of the last of her kind. You can hardly see the Penobscot blood in her, but you feel it when you see her at home."

"Her home? On Heart Pond?"

Garth inhaled deeply through his nose. He swept his arm in a wide arc from the black-growth forest side of the road to the rushing river and wetland beyond. "Here, this is her home. This river, these lakes and streams—the drainage basin forms one branch of the Penobscot River." He dropped his arm. "By ancestral rights, it should all be."

"Is Charlotte the reason you became a park ranger on Pyke Island?"

"She's pretty much the reason I did anything."

"Why didn't you marry her?" Del said as she moved a few steps closer.

"The old man would never allow it. I thought maybe after he died, but then once the sickness came, she just wouldn't. Just wouldn't hear of it." He climbed onto the ATV.

"Rubin, did you kill George Tozur?"

He sat squinting at the sun hanging over the river. "Dark in an hour. Down in the fifties tonight. You can stay here and wait. Maybe they'll find you before dark. If it was me, I'd follow the river upstream. You'll see the lake in forty minutes. There's always boaters. If not, take the right shore aways to an empty cabin. You can build a fire and stay warm until morning. They'll find you then."

"Did you take the earthquake reports? Drive Lucy off the road?"

Garth shot her a quick glance but wouldn't meet her eyes. "Why would I do that?"

"Fear. Maybe someone reading it will figure out what you found?"

"I got nothing against Lucy."

Del waited for more, but he just sat there in silence.

She took a few more steps toward him. "Who else knew about the cave?"

Garth pulled on his helmet and started the engine. "You tell them, tell them I killed George Tozur. I brought him to see the art in the cave. I thought him being a Native himself … But … but that's it, just tell them."

"What'd you use for a weapon?" Del wanted the details. "Tell me how you did it."

"Don't matter."

"It does matter if the police are going to believe you really did it."

"The man needed killing." Garth made a multipoint turn on the narrow road.

"You're just going to drive away? Why did you follow me here?"

He shouted over the engine and crunching of tires on gravel. "I wasn't sure what to do next. Now I know."

Del had to back off to avoid getting sprayed by flying pebbles. She watched his dust cloud settle on the road and decided to follow the Wapaton River upstream to the lake as Garth had recommended.

It was already dusky in the forest. What was left of the sun flickered through the wind-dancing branches. She felt a chill in her wet clothes even after she took off her shirt and pants and wrung out what water she could. She thought about Janie's sweatshirt submerged somewhere in the river. She thought about oatmeal cookies.

FORTY-ONE

Complete bedlam broke out in the Community Center's gym after the shotgun discharged. Pale Moon screamed and screamed, louder than the fire alarm. The sheriff and officers stormed in through every entrance. Ty realized the bits that were still falling came from the buckshot-shattered plastic material lining the ceiling. Josh was holding the gun away from Charlotte with one arm and cradling her sobbing, collapsed form with the other. Deputy Jessica Ouellette doused the flames with a chemical fire extinguisher just as the sprinkler system came on, sheeting water down on everyone. It took a few minutes before someone found the shutoff.

Mike's officers escorted everyone out of the gym. Charlotte and Josh were taken to the parking area, and one of the cops started reading them their Miranda rights. Ryan and Pale Moon were taken to her office. Mike let Uncle in after he insisted he was their spiritual counselor.

Outside the building, Mike took Ty aside. "I need a copy of the video to document everything that happened. Is it secure?"

"There's two copies of everything. I'm the only one who knows how to purge the backup files."

"I'll have to get a court order," Mike said, walking back inside with Ty behind him. "Something tells me Pale Moon is not going to volunteer a copy and would just as soon it was *accidentally* erased."

"No chance of it disappearing, not even if they burn down the building," Ty said. "One copy is on the backup file server in the schoolhouse. Why're you arresting Josh?"

"Assaulting an officer. Unauthorized entry to a closed emergency area. Failure to obey a lawful police order. I could go on."

"He prevented a murder."

"That's up to the DA and the judge now. But we can talk about that later. You must be eager to get to Lake Awasosee."

"I should check in with Del first."

Mike pulled his phone out of a pocket. "You didn't get the message from Gabe? Came in a while ago."

Ty stopped short, reaching for his phone. He had silenced it before he climbed into the security equipment room.

The text was: *DEL IS MISSING. GARTH TOOK OFF. WARDEN SERVICE ORGANIZING SEARCH. COME ASAP.* He'd never seen Gabe use all caps in a text before.

FORTY-TWO

From Buck's Village, Ty caught a ride with a no-nonsense woman named Janie who was delivering sandwiches to the Wapaton Bridge. It was close to sunset, and the sky above was very dark blue, the remaining daylight just a yellow glow near the horizon. Janie explained that volunteers had already covered all the dirt roads in a ten-mile radius from the village. When they found Buck's pickup on its side under the collapsed bridge, the search headquarters moved there. They didn't find Del's body in the truck, but no one could explain why she hadn't stayed with it. Janie thought Garth wanted to go after Del, but everyone had seen him leave in his boat, heading down the lake. His truck was still parked in the village. A couple of local sheriff's officers checked out his cabin, but he wasn't there. Garth had disappeared. The consensus was that he must have had another vehicle stowed somewhere and was making his way to Canada.

At the bridge the guy in charge was from the Maine Warden Service, the police agency responsible for the enforcement of fishery and wildlife laws and the coordination of search and rescue in wilderness areas. He asked Janie to come look at a handful of damp, dirty bandages they'd found on the riverbank next to the bridge. She confirmed they were probably the ones she had applied to Del's feet and knee. Searchers were already assigned to the channels and islands downstream of the bridge and the snowmobile trails leading off in several directions. A while ago, a searcher had come back with a magenta flip-flop he'd found in the water a half-mile down. It matched one they'd found in the truck. They were working on the idea that Del had been swept downstream. Janie insisted Del was a strong swimmer but admitted she was probably also very tired.

After he reported in, Ty got some disappointing news. The warden said they were going to call off the search at dark. Moonrise was not till after midnight, and he didn't want anyone to be tramping through the forest or wetlands after sunset. Ty explained he was planning on searching all night. The warden gave him a copy of a topographic map of the lake area with instructions (which Ty took to be a recommendation) to be back before ten to catch the last ride back to the village.

"I've got clothes, food, sleeping bag, flashlights," Ty said. "If I can't search effectively, I'll just camp until morning." He showed the warden his handheld GPS.

"The bulk and weight of that pack will be a hindrance in the forest," the warden said. "It's better to travel light."

"I'll take my chances."

"Stay away from the riverbanks. They're undercut in places." The warden took a final long, hard look before dismissing him. "I'd really hate to have to conduct *two* rescues tomorrow." He turned away as a pair of searchers moving awkwardly in hip waders reported in.

The warden hadn't seen the outline of the Glock hugging Ty's spine, tucked in his waistband. If he had, he would have asked to see a concealed carry license, which Ty was ready to show. But nothing said was better. Ty knew that some portion of the forest around them was a wildlife management area where firearms were off-limits.

He walked to the edge of the bridge, where he could see the silhouettes of another pair of searchers in the distance downstream. If the warden already had multiple volunteers in that direction, there was only one way for him to go. He turned to the right to follow the river upstream and entered the forest. The bandages they'd found meant Del had gotten out of the truck and onto dry land. This river drained the lake, and after talking to Janie, who saw Del examine an area map, he was pretty sure Del would know that and try to get back to a familiar place.

As soon as the canopy of trees closed in, Ty moved the Glock to his windbreaker pocket so it didn't interfere with his backpack. Even before it was complete darkness, he strapped on his headlamp and turned on a handheld flashlight. After a few minutes, he realized just how difficult the search was going to be, because even with the high-powered light, he couldn't see more than a few feet in any direction. Del could be unconscious, lying just outside the beam, and he would walk right past her. Ty found it easier to stay close to the riverbank where there was less undergrowth. He swept the beam of his big flashlight back and forth, examining all of the river and a narrow strip of forest. Once he got to the lake, he would pace off twenty feet and then turn south, heading parallel to the way he had come and thereby covering the next swath. He was prepared to do that all night.

Every fifty feet or so, he blew the whistle hanging around his neck and listened. Sweep a wide arc with the flashlight, blow the whistle, and listen—he repeated those steps over and over. The forested land rose steadily. In three places he climbed steep rocky outcrops where the river echoed with a cascade of white water. Ty struggled on, scrambling over downed trees, working around boulders. It seemed that with every ten steps his pack snagged on low branches.

It was an hour before he saw the lakeshore. A cold breeze drove little waves that lapped at his feet. There was no moon, but coming out from under the tree canopy Ty could see a river of brilliant stars above and their reflection on the water. He followed the edge of the lake fifteen steps north and checked his GPS position on the map. He stopped blowing the whistle. His shoulders were sore, and he took off his pack for a water break. He needed a breather, preparing himself for the long slog back through the woods.

A rustle and crack along the shore farther north made him shout

out, "Hey? Someone there?" and head toward the source. He jogged as quickly as he could, holding the flashlight high and pushing away the branches with his free hand. He caught a few brush slaps to the face before he broke out into a small clearing. Another rustle, close by, and then a black shape with the reflection of two small, yellowish eyes—a bear cub.

Another appeared. Ty froze but kept the light on them. A loud snort came from somewhere behind the cubs. Before he could move away, the mother bear charged.

Caught off guard, Ty jumped back. Catching his heel on something, he tumbled into the branches of a spruce tree, which knocked his headlamp to one side and ripped the flashlight from his hands. It bounced toward the bear, who stopped short as the light rolled near her enormous paws. As she lowered her head to inspect the light, he could clearly see her massive skull and narrow muzzle. She sniffed and snorted at the flashlight.

Ty watched her rise up on her hind legs, a huge dark shadow that blocked the starlight. He fumbled for the Glock but couldn't pull it out from the pocket of his twisted jacket. The bear moaned long and loud, then dropped to all fours, snorted again, and took off the way she had come, followed by her cubs. He could hear more crunching sounds as they retreated.

Ty was hauling himself out of the tree branches when he heard, "Is someone there?" The voice was weak and trembling, but he knew it was Del.

FORTY-THREE

Ty adjusted his headlamp and grabbed his flashlight. Swinging the light away from the lake to where he'd heard her voice, he found her huddled in the pitch-black on a porch outside a small, shingled cabin. Hugging her arms around her shins, Del was shaking hard and could barely talk through chattering teeth.

"T-T-Ty? How d-d-did ya find me?" She blinked and turned her eyes away from the headlamp's brightness.

He ran his hands over her face. Her lips were gray, her skin ice-cold. "Let's get inside," he breathed. "This is hypothermia. Get inside."

"D-d-door's p-p-padlocked," she sputtered.

Ty stepped back and was about to kick in the door when in the glow of his headlamp he saw letters scratched in the wood that said, "Pilgrim, don't break down the door. Key behind shutters. Use what you need to stay safe."

Inside the cabin, the temperature was just as cold as outside, but they were out of the night wind. There was a cast-iron woodstove in the far corner.

Leaving Del huddled in the cabin, Ty ran back along the shore to find his backpack. It was farther than he thought. If the bears hadn't drawn him to the clearing, he would have missed her and instead would have headed back into the woods. In fact, he might not have found Del for hours, not until his third or fourth pass. Ty took a moment to thank the bears, the stars, or whatever beautiful, blind luck had led him here.

On the way back to the cabin, he stumbled over a fallen branch covered in dried spruce needles; the branch would be enough to start a fire. He dragged it back to the cabin.

Inside, he laid out the sleeping bag and insisted Del take off her damp clothes and crawl in. Del told him where to find more firewood under a lean-to behind the cabin.

In no time, there was a roaring fire visible through the stove's glass doors. On the floor, staying as close to the front of the stove as she dared, Del sat hunched in the sleeping bag. She drew it completely over her head so that all Ty could see was her face. Her clothes were spread out on the floor on either side.

Ty found two steel camp cups, which he filled with water and set on the stovetop to boil. He pulled packets of dried food out of his backpack. They shared a dinner of broken energy bars, dried fruit, and powdered breakfast drinks mixed with hot water. At first, Ty didn't want her to take her hands out of the sleeping bag and insisted on feeding her. He was a fairly clumsy nursemaid. After there were more dribbles on the front of the sleeping bag than in her mouth, Del claimed she could handle exposing her hands.

Even though she was still shivering, Ty could see the color coming back to her lips. He plucked a couple of broken twigs from the hair matted around her face. One of her cheeks was scratched but not bleeding. Ty noticed areas of dried blood on the socks drying by the stove. He chuckled to himself, knowing Del would be embarrassed to see what a dirty, disheveled mess she was. Somehow, at the same time, she was beautiful.

"This time *you* saved *my* life," Del said, referring to a rescue she and Marco had made in the winter that had saved Ty from a sure death by explosion. "Was that you moaning?"

"That came from a really pissed mother bear." He described his encounter with the charging black bear. "There was a moment I was pretty sure I had bought it."

"Thank you, mama bear," she said, clinking his cup in a toast. "Is Grandpa looking for me too?"

"When I left Buck's, he was on his way to the airport to pick up your parents."

"Oh, shit!" Del choked on a swallow and coughed. "Don't get me wrong. I'll be glad to see them, but I hate it when I become an emergency."

"It's not your fault. Charlotte and Garth cooked up this mess."

They traded stories that covered the last few hours. Ty mused, "Now we have two confessions to the same murder."

"My working theory is that they were both involved."

"Any idea why Garth followed you? Why was he driving an ATV?"

"He didn't say. Probably had one stowed somewhere so he could get away." Del yawned. "Imagine loving someone from afar for over twenty-five years."

"No." And he meant it in more ways than one.

"Don't let me fall asleep yet. I'm still too cold. I'm afraid to go to sleep." She leaned against him and yawned again.

Ty hugged her to his side. In the sleeping bag, she looked a little like a giant stuffed animal. Underneath a layer of down, he could feel quivers run along her arms and shoulders.

"We'll sit here together and wait until you stop shivering. I'll heat more water."

"Tell me a story," she said after he brought her a steaming cup.

"Any special request?"

"The story of your family Christmas picture, the one where no one looks very happy." She was asking about the portrait she had seen in his apartment showing his family—his mother, father, and two brothers—in front of a slightly faded and crooked Christmas backdrop, an image where he was the only one smiling at the camera, and everyone else just wanted to leave.

"Sure, right, you want to meet the unhappy family," he said. "I knew you would get me to talk about it someday."

"Just tell me whatever feels good."

With determination, Ty closed his eyes and thought about how none of those memories ever felt good. When he opened them again, he was ready to start. "The picture of the unhappy family is courtesy of the Indiana Juvenile Justice System. It was taken at a detention facility we nicknamed the DD, short for the 'Dungeon for Delinquents.' I was fifteen."

"Sounds awful. You were a delinquent?"

"I helped my older brother Mitchell steal cars. Actually, the place wasn't as bad as we made it out to be. The staff tried hard, but it was filled with many very bad dudes. And ..."

"And?"

"And Mitchell turned into one of them."

"I'm sorry. What about your parents?"

"As far back as I can remember, Dad disappeared for long periods of time. I never knew why. Sometimes, when he did come home, his pockets were stuffed with cash and we all got presents. My parents loved their alcohol, drugs, and partying. Mitchell and I raised ourselves and even took care of the baby, our youngest brother Andrew—Drew. Everything fell apart when we both went to the DD. Just after the picture was taken, my mother overdosed and Drew was put in foster care because no one could locate good old Dad. They let the three of us attend the burial. I've never been able to track down *Dad*." He found himself saying the last part through clenched teeth. "What kind of man abandons his children?"

Ty couldn't meet Del's wide-eyed gaze.

"I can't imagine trying to deal with that," she whispered. "You overcame a lot. What happened to Mitchell?"

"He's dead."

Del took in a sharp breath. "I'm sorry. I don't know what to say."

"No need to say anything." He hugged her close.

"Why do you keep that picture?"

"It's the only one I've got."

"I really am sorry."

"I know I shocked you with the story of the unhappy family. I haven't had much practice telling it." He paused, staring into the fire. "I'll work on coming up with a happy ending."

"You're here," Del said. "I can't think of anything happier than that."

He kissed her on the cheek. She smelled like the piney woods.

"I'll listen as much as you want." The last word was caught in a long yawn. "I'm feeling warm now, not shivering at all. Do you think we could lie down here in front of the stove?"

While he opened the stove and added two more pieces of wood, she curled up in the sleeping bag, lying on her side with her back to the fire, her hands tucked under her chin. He lay down next to her and propped his head up so he could see her face and keep a watch on the fire.

He talked for a while longer about the social worker who convinced him to finish high school, the patient teachers who helped him cram four years of schooling into two, the sympathetic judge who agreed to expunge his record after six years of honorable military service. Her eyelids flickered and closed before he was done, but he kept on talking. He laid his face close to hers so he could feel every breath and wait for the next breath, making sure they were regular and strong.

He skipped the part about how Mitchell almost killed him, how the brother he had looked up to his whole life tried to cut off the left side of his face. Years ago, Ty had lost the words to that story.

"After my service, I went back to Indiana to make sure my criminal history was wiped off the books. I worked for a security company, worked on my PI license. I tried to find Drew," he continued in a low voice. "A year later, homeless and overdosed, he turned up in a hospital in Portland and they found me. Before that, if you'd asked me to point to Maine on a map, I wouldn't have found it. A sixteen-hour drive and I saw him for the first time in over seven years. He looked like a death camp survivor. We're the same height, look a lot alike, except he weighs about a hundred pounds. Two days later, barely able to walk on his own, he disappeared again."

Ty reached over to brush a lock of hair away from her face. She was fast asleep.

He turns up from time to time. When the Portland cops or the shelter see him, they call me. Sometimes he lets me buy a meal or bring him some clothes. It's the best I can do. Really all I can do.

Del stirred. She flexed her hands inside the sleeping bag and was quiet again. If she reached out to touch his scar now, he would let her. He would let her touch the deepest wounds in his soul.

FORTY-FOUR

Del woke hot and sweaty. She pulled the sleeping bag off her shoulders. The cabin floor around her was checkered in squares of pale blue moonlight coming through the windows. The embers left in the woodstove gave off a deep orange glow. On the bare floor next to her, Ty was asleep, curled up on his side with his head resting on one outstretched arm. Without disturbing him, she scrambled out of the sleeping bag and quickly pulled on her clothes, now dry and warm. She checked his cell phone. It was after one a.m. She put two more cups of water on the stove to heat up.

In his sleep, Ty moved his free arm and touched the floor where she had been lying. He jolted awake, turning his head left and right. Del put her hand on his shoulder and sat down next to him.

Ty rolled onto his back, inhaled deeply, and stretched both arms over his head. "What time is it?" he said on the exhale.

"One twenty."

He stretched again and sat up. "Why are you dressed?"

"I want to start for Buck's now. I've recovered."

"It would be better to wait until dawn."

"Every hour that I'm missing is causing my family heartache. Not to mention wasting a lot of others' time and energy."

He shook his head. "It's a long, dangerous walk in the dark woods."

"Then how about a nice, smooth paddle? Show me the map. We can canoe about three miles an hour without breaking a sweat."

"What canoe?"

"The one stored up in the rafters in the lean-to. The paddles are on the wall," she said, pointing over her shoulder.

Ty flexed his shoulders and neck. He pulled the map from his jacket and measured off a distance of five miles.

"See, maybe ninety minutes if we work at it." Del said as she mixed up the last of the breakfast powder.

He was clearly skeptical. "Sunrise is in four hours. They won't be searching again until then."

"In less than two hours, way less if Jules and Janie are in their cabin, we'll be at Buck's and they won't need to search at all." Del handed him the cup of watery breakfast mix.

"What if I told you I've never been in a canoe?" he asked.

"Not a problem. You can learn in about five minutes. Summer camps in Maine, they let children do it by themselves."

"Probably only in the daytime. And how about life vests? I don't see any of those around here."

He was right about the life vests. Del scratched her itchy head and plucked out another pine needle. "Some people leave them with the canoe."

They finished their drinks and went around back to the lean-to. The eighteen-foot aluminum canoe was upside down in the low rafters. It was easy to lift it down and clear out the cobwebs and the one bird nest. They found very dirty, mildewed life vests and kneeling mats hanging from hooks on the wall behind it.

"We don't even know if this will float," Ty grumbled.

They carried the canoe to the edge of the lake. Holding a line attached to the gunnel, Del shoved it into the water. They watched it floating calmly, and she declared it "seaworthy."

While Ty put out the fire in the woodstove, Del washed their cups under the hand-pump faucet. He gave her a sweatshirt to wear and put on his jacket. She saw him tuck a handgun into the back of his waistband, but didn't say anything. He had carried it all last winter when he was acting as her security detail, but she still wasn't used to it. Ty repacked his backpack and secured the rolled sleeping bag to the top with elastic ties. After locking the cabin, they carried everything to the canoe, which was still floating, mirrored in the glass-like surface by the silver-blue light of a half-moon. The night wind had died down to a whisper.

At one time, the canoe had webbed canvas seats, but most of the material was torn or missing, probably lining all the mouse nests around the cabin. After putting the life vests on and cinching them tight, Del helped Ty into the front and showed him how to kneel on the mat, rest his butt on what was left of the seat, and hold the paddle. He turned on his headlamp, and the large flashlight was near his feet in case they needed it.

"Our biggest risk is hitting a rock just under the surface," she instructed. "You're on lookout. If you see any sudden change in the water, yell out 'back-paddle.'"

"Got it."

She placed his backpack in the center and took her kneeling position in the stern. With a gentle push, they were off. At first, Ty's movements were too upright and rigid because he was trying not to shift his weight while dipping his paddle.

"Relax," she said. "If you stay a little loose, the balance will come naturally."

"There's nothing natural about what I'm doing," he muttered.

"Put your paddle in the water without making a splash. It's more efficient."

After a while, they found their rhythm and paddled with ease. At least Del was at ease. She could see Ty was unhappy. She steered them to the middle of the lake, which was about two miles wide at this point. She knew Garth's island would be coming into view soon. Just north of that was the field of boulders. They would have to work around those on the east side, then pass Jules and Janie's camp. If they saw the Whaler tied up to the dock, they would ask them to help. After that, the shoreline would close in some and they would pass into the middle lobe of the snowman-shaped lake.

They traveled many minutes in silence except for the softest dip of the paddles in the water and the barely audible drips as they pulled them out. Then on the left, as expected, the shoreline and trees appeared much closer. Del thought this must be the southern end of Garth's island. A few more minutes and she could see his dock in the distance as a black outline in the moonlight. She stopped paddling when she saw a silhouette, the hulking shape of a large man moving from the dock to the shore.

"Shut off your headlamp," she said with a breathy voice. "Stop paddling. Don't move."

She crawled forward in the canoe, making it rock a little, until she was in the center right behind Ty, who had seen the silhouette too. "It's Garth," she whispered. "I'm sure of it."

They watched the dark shape walk back to the dock, step into a boat, and then out again carrying something to the dimly lit cabin. He stayed inside and they didn't see any more of him even as the canoe slowly drifted closer.

"I don't get it," she whispered. "He looks like he's moving stuff in."

"We should back off and let him be." Ty started to paddle backward, causing the canoe to turn. "We don't want him to hear us."

She crept back to the stern and steered away to the east. They were about halfway to the eastern shore when they heard a loud *whoosh!* behind them coming from the island. On all sides, the water suddenly burst with the reflection of leaping orange flames.

Del spun the canoe around.

FORTY-FIVE

"**P**ut your back into it! Paddle hard!" she shouted.

Ty obeyed, even though he wasn't convinced they should go back to the island. In a few minutes they were approaching the dock. Del pulled the canoe around Garth's bass boat and climbed out. Ty scrambled after her as she tied off the rope. She tore off her life vest and started for the cabin, which was burning brightly on the inside, throwing waves of yellow light from the windows and doorway. He could hear the roar and crackle of the flames. It was loud enough that they had to shout.

Ty grabbed her arm. "We need to talk about this first. If he wants to burn down his cabin, why should we stop him?"

"It's not just the cabin," she answered, shrugging off his hand. "Don't you see? He wants to burn *with* it. We need to stop him."

"And how do you expect to do that? Did you bring the fire department?"

"I don't know." She took off in a jog along the dock and onto the dirt- and grass-covered shore.

Throwing off his life vest and pocketing the headlamp, Ty stayed right behind her as they climbed the slope to the front porch. When they were within six feet, he could feel the heat of the fire on his face. Del must have felt it too and stopped moving forward; instead, she changed to pacing back and forth.

They were close enough to see him. Rubin Garth was a backlit silhouette sitting in a rocking chair on the porch, toying with a large-framed picture, turning it this way and that. He didn't seem to notice their approach, but then they heard his distinctive low growl. "Go away. Just go away."

Inside the cabin, the flames crept up the back wall. Smoke curled out from under the eaves.

"They stopped Charlotte from killing anyone. She's been arrested," Del shouted over the roar.

Garth didn't respond.

"You can't end it here." Del stopped pacing. "She needs you now more than ever."

He slammed the picture onto the porch floor and kicked the frame. Shattered glass pieces lying around his feet reflected the light of the fire. He spoke to his feet. "I can't help her. I'll be in prison the rest of my life."

"Rubin, listen to me." Del took a step closer. "Prison doesn't mean you lose contact. You write. You phone."

He pushed his bulk out of the chair and, standing, shook his fist. "Go away!"

"She needs the only person who ever understood her."

Del's arguments weren't working.

"You're a coward, you selfish bastard!" Ty shouted, hoping he could use Garth's anger to lure him off the porch. "You know what we'll tell them about the way you checked out? Rubin Garth took the easy way. Suicide is always the coward's way out."

Garth wasn't buying it. His head was thrown back. "You can't stop me," he roared, but seemingly not to them.

He was still standing, but swaying like he was in a trance. The window on the other side of the door exploded. Flames shot out and curled toward the roof. Del and Ty both ducked and jumped back. Ty couldn't understand how Garth could be that close to the fire and not faint from the heat.

"Rubin, if you kill yourself, Charlotte will never forgive you," Del said, reaching a hand out to him. "Please. Come down from the porch. Please."

They heard a loud crack as the first flames shot through the roof, releasing an intense wave of heat. Del and Ty were forced to step farther back. Garth sagged against a porch column. With head hanging and chest heaving, Ty thought he might be sobbing.

There was no more time to lose. Ty reached for his Glock.

"Yes, shoot him so he can't stand or fight us," Del said. "We can pull him off the porch."

"I might kill him," Ty said.

"Do it," she said, pulling off her sweatshirt. "Give me your jacket." She ran down the slope to the lake.

In his best target practice stance, Ty aimed the Glock at Garth's large thigh. At this range, he might destroy the femoral art, and Garth would bleed to death in minutes. He shifted his aim lower. Of course, a muscular guy like Garth would be able to walk with a lower leg wound. He moved his aim higher to his belly and thought about all the organs he could damage. He lowered the Glock, reset the safety, and stuffed it into his waistband. He wasn't ready to shoot anyone.

The inferno in the cabin blasted another hole in the roof that sent embers flying through the night sky. Garth swayed and, with a spasm, fell to his knees. He fell on his side in a second convulsion. Immediately, Ty understood he was watching a man overcome by heatstroke. He was sure that had been Garth's plan all along. It would have been too risky to walk your own flesh into the flames. The pain might be too great and your will too weak. But once you're unconscious from the heat your organs fail, guaranteeing death, so that by the time the flames lick your feet, there's no one left to scream.

Del came back from the lake with the soaked garments. They wound them around their heads and shoulders like hijabs, and together they made a dash for the porch. Dragging and rolling the unconscious

Garth, they managed to haul him to the edge of the lake near the dock. The top of his hair was singed, his skin hot and dry to the touch, his breath rapid and shallow. They soaked the jacket and sweatshirt in the lake and laid them over him. The shirt on his back was so close to burning that when they applied the wet cloth to it, it sizzled. As soon as the wet garments felt warm, they soaked them again. Garth remained unconscious.

With another explosive crack, the inferno ate through another section of roof, which collapsed and released a shower of embers. Ty and Del dragged Garth to the end of the dock with the intention of laying him in the bass boat.

They never heard Jules and Janie approach in the Whaler until it bumped against the wooden pilings on the other side. Del greeted them with huge hugs and a rapid-fire explanation of what had happened. They laid Garth on the bow seat of the Whaler. Janie and Del continued to apply cold water to his unmoving hulk. Ty grabbed his backpack. Standing next to Jules at the center console, he was assigned floodlight duty with a warning to keep a lookout for submerged rocks. Jules deftly steered the boat around the boulder field and headed straight for Buck's Village.

FORTY-SIX

For Sunday dinner, the day after the excitement ended, Del's father organized a celebration by reserving the entire dining area and bar at Pepper's Pub, the only full-service restaurant in the village of Ferry Landing. Lately, Pepper had been keeping the pub closed on Sundays due to lack of staff, but he must have made Pepper and her cook a financial offer they couldn't refuse, not to mention that Del, having worked there part-time for two years, was almost family. They set up one long table to hold the Corriveaus and friends, including Del's parents, Philip and Julia, her brother Ben and his soon-to-be official fiancée, Marilyn, her brother Patrick who had just flown in, Grandpa, Evie, and of course, Marco and Ty sitting on either side of Del. Grandpa had also invited Sheriff Mike, who said he would stop by.

Both Marco and Del were using crutches to get around. Marco's surgery had gone well. His knee was in a brace, and he was under orders to keep the weight off for at least a month. Grandpa had picked him up late yesterday from the hospital after returning from Lake Awasosee. Marco was spending one more night in the bunk room, and then his roommate and a friend planned on driving from the university to take him and his car back. He said he had a lot of writing to do.

Also, late Saturday, Del's parents had taken her to the emergency room in Ellis Junction after her mother noticed she was limping. Two of the cuts on one foot had become infected. The ER doctor opened the wounds and drained bloody liquid from them. She cleaned, sutured, bandaged, and advised Del to stay off the foot until it healed. The use of crutches was no mystery to her—she had learned to navigate with them one spring in high school after a soccer collision put a gash in her shin.

As they assembled at Pepper's for dinner, Del noticed Marco was mostly trying to hop on one leg using the crutches like a cane. She took some time to demonstrate how to swing his weight, how to negotiate stairs, ramps, and tight turns on three points. She led him on a practice tour in and out of the building, down the stairs and up the wheelchair ramp, then a tight turn in the doorway and the course in reverse.

When they came inside, her family was huddled around her brother Patrick watching a video on his phone. He had recorded them, sped it up, and added an old-time, black-and-white movie effect so that now their lesson looked like a Keystone Cops chase on crutches.

Marco and Del almost fell over in hysterics, which, as they passed the video around, infected everyone and relieved much of the tension of the last three days.

At Buck's Village, Del's middle-of-the-night reunion with her parents and Grandpa had been tearful—a mixed emotional brew of joy, relief, and guilt. Soon after they arrived, Rubin Garth was taken away in an emergency van accompanied by a county officer. As the EMTs injected him with saline to bring down his temperature, he showed some signs of life but was still unconscious. Janie and Jules agreed to take care of returning the borrowed canoe. While it was still dark, they motored away, leading a crew of volunteer firefighters who brought a pump and hoses to put out the inferno on Garth's island.

Del and Ty were interviewed at length by the local sheriff and the Maine warden who'd organized the search. Buck insisted he had given Del permission to use his pickup. Her father threatened to sue the bridge's owner (no one knew who that was) for not posting a weight limit. He told Buck he would help pay for a new truck if his insurance didn't cover it all.

Buck fed them all breakfast and lunch. At some point between their arrival Friday evening and the wee hours of Saturday morning, her parents and Buck had become fast friends. They learned Buck was often in Boston, where his son attended medical school. They gave him an open invitation to stay with them whenever he was in the area and set up a date for a visit after he closed the cottages for the season in September.

There was a lengthy discussion among the police about which charges should be brought in Prescott County by Sheriff Mike versus which charges were under the jurisdiction of the local sheriff. Del didn't care. She really wanted to go home.

Her exhaustion showed itself on Sunday morning when, after sleeping for ten hours, she woke up at seven, drank a glass of water, and went back to bed for three more, finally waking up when her parents came by in the afternoon. Later, Grandpa told her he'd heard the guys in the bunk room talking until midnight and he hadn't seen or heard them again till after lunch. She exchanged texts with Ty and Marco, who both asked how she was doing. They each sent the others *I'm sleepy* emojis. By dinnertime, Del was absolutely starved and the delicious smells coming from Pepper's kitchen gave her hunger cramps.

After a round of drinks, dinner started with Pepper's best fish chowder. It was filled with chunks of fresh haddock, onions, and potatoes, all cooked in a seafood broth topped off with some light cream, a sprinkle of fresh thyme, and freshly ground pepper. That was followed by Pepper's famous lobster pie, a concoction of chunky lobster meat in a pink broth topped with buttery crackers, accompanied by cornbread, salad, fresh tomatoes with basil—the vegetables all grown by Settlement Creek Farm. Everything was served family-style. Bowls and casseroles filled the center of the table.

With the great preponderance of legal minds in the room, the dinner discussion centered on the mystery that had started with a hike up Monks Head. Del, Ty, and Marco took turns recounting a month's worth of experiences, more or less in chronological order. The group around the table listened attentively between sips and bites, punctuated with nods of understanding and interrupted by more than a few comments. Evie, on Ty's left, did throw a little elbow jab his way when he described finding the cave on their first hike.

Sheriff Mike arrived while the serving dishes on the table were still half full. They made room for him next to Grandpa. Pepper brought a place setting and a beer to go with it.

Del's father asked the sheriff to just frown if any of the speculative talk was way off base. "I know you can't tell us anything about an ongoing investigation, but you can wrinkle your forehead. We'll just have to figure out what it means." Everyone but the sheriff laughed. He was already into his first bowl of chowder.

"The only time I make a face around here is because Pepper sometimes burns the cornbread," Mike said.

Pepper gave him a pretend slap on the shoulder. "No complaints, Michael, just put more butter on it." She tossed her head and said to the crowd, "I get away with that because we went to high school together."

"Sheriff, how's Lucy doing?" Del asked. "The hospital said she's been discharged."

"She's making a great recovery and could be back by September," he answered. "But she doesn't have a clear memory of who ran her off the road. She remembers the jolt, the sound of metal tearing, and how she lost control of the vehicle."

After the trio finished the entire story—the skeletal remains, the Wilsons, the earthquake report, Lucy's accident, the hostage crisis, the kidnapping, the escape, and the rescue—their audience debated the most likely scenario, and there was no lack of disagreement.

"I'd like to come back just to hear the prosecutor's closing arguments," Ben said. "Even if we don't know the truth, he, ahem, or *she*"—with a nod to Marilyn—"can tell a story of how Charlotte crafted revenge with a touch of irony, murdering George, the fake Native American, in front of a real native work of art." He stood, took a step back, and addressed the table.

"Ladies and gentlemen of the jury, the evidence points to the murderer, Charlotte Wilson, who, driven by hatred, exacted revenge on George Tozur in an attempt to wipe out the humiliation of sexual abuse that he perpetrated on her when she was an innocent fourteen-year-old and the years of shame as she helplessly watched him manipulate and swindle her Aunt Ella. The opportunity came with an earthquake and the opening of a cave that Rubin Garth found in his examination of the rockslides. Rubin Garth would have understood the significance of the prehistoric petroglyphs, and out of respect for her native heritage, he contacted Charlotte. She saw the opportunity and carefully planned the trap, sending word to Chief George to meet someone there—perhaps it was anonymous, just directions and a specific time.

"Of course, George Tozur would want to see it. At the appointed hour, he lowered himself into the dark opening and saw nothing but a bright light focused on the petroglyphs. He walked toward the wall of art and stood there with his mouth open in surprise and awe. Charlotte stepped silently out of the shadows, and with all her power, smashed a hole in the back of his head. And what was the murder weapon? You heard the coroner's testimony that the blow that killed George came from a pointed object swung with significant force. Charlotte had easy access to a weapon like that—for example, the rock hammer she often carried in her father's quarries. We don't need to find the exact murder weapon. Just imagine the years of hatred behind that first blow. George fell face first and slowly bled to death. Did she weep for him? Yes, I expect in the release of emotion, she did. It was likely the last sound he heard.

"The next task was to hide the cave entrance—which Charlotte asked Garth to help her with—to wedge a rock in the triangle opening and place a log over the crescent hole above, thereby creating a tomb for Chief George that only they knew about and that they never expected to be found again. I ask you, the jury, to look at the evidence and find

Charlotte Wilson guilty of premeditated murder." Ben made eye contact with everyone around the table and then, with an air of dignity, sat down.

Del was impressed. There was a long pause before the jury of Corriveaus and friends applauded. She came to the conclusion that Ben was going to be a hell of a prosecutor.

Patrick chimed in, "Nice job. I'll vote to convict."

Her father was scratching his chin. "I hate to disappoint you both, but as long as there are conflicting confessions, the DA may never bring murder charges. No reason to; there are plenty of crimes with witnesses to convict them on."

"The murder should have been a perfect crime," Marco said.

"Except for nature's way of eroding tombs," Del countered. "Granite blocks eventually tumble and all logs decay."

"Let's give credit to the curious geologist," Ty added. "She knew the giant slab of rock would make a shelter and did not hesitate to explore."

Everyone clapped. Del stood awkwardly on one leg and took a quick bow.

"The crime should have been *perfect*," Marco said with new emphasis. "Even after you found it, there was no reason to suspect Garth or Charlotte. Time had erased any evidence, including DNA that they might have left. Then the probate filing happened."

"When Charlotte learned Ryan was also George's son, she must have been beyond mad as hell," Ben said. "That's when she crafted another revenge."

Del played with a leaf of basil stuck to her plate. "Not sure if revenge is the right word, but a punishment, for sure. With a way-too-complicated plan. Kidnap me to get the police and Ty off the island? She could have phoned Pale Moon and said 'we need to talk' and invited her over for lunch."

Ty disagreed with her. "She wanted Ryan for a hostage while she abused Pale Moon. She wanted to burn the lovefest memorabilia. She wanted to show everyone what a scumbag George was and how guilty Pale Moon was for covering for him."

"Charlotte shares responsibility for not stopping him sooner," Del said.

Her mom spoke up. "Don't judge her too harshly. She was so young. It's a pattern with many victims of sexual abuse. They won't come forward because of how often we blame the victim."

Ben was tapping the table softly with his fork. "I don't understand how Charlotte knew she would find Pale Moon and Ryan alone. That could have backfired," he said. Marilyn reached over and trapped the fork under her hand.

"It wasn't luck. She's been communicating with Ryan since the memorial service," Marco announced.

"What was he thinking?" Ben asked, chuckling. "Hey, let's invite that lady over for tea, you know, the one Mama kicked off the property."

"Yeah, kind of like that," Marco answered. "I know he felt really bad for her and was embarrassed by the way Pale Moon behaved. Charlotte is an expert at getting people to feel sorry for her."

"Now you need to tell us how you know," Ty said.

"I hooked them up," Marco said. "Ryan contacted me after we first met him and Pale Moon. I asked some questions about the Wilsons and the lawsuits. He was curious. We went back and forth. I found out later, when I had dinner with Charlotte, that it was Ryan who sent her the invitation to the memorial service. I'm sure he didn't realize where it would lead."

They all looked to Sheriff Mike for confirmation, but he just smiled at them with cornbread crumbs on his lips and dismissed any concern with a wave of his fork.

Ben was helping himself to more lobster pie. "The real interesting character to me is the truly lovesick Rubin Garth. Who covers up a murder and commits multiple assaults and a kidnapping out of unrequited love?"

"So? Not the best way to win over your sweetheart?" Marco added, with a wink at Marilyn.

There were murmurs of agreement and quiet laughter around the table. Ben and Marco were enjoying the game of bouncing clever comments off each other like ping-pong balls. Del could see a lot of the same personality traits—how both seemed to work their way into the center of attention and lit up in response to laughter.

Then Ben's last remark hit her. "Wait. How many are you counting as multiple assaults?"

"Marco, you, and the one driven off the road, Lucy," Ben replied.

Del shook her head. "I'm sure Garth had nothing to do with Lucy's accident."

Sheriff Mike raised his eyes quickly. The spoonful of buttery lobster he was holding to his lips was lost to gravity and plopped back onto his plate.

"You think it could have been a random event, a coincidence?" Marco asked.

"No," Del answered. "It was a different fear, not the fear of what someone knew about the rock shelter, but the fear of bringing too much attention to the earthquake damage."

"Okay, Sherlock, you're going to have to explain," Ty said.

"Kay Levant was in the office when I went to pick up the report. We know her as a respected naturalist and ranger. She authored a detailed, professional report. Why wouldn't she be proud of doing something that brought needed money to the park? Instead, ever since Lucy's accident, in every conversation she distanced herself from it and tried to minimize her role. Ty said she didn't want to physically touch it."

Ty nodded once thoughtfully. "Right, she overheard your conversation with Lucy. She could have easily removed the rest of the copies before anyone else got to the files."

Sheriff Mike was wrinkling his forehead like an accordion. "She has an alibi. We checked her vehicle and there's no evidence it was used in the accident."

"Kay was really scared after you interviewed her with the other staff at park headquarters," Del added. "When I saw her, she was on the phone but put it down quickly like she didn't want me to see. Find out who she was talking to that day, and I think you'll find someone who was even more scared."

"Scared of what?" came from several voices at the table.

Ty was the first to make the connection. "Fraud."

Del smiled and directed a single, thoughtful nod his way. "Someone should audit the grant they got and how they spent the money."

"Sweet Jesus." Marco slapped the table. "Another almost perfect crime. There really was an earthquake. It was a big deal for weeks. An opportunity for some significant exaggeration and a windfall of cash. I like it."

"Fraud with taxpayer money is a career killer," Ben observed.

Looking over his glasses at Del, Grandpa was grim. "I'd be very sorry to hear that Hiram Lemuel, our long-time director of Granite Coast Park, had any involvement. For two decades, he did a lot of good for this island. When they announced he had been appointed state DEP commissioner, dozens of county and island organizations gave him recognition awards."

"Fraud with taxpayer money is also a reputation killer," Marco echoed.

Her father added, "The investigators will want a subpoena for her phone records."

Wiping his mouth with a napkin, Sheriff Mike pushed back in his chair and stood up. "Great dinner, Pepper!" he said loudly in the general direction of the bar, where Pepper was loading glasses into the dishwasher. He made the rounds at the table shaking hands. "Thank you, Philip and Julia, Gabe. Nice meeting you all. Sorry, got to run. I've got another appointment." He leaned close to Del's ear and whispered, "Come see me any time you're thinking of a career change."

He clapped Ty on the shoulder, and Ty followed him to the door, where Del could see them having what she called a *bro-chat*, one that involved more body language than words. It was punctuated with lots of short nods. Then the sheriff left.

Pepper asked everyone to clear the table to make room for a blueberry cobbler dessert. There were several minutes during which the room was transformed into a slow-motion merry-go-round while the diners carried dishes to the kitchen and returned with refilled drinks, all except Marco and Del, who were pretty useless except for moving themselves around on crutches. Del sat alone at the table. Marco had limped off to the restroom, on the way exchanging a few more quips with Ben. Ty, carrying dishes, paused to talk with her parents. He disappeared into the kitchen, and on his way back with a stack of dessert bowls, stopped for a word with Grandpa.

Making sure everyone had either coffee or after-dinner drinks, Pepper asked the crowd to find their seats again. Ty slipped into his chair next to Del, wearing his shy smile. The man sitting next to her was a different Ty Holden in so many ways she could hardly recall the smug and distant private investigator she'd met in January. He started to talk to her about "something's come up in Portland" when Marco lost his balance, landing on the floor behind them with a grunt. Ty jumped to the rescue. With Patrick on the other side, he helped Marco to stand, made sure his knee brace was still in place, and steered him back to his seat.

Pepper and the cook made a grand entrance with two baking dishes of blueberry cobbler, the steam rising from the segments of golden-baked biscuit crust floating on top of a bubbly, dark-purple filling. They placed a dish near each end of the table with a gallon container of vanilla ice cream in the middle.

"Hey," Del exclaimed. "Cobbler might be a model for plate tectonics. Look here, the filling is bubbling up, pushing these parts of the crust apart, and here one section of crust is getting pushed on top of another because of the expansion. The dynamics are perfect, like earth's crust floating on a mantle of magma." She flashed a Cheshire grin at Pepper. "Except a red cherry filling would be more realistic."

There was a moment of silence. Then Del's brothers roared with laughter, her father was holding back and covering his mouth with a napkin, her mother giggled, and Grandpa chuckled. Evie laughed along but Del could tell she didn't get the joke.

"You mean she was always like this?" Marco asked.

"Always," Ben said. "Ask her about the spearmints!" That caused Ben and Patrick to go into knee-slapping convulsions. Del stuck out her tongue at them. She wanted to give them the finger but couldn't do it with her parents and Grandpa looking on.

Ben recovered enough to start. "Our family dinner table is always the center of loud debates on points of law and politics." Del knew the story well, and she also knew that Ben and Patrick liked to tell it like a wrestling tag team, each taking a choreographed turn in the center ring.

"Even when we were in grade school," Patrick said in his turn.

"And loud is an understatement," her mother added. "Philip would egg them on, and the boys responded with passion. Most of the time, Del and I ignored it all."

"One time, she was about six," Patrick said. "I remember because her front teeth were missing. Ben wouldn't listen to something I said even though I was right. So I kept repeating it over and over, getting louder each time."

"You were dead wrong, which is the reason I ignored you," Ben added, as if it still mattered some twenty years later.

"Del suddenly starts pounding her fork on her plate yelling, 'Stop shouting! Stop shouting!'" Patrick said. "We were so shocked, we did stop shouting. Then she said, 'Shouting something over and over does not make it truth.'"

Ben curled his upper lip like a nervous baboon and pointed at his front teeth. "Except she had no front teeth so it came out 'troof.'"

"Dad asked her how we can find out the truth," Patrick continued. "She answered, 'Spearmints. Scientists know the troof with spearmints.'"

There were chuckles and giggles around the table. Del rolled her eyes.

Ben's turn next. "Then Mom leans over to her and says, 'You mean *experiments*, don't you, Adele?'"

"And Del gets this faraway expression. She doesn't move or answer for so long that we forgot about her and started eating again," Patrick said.

"Finally," Ben said, demonstrating with a flourish of his own utensil, "Del waves her fork like a conductor and announces, 'No, it's *spearmints*!'"

As it swept by her face, Marilyn grabbed the fork out of his hand.

FORTY-SEVEN

The hearty laughter at Del's early understanding of the role of "spearmints" in the scientific method died down as Pepper served the cobbler with ice cream. The diners passed the bowls around until every place had one. They put a bowl for Ty in front of an empty seat. Del hadn't seen him get up.

The cobbler received many compliments, even as there were a few more jokes about how much tastier it was than molten rock—at least that anyone had ever tried. Del watched Ty's ice cream melt into a milky white puddle.

She put her hand on Marco's arm to get his attention. He was still engaged with Ben and Patrick. "Do you know where Ty went?"

He shrugged.

Del pushed herself up and grabbed her crutches. She swung her way to the restrooms, which were in a corridor at the end of the bar. There was no one. As she pivoted to head back to the dining area, the phone in her cargo pocket chirped for an incoming text.

It was from Ty: *Sorry didn't get to say goodbye. Need to be in Portland. Spoke with Marco long time last night. He really loves you. Give him a chance.*

With the crutches in her armpits, Del leaned her back against a wall outside the restrooms and started texting with both thumbs like mad. More than like mad, like *furious.*

Her first one said: *FKU Where do you get off? So you guys have a nice chat and decide who gets me? Glad you worked out a solution. Did you grab the short but noble straw? Why are men so F-ing stupid?*

She erased it.

Her second one: *FKU. He's a grownup. He knows how to talk.*

She erased that one too.

Her third one: *Why is no one asking me?* She deleted it slowly, one character at a time.

The message she finally sent: *F-ing coward. Worst NOT break up text ever.* She knew they really had nothing to break up, but she felt better having sent it. Maybe he would take it as a joke, a joke with a jab, only funny if you think it cuts at the truth.

His response: *Driving now. Will call tomorrow.*

Del hobbled back to the dining room still buzzing with chatter. She stopped at the periphery, outside the noise and laughter of the celebration, balancing on crutches and one leg, to watch her family enjoying themselves. Her parents—both successful, handsome, wealthy—were in their prime. Her brothers were on their way to lucrative careers. Even Grandpa and Evie had found each other and were making plans. As she looked around the room, Del counted herself as the odd girl out.

Her reflections were cut short when she felt a nudge on her arm. From somewhere, Grandpa had come to stand next to her. He gave her a warm smile and put a hand lightly on her back.

"Are you tired?" he asked. "Want me to take you home?"

"No, I'm fine."

"Okay, then. Just say the word." He dropped his hand and took a half step toward rejoining the party in the dining room.

"Grandpa, you and Evie decided what you're doing this winter?"

"At my age I don't make plans that far ahead."

"Oh, don't tell me you haven't talked about it."

"We talk about how lucky we are to wake up every morning with all essential functions intact." He chuckled, turning to face her. "What about you?"

"Finish my independent research project. Start a master's degree here. Check out doctorate programs in geologically interesting places."

"Sounds like a plan." He tilted his head toward the dining table. "Make sure you write down why you think it's a good one and keep it somewhere safe. I'm betting someone at some point will try to get you to change it."

"Good advice," she said.

"Here's more." Eyeing her over his glasses, Grandpa lightly clasped a hand on each of her upper arms. "Get a room on campus for the fall and spring semesters. You're taking a full course load. The ninety-minute drive one-way from Pyke Island is bad for the car and worse for you."

"But—"

"No buts." He tightened his grip. "It only makes sense. Remember the plan you just told me."

The next seconds passed while she sifted through memories of how they had become a team—Grandpa and the odd girl out working together—remodeling projects, fishing, digging clams. Since Grandma Marjorie's death, they had grown very close. And now he was moving on and urging her to do the same.

"Will you water my plants?" she asked.

"I can do that." He gave her a warm smile and a soft kiss on the cheek, turned away, then stopped short. "Since when do you have house plants?"

"I'm thinking of buying some to get a jump start on your garden next year."

With a finger wag that said "you got me," Grandpa walked away to join the celebration.

It was Marco who noticed her standing by herself. Using the table for balance, he half rose, pulled out her chair, and with a radiant smile that highlighted his dimples, waved her over. When she hesitated, he waved with more vigor and almost lost his one-legged balance. He never took his adoring eyes off her until she came back to her seat.

CODA

Rubin Garth recovered from minor burns and was left with nothing more permanent than mild kidney damage, requiring him to forevermore pay attention to his diet. He was transferred from the hospital to the Prescott County Jail to await trial. Josh Wilson was released on his own recognizance, and Charlotte was placed under home confinement and electronic monitoring, at least until her day in court. Following her arrest, Charlotte's strength declined precipitously until she was completely wheelchair-bound and needed round-the-clock care. All firearms were removed from their home on Heart Pond.

Home confinement meant she could only travel for medical treatment. However, after appealing to Sheriff Hodgkins and the district attorney, Charlotte was allowed supervised one-hour visits twice a week with Garth in the county jail, where they spent their time together in the visitation room quietly holding hands. The charges, covering the two separate kidnapping events, were written so they would not be considered codefendants, as that would have forbidden any contact between them. According to his attorney, the visits improved Garth's mental health, and they were beginning to work on his legal options. Because he had released Del unharmed, his defense could have the punishment reduced to a Class B crime.

Technically, the murder of George Tozur remained unsolved. There was no feasible way for the DA to try either one with conflicting confessions and no hard evidence.

Pale Moon Smith resigned from the elder council of Settlement Creek Farm. By unanimous vote, she was replaced as president by their medicine man, William Crockett Brady, often called Uncle. She remained a member of the farm cooperative as supervisor of the organic vegetable division.

By the end of August, the council announced that they had met the requirements for a Maine license to grow marijuana in their new state-of-the-art greenhouse. It was revealed that, through Uncle's financial ties to a Colorado cannabis firm, they were well-positioned to be the largest grower in Downeast Maine. For the last few years, cash from the Colorado firm had been keeping Settlement Creek financially afloat, and as a result, that firm now had majority ownership in the farm.

Meanwhile, the Town of Pyke Island had yet to vote on whether to allow marijuana operations anywhere on the island. The town council expected the tax windfall to be substantial, and most townsfolk had already changed their attitudes about a bunch of hippies—now professional farmers—who wanted to grow pot. The agricultural easement required that the ten acres of Settlement Creek were dedicated to farming in perpetuity, but there was no restriction on the crop.

Probate Court acknowledged that Ryan Smith and Joshua Wilson were half-brothers and equal heirs to George Tozur's estate, but the judge delayed for a few weeks to ensure there were no other Tozur offspring with valid claims. No one else came forward.

While hardly friends, Ryan and Josh were on speaking terms, and with lawyers present, discussed a joint solution on the rock shelter and petroglyphs. They agreed to give Granite Coast Park the rest of Monks Head and enough of the encircling acres to create an access road and interpretive center. They signed a memorandum of understanding stating that the highest priority was to preserve the site. As a follow-up, Abby Wilson kicked in her forty acres along the coast, making for a significant and valuable expansion of the park.

As there was no longer a murder mystery hanging over Monks Head, an archeological team, under a state-approved principal investigator, began work in August. Ryan was invited to join the team and took an indefinite leave from his post-graduate work at Wisconsin. He and his mother reconciled after several meetings with a family therapist.

Ryan canceled his August birthday drunk, instead meeting Del in Summer Hill Harbor over beer and peanuts. He gabbed brightly about the laboratory they were planning to build as part of the Monks Head interpretive center. He said he couldn't remember much about the incident when he'd lost the car keys, but told her what happened after the local constable found him asleep in his car and called his mother to drive him home. Pale Moon sent Uncle to retrieve him. Getting into Uncle's car, Ryan threw up on himself and the car's dashboard. Uncle dragged him out, walked him to the end of the dock, and threw him into the harbor. Uncle called it a character-building experience. Something about the entire incident had left Ryan with an extreme distaste for bourbon. By the end of the evening, Del came to the realization that Ryan really did know his way around chemical analysis equipment, and she recognized the seedling in him that could grow into a mature adult. He invited her for a tour of the dig, only this time he was sober.

The Maine attorney general began an investigation into alleged misappropriation of funds for Granite Coast Park. For her testimony, Kay Levant was given immunity. Shortly after the start of the investigation, DEP Commissioner Hiram Lemuel resigned. Kay applied to the National Park Service and moved to California for a position at Yosemite.

Under oath, Lemuel confessed to sideswiping Lucy Irwin's car, but insisted he never intended to hurt her. He explained that he only wanted to talk to her, to ask that she stop making an issue about the missing documents, hoping to convince her they were completely unrelated to George Tozur's death. He had driven from Augusta early that morning with a plan to catch her at home, but as he arrived, she was backing out of her driveway. He followed her. When they crossed the bridge, he began to panic. He knew he couldn't have a conversation with her at park headquarters without raising suspicion. He passed her car, giving it a little nudge and thinking she would stop for an accidental fender bender. He didn't expect she would lose control. He said he still had nightmares that replayed the moment when her car flew off the road at the end of the guardrail. Hiram Lemuel was indicted on a long list of charges.

The extended Corriveau family reserved five cabins at Buck's Village for the week of July Fourth the following year. Del wrote a long thank-you letter to Jules and Janie. She sent it packed with a University of Maine sweatshirt, a pair of hot-pink flip-flops (the closest color to magenta she could find), organic dog treats, and a hand-painted multicolored silk scarf that she thought would look gorgeous with Jules's yellow dress.

In August, Del made two more trips to explore the pink granite outcrops in the old Wilson quarries, both times in an ATV driven by Josh Wilson, who was curious about her interest in geology. He told her that, despite everything his mother had done, he was grateful to be with her because he wasn't sure how long she had. He was reconciling himself with the idea that she would never make it through a trial. They were meeting regularly with a therapist to address issues with forgiveness and communication. Charlotte revised her will to include significant sums to her loyal staff, in particular Marissa and Bruce. With all his years of boarding schools and army service, Josh said he never really thought of Pyke Island as his home, but now he intended to stay.

Del's university advisor came along on the second trip to the quarries. He was more than delighted, as the early bedrock mapping done on Pyke Island had not included any of the historical Pyke/Wilson property. With the required permissions, he and Del made several more treks to examine every cliff and outcrop. As a result of their findings, they planned over the winter to copublish a revision to the bedrock map of the island. He told her that having her name associated with the fieldwork and publication would open doors to other grants and possibly graduate programs.

The trips to the abandoned quarries led Josh to a new interest in the history and preservation of the granite industry. He started consulting with the Pyke Island Historical Society on an exhibit displaying many of the artifacts left in the quarries and old photos stored in the attic of his house.

Ty Holden called her the morning after the worst not-really-a-breakup text ever. He even offered to drive back and ask her forgiveness in person. Del told him that there really wasn't anything to forgive. She had already decided that choosing between Marco and Ty was a false choice. She wanted to keep them both as friends—extraordinary, wonderful friends. Del explained her feelings to Ty and later at the university to Marco. She didn't want anyone to be in love with her. She wasn't ready for that kind of love herself.

Someone had once told her that three friends never seemed to work. Even if it looked like an unstable compromise, she was determined, without betraying Marco or Ty or herself, to prove that someone wrong.

She completed her independent study with a thesis entitled "The Monks Head Granite Formation, a Later Intrusion in the Pyke Island Magma Reservoir." In the introduction, she wrote the following, and as she finished, she realized that if she replaced the word *science* with *love*, it would still be true:

> In science, new understanding comes from new discoveries and observations. It is progress built on the foundation of previous observations and measurements, but still incomplete, and to some degree, flawed. There is always more to learn. After a summer of fieldwork, sampling, measurements, data gathering, and analysis,

we come to the writing, offering a hypothesis that seeks not just to document but to explain. While the arguments presented here are based on data, criticism and debate over the conclusions are part of the process.

Del got an A.

As for the memory of Chief George, it quickly turned to dust. His name was erased from all public information on Settlement Creek Farm. No bronze plaque ever materialized. Some of the early members of the cooperative, including Pale Moon, still honored the values that had brought them together, but they acknowledged that they had given them the wrong face.

After many discarded drafts, Marco finally gave up on publishing an article that would set the record straight on the real George Tozur. The problem was that there was no one to be found in the story, only a dim reflection collected from the gossamer memories told by those who thought they knew him.

No one even knows what happened to his bones.

Coming Soon
Book 3 in the *Pyke Island Mystery* Series

by
Moe Claire
Black Veil, White Rose

Eager to enjoy the few waning days of Indian summer, Del Corriveau and friends Marco and Ty take a boat trip to a quiet, pristine cove nestled in a peninsula just east of Pyke Island. The property, with a long history of disappointment, was once considered an ideal place for a shorefront campground but that went bankrupt, and the property was abandoned. Then the squatters moved in, leading the good neighbors of Des Isle, an exclusive summer community, to do everything in their power to remove them. All that happened years ago and was resolved when the squatters left voluntarily. Or did they? Under the cove's placid surface, a mystery lies on the gravel and sand bottom waiting to be snagged. No one is surprised when Del and friends find it and then along with it, raise a swarm of ghosts—some long dead, some still living.

Acknowledgments

I am immensely grateful to my alpha readers (you know who you are), who are fearless in their criticism and helpful in their suggestions. Thank you all. Special thanks to 12 Willows Press for making this edition better than the original (Thanks, Tessa and Steven!) Every reader and every editor made this a better book.

As Downeast Maine, with its granite and volcanic bedrock, is my muse, it seemed fitting for Del to explore old quarries. Quarrying granite was an important industry in Maine, particularly in the late 1800s and peaking around 1900. Many large public buildings, such as libraries, post offices, and museums in the cities of the east, including New York City, Philadelphia, and Washington, DC, are made of Maine granite. The coastal region of Maine is dotted with abandoned quarries. A handful are still active. The Maine Granite Industry Museum on Mount Desert Island is a one-of-a-kind resource preserving the history, tools, stone samples, and stories of quarry workers. See https://www.mainegraniteindustry.org/.

While I was writing this story, I also took inspiration from a small book with fascinating tales: *Giants of the Dawnland: Ancient Wabanaki Tales*, collected by Alice Mead and Arnold Neptune (2010). In a time of receding glaciers, these oral history lessons tell us how to survive long, cold winters, how to treat one another with generosity, and how to show respect for the land—lessons whose meanings are just as valuable now as they were in centuries past.

Do we think of the stones we walk on? Do we think of the people before us who placed their feet there in exactly the same way?

About the Author

Moe Claire lives and writes in Downeast Maine. She is the author of the Pyke Island Mysteries, in addition to short stories, community theater plays, and some poetry. Retired from a career in computer science, she describes herself as an insatiable reader and a lifelong learner who is fascinated by the natural sciences and geology. When not writing, she enjoys summer and winter in Acadia National Park, and volunteers for several local nonprofits, including community theater, garden club, and the Maine Granite Industry Historical Society. For many years, she and her husband have explored Downeast Maine islands and harbors in their old Cape Dory cruiser but are currently between boats. They continue to explore Maine mountains, wild places, and park lands on foot.

9 781961 905504